The ... Future

- Identify the boundaries of the human soul
- Fly to the stars on beams of light
- Climb a magic beanstalk into space
- Soar through the solar system on magic matter
- Defy gravity

From dazzling engineering feats and ultrasophisticated forms of space transport to conquering intergalactic phenomenon, distinguished scientist Dr. Robert L. Forward says there is truly magic in our future.

Explore that wondrous world with him.

FUTURE MAGIC

Dr. Robert L. Forward

AVON BOOKS ◆ NEW YORK

FUTURE MAGIC is an original publication of Avon Books. This work
has never before appeared in book form.

AVON BOOKS
A division of
The Hearst Corporation
105 Madison Avenue
New York, New York 10016

Copyright © 1988 by Robert L. Forward
Front cover illustration by Rick Sternbach
Published by arrangement with the author
Library of Congress Catalog Card Number: 87-91459
ISBN: 0-380-89814-4

First Avon Books Printing: June 1988

Printed in the U.S.A.

K-R 10 9 8 7 6 5 4 3 2 1

Clarke's Third Law

"Any sufficiently advanced technology is indistinguishable from magic."

—Arthur C. Clarke,
Profiles of the Future

Introduction

Each day we see on television or read in the papers about some new advance in technology. In most cases we take the news in stride, for we have heard of similar things. But for our ancestors of only a few generations ago, these new technological achievements would have been thought to be magic.

It *is* magic—future magic—and we live with and use it daily. Direct-broadcast satellites that instantaneously bring us pictures of events from anywhere on the globe, like the magic crystal ball of the Wicked Witch of the West; powerful laser beams that destroy the missiles of our foes like a bolt of lightning from the hand of Zeus; air-cushion boats that magically levitate and walk over the surface of the water; genetically tailored microorganisms that produce insulin, eat oil spills, and leach copper ores, like miniature golems animated by our biological magic; radar—a magic that lets us see beyond what the unaided eye can see.

The wonders that take place every day of our lives would have amazed our parents 30 years ago, bewildered our grandparents of 60 years ago, and would have raised cries of "Black magic!" a century ago. The now-prosaic microwave oven is an excellent example of future magic. If you want to cook a large beef roast with heat, it takes four hours. It doesn't matter if the heat comes from wood, electricity, nuclear energy, evaporating black holes, sunlight, or cow dung—it takes four hours to cook a roast with heat. An ancient cook brought from the caves a million years past might not understand the source of the heat in your "black hole" oven, but after a few minutes of watching it cook a beef roast he would be able to prepare an auroch roast that would be done to perfection. Yet show him a microwave oven cooking a roast in a half hour and he would be bewildered by its magic.

The technology that produced the microwave oven did not develop a new source of heat; it developed "magic" heat—heat that is generated *inside* the roast, not applied to the outside, so the roast gets done in the magical time of 30 minutes instead of four hours.

A number of years ago the famous science-fiction author Arthur C. Clarke propounded what is now known as Clarke's Third Law: "Any sufficiently advanced technology is indistinguishable from magic."

It used to be that technology evolved slowly, and generations could go by with almost no change in the way things were done. Every decade or so, however, something new would be added to the existing base of technology. A blacksmith would find that a blade would take on a different temper if it were quenched in oil instead of water. A sea captain would find that his crew didn't come down with scurvy if he took along a few barrels of limes. A doctor noticed that he never saw a milkmaid among his smallpox patients.

In those days, the words *sufficiently advanced* meant hundreds of years in the future. For back then there was time enough between those new advances in technology to allow people to accept them and absorb them into "the way things are done." But even then, there was a resistance to change. It took the Royal Navy over a century to make limes part of the normal diet of a seagoing "limey"—and Edward Jenner's 1798 introduction of the concept of vaccination is regarded as magic by the ignorant even today—"How can you possibly make someone well by making him sick?"

Events move much faster these days. There are more scientists, doctors, and engineers active now. The rate at which they produce new technology has been accelerated by the prior technological inventions of the printing press, radio, television, and now the communication satellites and data links that spread the information about each new technological advance rapidly around the globe, making it almost instantly available to other researchers. The power of each researcher is also magnified a thousandfold by the electronic slaves they created, the computers. These range from the hand-held pocket wonders of the engineers to the giant electronic genies that serve a hundred masters at one time.

Nowadays, the distance in time where future science fades into future magic is only decades away. The best example is spaceflight. Who, in 1929, in the bleakest days of the depression, would have thought that in four decades there would be a man walking on the moon?

Here we are today, living among and using those magical wonders that were so impossible that our parents and grandparents couldn't even imagine them. What will be the magic in our future? It is impossible to predict, because as soon as we can tell exactly how it can be done and when it will be done, then it is no longer future magic, but future technology.

There are, however, some magical things coming in our future that can now be glimpsed, although dimly. Aided by existing theories, we can guess at these magical wonders, but we are very uncertain of how we will attain the technologies that will be needed to turn them from wishful magic into hard reality. Whether they will come true is not known. The theory on which some future magic is based may be wrong and it could never come to pass. The theory may be correct, but the technology needed to achieve the goal may require a material that just doesn't exist. It may be that the theory is correct and the technology is possible, but we decide that the effort involved is more than it is worth. Or—it may be we will be too busy exploring other realms of future magic.

In the following pages are some of the magical things that I can see through the uncertain curtain of the future. Things that are theoretically possible, but so far from our present technical capabilities that they seem almost magical. In the next pages we will visit that black magic marvel of gravitation, the black hole, travel in time and space, and float through the air without wings—defying gravity. We will climb a magic beanstalk into space, fly through the solar system using magic matter, and then go off to the stars on beams of light.

There is magic in our future. How and when it will come we can only guess. But come it will—and sooner than you think.

Future Talk

One of the most magical technologies that we have today is used in the machines by which we talk to each other. These machines would be magic not only to cavemen, but in some cases, even to our parents or grandparents. The simple telephone, the "magic talking box," which sends your voice from one side of town to another, is only a little over 100 years old. You can still use one of those old crank phones to hook into the present telephone network. Now, however, instead of traveling around town by wire, your voice skips across mountaintops on beams of microwaves carrying hundreds of other conversations at the same time; hops up to a communications satellite hanging in the sky, where it is bounced down again to a distant continent; and there, through the magic of international direct dialing, all without human intervention, activates the phone of some person on the far side of the Earth. Sometimes the connection doesn't involve talk between people, but one computer automatically dialing and "talking" to another computer in their arcane language of ones and zeros, transmitting scientific knowledge, the latest stock prices, or even billions of dollars' worth of intangible "money" from one bank account to another, which is then "signed for" by secret one-way passwords.

Then there is the magic of television, just over 50 years old. This "magic picture box," having opened a window onto the world, has not only entertained and educated us, but insidiously has taken us out of the parochial surroundings of our little towns and petty states and made us citizens of the world. We, sitting comfortably at home, now anguish with victims of catastrophes around the globe, exult with victors of all nations during the

4

Olympics, and thrill with explorers as they take the first step on the moon.

These are true examples of future magic that have come into being in just a few generations and have revolutionized our world. Are there more possibilities of future magic in the field of communication? Or are we just limited to modest improvements in the present capabilities of transmitting information around the globe?

I think there is a lot more in store for us. In the research laboratories of the universities and industrial facilities around the world, thousands of scientists and engineers are busy exploring new ideas and concepts for communication. If these new concepts can be made to work, they would make as profound a change to our present way of communicating as the telephone and television did to the letter and the newspaper. Not all of these revolutionary concepts for future talk will come into being. Some will never work because of fundamental difficulties. Others will be a technical success, but will fail because of more pragmatic reasons, such as not being cheap enough to compete with existing communications technology. There are some concepts that will almost certainly come true, such as replacing the present wire and microwave interconnections with high bandwidth optical fibers, and three-dimensional holographic wall television. Since they have already been anticipated in the popular science magazines, however, they are not really good examples of future magic.

But there exist more exotic possibilities for future talk. One possibility would use black boxes that can communicate without wires between any two points on the Earth, even if it means going right through the Earth. This form of future magic just might come true in the next few decades. Then there are even more speculative forms of future talk, where it may be found possible not only to communicate between two different points in space, but two different points in time.

One possible way in which we can talk directly from one point to another on Earth would be to communicate using gravitational waves. Gravitational waves are very much like radio waves except they are made of gravity forces instead of electromagnetic forces. (Unfortunately, water waves in the ocean and air waves in the atmosphere were given the name "gravity waves" a long time ago, since their wavelength is proportional to the strength of the gravity field of the Earth. To avoid confusion, I will use "gravitational waves" to describe waves made of gravity forces.)

We know that gravitational waves exist. Astronomers watching the motion of a pair of co-rotating stars have concluded that because the orbital distance between the star pair is shrinking, they must be emitting waves made of gravity. Dozens of detectors for these gravitational waves are now in operation around the globe, hoping to be the first to detect these elusive weak carriers of gravitational energy. Gravitational waves are not affected much by anything and can pass right through the center of the Earth with ease. If we could find ways to efficiently transmit and receive gravitational waves, then we could build a future-magic graviphone that could allow talk anywhere on Earth without concern for interference from any object.

Gravity has a great deal in common with electricity, except that it is much weaker. Practically everything you can do with electricity you can do with gravity, it is just harder to build the machines. Because of the many similarities between gravity and electricity, it is easy to predict how one might make a communication system based on gravitational radiation. We just examine the techniques by which we communicate using electricity, and then attempt to duplicate those techniques using gravity. Since we are still beginners in the field of gravitational communication, we should not attempt to duplicate our present sophisticated electronic communication technology. Instead, we should look at the fundamentals of the electromagnetic interactions and attempt to duplicate some of the simpler experiments carried out in the early days of electromagnetic research.

The basic starting point for the understanding of the generation and detection of electromagnetic waves is the electric charge. For some yet unknown reason, the electric charges made in nature come in discrete amounts. One particularly useful particle, called the electron, has one unit of negative charge, while other particles, such as the proton, have one unit of positive charge. There are many other particles of different masses and lifetimes, some charged and some not charged. Among these are the mirror particles of the electron and proton, called the positron and antiproton, whose masses are identical to their mirror twins, but whose charge (and magnetic moment) is reversed. There are even speculations about particles with a charge that is one-third or two-thirds that of the electron, but they have yet to be observed.

To make our electrical machines we use the two carriers of charge that are present in enough abundance and last long enough to be useful, the electron and proton. Usually, the two types of charge are bound together in atoms. The protons (along with some uncharged neutrons) form into a positively charged nucleus. The protons are positively charged and repel each other, but the neutrally charged neutrons strongly attract both protons and other neutrons, and thus act as a "glue" to keep the nucleus together despite the repulsive forces between the protons. Surrounding this nucleus is a cloud of negatively charged electrons that define the size of the atom.

If the nucleus is oxygen, then it has eight positively charged protons held together with eight neutrons, giving the nucleus a total positive charge of eight units. Orbiting around that nucleus are eight electrons. The resulting oxygen atom has no net charge and the electrons are bound fairly tightly to the nucleus, so they don't wander around.

There are other types of atoms, however, called metals, where the binding of the last few electrons is not so strong. While a single metal atom all by itself will hold on tightly to its electrons and keep them from wandering away, when that metal atom is in a wire with a lot of other metal atoms, the outer electrons are free to hop from atom to atom, as long as their places are taken by an electron from another atom nearby. Because nature was kind to us and gave us things like metal to make wires out of, we have been able to use the almost-free electrons in those wires to make machines, such as electric lights, telephones, radios, and video games.

The first experiments with electricity used static electricity. Positive charge could be made by rubbing a glass rod with silk; negative charge could be made by rubbing a hard rubber rod with fur. Using these early electrical "generators" to charge up pith balls hanging from silk strings, scientists demonstrated that like electric charges repel while opposite electric charges attract. Later they discovered Leyden jars (metal foil–lined bottles—now called capacitors) to store the electricity, then batteries that could generate electricity from chemical reactions.

Now that batteries could produce a long-lasting supply of electrical energy, other experiments were done using electrical currents made of moving charges. New effects were found. An electrical current moving through a wire created a magnetic field. If the wire were wound around a stick, then current moving through the coil of wire produced an ''electromagnet'' that could pick up pieces of iron just like a magnet made of lodestone. A connection between electricity and magnetism had been found that was unrealized before. Because that connection was found, it became possible to build all the future-magic electromagnetic machines we use today. What kind of future magic would result if we could find a similar connection between electricity and gravity?

It was much later that scientists learned that the magnetism in a lodestone or permanent magnet is really caused by electrical currents. The electrical currents come from the rotation of the electric charge in the electrons and the nuclei. The rotating electric charge acts just like the circulating electric currents in a coil of wire, making each electron and nucleon into a tiny electromagnet with a magnetic moment. In magnetic materials like lodestone and Alnico™, the atoms are aligned so that some of these little tiny magnetic moments add up, while in most other materials, the magnetic moments point in opposite directions and cancel each other out.

Later it was found that when a magnet (either a bar magnet or a newfangled electromagnet) was inserted into a loop of wire, a momentary surge of electrical current was generated. When the magnet is removed, another surge of current occurs, but in the opposite direction. Then it was found that if you ran current first one way, then the other way, through an electromagnet inside a loop of wire, that the outer wire would respond with opposing surges of current. This was the first transformer, a device that allowed electrical energy to be transmitted from one wire to another without the wires touching. The electrical current had to be alternating current (AC) rather than direct current (DC).

It wasn't long before even higher frequencies of current oscillation were tried and the coils were moved farther and farther apart to demonstrate transmission of signals by means of electricity. Then in 1865, James Clerk Maxwell took the four separate, experimentally determined equations for the behavior of electricity and magnetism and combined them into one equation that described the behavior of a new combined electric and magnetic force field, called the electromagnetic force field, that was made by stationary and moving electrical charges. The equation predicted that this electromagnetic field would propagate as a wave and the speed of the wave would be that of the speed of light.

In 1885, after a great deal of experimentation and effort, Heinrich Hertz was the first one to make and detect what he called "electric waves" in the laboratory. He generated the electromagnetic waves by causing large sparks to jump across a gap in a loop of wire and detected the waves by observing sparks appear in the gap of a similar loop of wire at the other end of his laboratory. He measured the velocity and length of the waves (they were very short—what we would call micro-waves today) and found that they traveled at the speed of light. He also showed that the waves could be reflected by metal and bent by glass prisms just as heat and light were. Soon it was established beyond any doubt that light, heat, and Hertzian waves were all just different forms of electromagnetic radiation that obey the Maxwell electromagnetic equations. The only difference was the length of the waves in the radiation and the means by which they were generated and detected.

Considering how difficult it was for Heinrich Hertz to make and detect his electric waves, he would have been astounded to know that within a few generations his discovery would be the force that animates the future-magic boxes that now bring music into our cars and MTV into our homes. To get to that point required many more inventions, however, such as sparkless transmitters that concentrated all the electric energy in a single frequency, better antennas that would couple all of the electro-magnetic energy into the air and direct it accurately to the receiver, and new types of narrow-band, supersensitive receivers that could sense currents consisting of only a few electrons oscillating back and forth in the wires of the receiving antenna.

Compared to the advanced field of electromagnetic commu-nication, the field of gravitational communication is in the pre-Hertz stage. We have an excellent theory that describes the behavior of gravitational waves, and have built some detectors for this gravitational radiation, but there are as yet no really good ideas for devices to generate significant amounts of gravi-tational radiation. We have to depend upon the stars to make the radiation for us.

The theory that predicts the behavior of gravitational waves is the Einstein theory of gravity, usually called the General Theory of Relativity. The Einstein gravity theory predicts that masses with a time-varying velocity give off waves made of time-varying gravity fields. These gravitational waves have the same velocity of propagation as that of light or electromagnetic waves. Although gravitational waves have many similarities to electromagnetic waves they also have some differences.

If you take an electron with its one unit of charge and move it rapidly (by using electric forces to shove it up and down the radio transmitter tower as an electrical current), the Maxwell theory of electromagnetism predicts that electromagnetic waves will be generated. If you take an object with mass and move it rapidly, the Einstein theory of gravity predicts that gravitational waves will be generated.

The difference is that to move a massive object rapidly, you must apply a force to it, and that force has to be applied by a machine; and that machine, in its attempt to move the object, will respond by moving in the opposite direction; and since the machine has mass, it will generate gravitational radiation that is of *opposite* phase to the gravitational radiation from the object that the machine is moving. The amount of gravitational radiation generated by a moving object is proportional not only to the mass of the generating object but the amplitude of its motion. Because of the Newton Law of Conservation of Momentum (the law of equal and opposite reaction) the small object moves faster and thereby generates just as much gravitational radiation as the larger machine moving more slowly. Since the two sources generate the same strength of gravitational radiation, but their phases are opposite, it turns out that any currently conceivable method for making gravitational waves involves two sources that almost cancel each other out!

Since the transmitting object and the machine that drives it are not at the same place in space, however, there is a slight difference in the phases of the two gravitational waves in certain directions, so that gravitational radiation does get emitted. The amount of radiation generated, however, is but a small fraction of what would be generated if it were not for the effect of the Newton Law of Conservation of Momentum.

According to the Einstein theory of gravity, the simplest generator of gravitational waves would be two massive objects that either vibrate back and forth or rotate around a common center. To get the most radiation, the objects should be very dense so that the gravitational fields they generate are strong (miniature black holes would be nice), moving very rapidly (just below the speed of light would be nice), and very strong (so they don't distort or disintegrate under the forces being applied to them).

Unfortunately, all we have available to us for the manufacture of a gravitational radiation generator is ordinary matter like steel and tungsten. The speed of vibration or rotation of ordinary matter is limited by the rupture strength of the materials. This is roughly the speed of sound in the metal, which is about 3,000 meters per second, only 10^{-5} the velocity of light. The amount of gravitational radiation emitted by a rotating or vibrating object can be shown to be proportional to the sixth power of the speed of rotation or vibration. Thus, if the speed of a gravitational wave generator is limited by the velocity of sound, the gravitational waves emitted will be 10^{-30} of the strength of the gravitational waves that would be emitted if the machine could be operated at speeds approaching that of light. To give some examples of where we are in this pre-Hertz era of gravitational communication, a massive rod of steel a meter long and weighing a ton, spun to its breaking point, would emit a mere 10^{-37} watts of gravitational radiation. This is far too weak to detect with any known gravitational wave detector.

One of the early pioneers in gravitational radiation, Joseph Weber, found a way around the speed-of-sound barrier by proposing that strong electric fields be applied to a large cube of piezoelectric crystal. The electric fields would set up stresses inside the crystal. In the Einstein theory of gravity, not only moving masses but changing stresses can create gravitational waves. Weber predicted that a crystal cube a half-meter in size stressed uniformly by strong applied electric fields would produce 100,000 gravitons per second with a one-meter wavelength. (A graviton is a single quantum of gravitational radiation, just as a photon is a single quantum of electromagnetic radiation.) This sounds like a significant accomplishment, but 100,000 gravitons per second at that wavelength represents a total emitted power level of only 10^{-20} watts. Unfortunately, present receivers for that wavelength are ten orders of magnitude from detecting that level of power.

To date, the only effective sources of gravitational radiation are two neutron stars or black holes orbiting each other at high rotational speeds with periods of hours to milliseconds (see Figure 1); stars or planets falling into a galactic-sized black hole; and the vibrating neutron stars or black holes created in the interior of an exploding supernova.

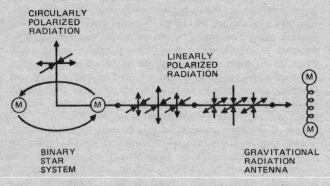

CIRCULARLY
POLARIZED
RADIATION

LINEARLY
POLARIZED
RADIATION

M

M

M

M

BINARY
STAR
SYSTEM

GRAVITATIONAL
RADIATION
ANTENNA

**Figure 1. Gravitational radiation from
a binary star system.**

Although we have no good ideas yet for transmitters of gravitational signals, we have many excellent ideas for receivers of gravitational signals. Most of these are due to Joseph Weber, who was the first one to look at gravitation from an engineering point of view. (Most courses on gravity are taught by mathematically oriented physicists, who, preferring economy of description, simplify their mathematical expressions by using an arcane system of units where the Newton gravity constant G, the speed of light c, and Planck's quantum constant h are all one—with *no* units! In this strange, nonintuitive system of units, both mass and time are measured in centimeters, a unit of length. This makes the equations easy to write, but removes any sense of the magnitude or importance of the terms in the equations. Weber teaches his gravity courses using engineering units so the student is constantly impressed by the extremely large masses and exceptionally high velocities that are needed to make just a few watts of gravitational radiation.)

In the middle 1900s, some of the more mathematically oriented physicists had even predicted that gravitational waves would be unobservable. They could prove that for every mathematical solution of the Einstein gravity equations that showed evidence of gravitational waves being emitted, they could transform the coordinate system (using specially constructed coordinate transformation equations) so that there was no energy left in the gravitational wave. In 1960, Joseph Weber used the Einstein General Theory of Relativity to show that not only did waves made of gravity carry energy, but that some of that energy could be extracted by a properly constructed gravitational receiving antenna. It turned out that the arbitrary coordinate systems that purported to show that gravitational waves did not have any energy were so artificial that the ad hoc coordinate transformations *themselves* carried energy and could be detected by the same type of antennas. By using operational definitions of masses connected by elastic springs and energy absorbers Joseph Weber cut through the mathematical confusion and showed how to make a gravitational wave receiver.

The basic concept for a gravitational radiation detector is to have two or more massive objects separated by a distance and coupled by some spring or energy-absorbing mechanism. As the gravitational wave moves through space it applies a gravitational squeeze to everything that it passes through. Since the forces that the gravitational wave applies are proportional to the mass of the object, big objects are pushed harder than small objects. Since the response of an object depends inversely on its mass, however, this means that all objects move the same amount, no matter what their mass.

This is not true for radio waves. If a radio wave goes by your car, the radio wave moves the electrons up and down in your car antenna, but they don't move your car. Since the car is standing still and the electrons in the antenna are moving, your car radio can detect the motion of the electrons with respect to the car and turn that detected relative motion into music. If a gravitational wave passed by your car it would move the electrons in the antenna just as much as it would move the car. Since the radio can detect only relative motion between the electrons and the car, it doesn't respond well to gravitational waves.

Joseph Weber showed that if two objects are separated by a distance, the passage of a gravitational wave would be observable by detecting the small change in the distance between the objects. If the two objects were in the same place, they would move together, but if they were separated, then the forces due to the gravitational wave would be slightly different in the two places. The two objects would move in slightly different directions and the distance between them would change. If the objects were connected by a spring, then the relative motion would cause the spring to be stretched, increasing the energy in the spring at the expense of an equivalent loss of energy in the gravitational wave.

The differential motion of the two detecting objects in a gravity antenna could be detected by any number of means. One way is to apply some kind of strain detector to the spring, like a piezoelectric crystal that produces electrical voltage when it is either compressed or stretched. This, in fact, was the first type of energy converter used in gravitational radiation receivers. Another is to measure the relative acceleration of the two masses. Supersensitive superconducting accelerometers are now the preferred method for detecting the response of gravitational radiation antennas. A third obvious technique is to measure the relative distance between the two masses with a laser.

I demonstrated the laser measurement technique in 1973 when I made the first laser interferometer gravitational radiation antenna. I used a high-power laser to measure the eight-meter distance between three massive blocks in an L-shaped optical interferometer to an accuracy of 10^{-15} meters. This meant measuring a distance that was one-billionth of a wavelength of the laser light we were using to make the measurement and one-thousandth of the diameter of the nucleus of an atom. A longer version of the laser interferometer antenna is now under study as a gravitational telescope.

I was also involved in the construction of the first detector for gravitational radiation. I was working as a graduate student under the direction of Joseph Weber and David Zipoy at the University of Maryland in the early 1960s. Instead of building an antenna consisting of two massive objects connected at the middle by a spring, we decided on a distributed version of the antenna consisting of a fat bar of aluminum five feet long, two feet in diameter, and weighing a little over a ton. The two ends of the bar would be the masses and the portion of the aluminum bar in the middle would be the spring. According to Weber's theory, a gravitational wave coming along at right angles to the axis of the bar would stretch and compress the bar, setting it into vibration.

I installed piezoelectric sensors along the waist of the bar that would respond to the vibrations and produce tiny voltages that were amplified by supersensitive cryogenically cooled amplifiers. This first antenna did not detect large gravity signals coming from space, but there were some small signals that looked interesting. The first bar antenna went to the Smithsonian Museum of Science and Technology where it can be found suspended from its wire harness in the middle of the floor, acting as a large aluminum rocking horse for the younger visitors.

Larger bars and disks of aluminum convinced Joseph Weber that gravitational radiation bursts from stellar objects had been observed. The signal-to-noise of his events was poor, however, and although similar results were obtained by a group in Italy, to this date many scientists do not believe that gravitational radiation has been detected. The work goes on. Joseph Weber and many others are continuing with designs for ever more sensitive detectors of gravitational waves, and one of these days, one of those designs will be sensitive enough to unambiguously measure the shape of a burst of gravitational radiation from the stars. It may be a short *chirp* coming from two black holes whirling about each other a thousand times a *second* in a furious do-si-do, or the multiovertone *bong* of a vibrating neutron star in its first few milliseconds of life at the center of a still-expanding supernova explosion. By examining the detailed structure of these signals, physicists expect to check the validity of the present Einstein General Theory of Relativity in strong gravitational fields (where it has yet to be tested), and astronomers hope to learn about the death throes of stars as they reach the end of their lives and shuck off great fractions of their mass and angular momentum to turn into neutron stars and black holes.

Despite the decades of work that have gone into constructing gravitational radiation detectors, they are still in a very crude state compared to detectors for electromagnetic radiation. For example, the bar antennas are too short. They are limited in length by the speed of sound through the metal, whereas it would be desirable for their length to be limited by the speed of light. So present bar antennas are 100,000 times shorter than they should be. The bar antennas are also lossy. If a gravitational wave passes through the antenna and puts energy into it, the energy shows up as vibrations in the bar. The metal in the bar has very little loss and the vibrations stay in the bar for many minutes before they turn into heat. The detector would be better if the metal had *no* losses and the only loss mechanism were the reradiation of gravity waves by the vibrations. This is true for our radio and TV antennas, but gravity detectors are some 10^{30} times short of this goal. In summary, trying to detect gravitational waves with the present bar antennas would be like trying to pick up a distant TV station by using a short stub of carbon as the pickup antenna for your television set, or an optical astronomer trying to take a picture of a distant galaxy using a pinhole for a telescope lens and blueprint paper for film.

Yet, if we look back to the early days of radio, with Hertz transmitting and receiving radio waves with loops of wire as antennas and spark gaps as detectors, we can begin to imagine the future improvements to come in gravitational waves. The basic problem, of course, is the weakness of the gravitational force compared to the other forces of nature. To make and detect gravitational waves we need dense masses and must be able to move them at high speeds. In electromagnetism we have the magic material we call "electrical conductors," which are full of free electrons that move at nearly the speed of light from one end of the metal wire to the other. (An electron pushed in one end of a piece of wire does not really travel to the other end at near-light speed; instead, that electron pushes on the next electron which pushes on the next electron until the last electron pops out of the other end of the wire a short time later. Since we can't tell one electron from the other, it is equivalent to having the electron travel from one end to the other at nearly the speed of light.)

For gravitational communication we need an equivalent magic material. We need a "mass conductor" that is densely packed with mass that can move at nearly the speed of light. Unfortunately, normal matter is not very dense since it consists of atoms that are mostly empty space with nearly all the mass in the small dense nucleus in the center of the atom. Then, the springy clouds of electrons that make up the outer portions of the atoms limit the speed of motion of the atoms to the speed of sound. If we could ever find and control miniature black holes, then it might be possible to excite vibrations or rotations in these miniature sources of strong gravitational fields to make significant amounts of gravitational radiation.

As Richard Matzner and others have pointed out, a charged miniature black hole is one possible way of converting electromagnetic waves into gravitational waves. Electromagnetic waves will interact with the charge on the black hole while gravitational waves will interact with the mass of the black hole. Since the electric charge on a miniature black hole is strongly coupled to the mass of the black hole, the electromagnetic field can be coupled to the gravitational field through this mutual coupling of the charge and mass. Matzner calculated the cross section and found, as expected, it was extremely small. But interestingly, he found that when the electromagnetic and gravitational wavelengths were much larger than the size of the miniature black hole (which would be much smaller than an atom), then it did not depend upon the details of the black hole; indeed, it didn't matter whether it was a black hole or not. Thus, a non-black hole object, like an electron or proton, that has charge as well as mass, can also interconvert electromagnetic and gravitational radiation. If a large number of electrons all act together, then the conversion efficiency goes as the square of the number of electrons.

Matzner ends by speculating on the possibility of an advanced technology uniformly illuminating a perfect crystal of electrons weighing ten tons with an X-ray laser with a wavelength of one angstrom and somehow suppressing all the electromagnetic radiation channels open for scattering of the X rays. With only gravitational radiation channels allowed, coherence in the crystal would lead to a substantial enhancement of the conversion efficiency to a small fraction of 1 percent, which would be more than sufficient. The resulting one-angstrom wavelength gwaser (gravitational wave amplification by stimulated emission of radiation) beam could in principle be detected by inserting a similar crystal in the beam path and detecting the electromagnetic X rays produced by the reverse process. It will be a long time before we can make powerful X-ray lasers and perfect electron crystals weighing many tons, but both topics are being strongly pursued today. We have all read in the newspapers about the classified efforts to make an X-ray laser for possible use in the Space Defense Initiative. What most of us are unaware of, however, is that other scientists are also active in attempts to make electron crystals. They are using strong magnetic field traps to contain, cool, and condense small clouds of electrons despite the natural repulsive forces between the electrons. Perhaps out of this fundamental research on X-ray lasers and electron physics will come the key to efficient generation and detection of gravitational radiation.

Then again, it might be possible that we will find some different way of controlling gravity. As advances in our understanding of science improve, one of the expected results is the discovery of the so-called "Unified Field Theory," which would describe all the known forces—electromagnetic, nuclear, weak, and gravity—as different aspects of a more fundamental force. Once we have that theory, it may be possible to build different kinds of machines that transform easy-to-make electromagnetic waves into gravitational waves, or allow us to combine electricity and gravity to make electrogravitic waves as we once combined electricity and magnetism to make electromagnetic waves. The machines to do this are magic to us now, but in our children's future, graviphones may be as commonplace as radiophones are today.

One of the most elusive particles in the ever-growing zoo of "elementary particles" is the neutrino. The neutrino is the nearest thing to nothing known to exist. The present description of a neutrino is that it is a traveling bundle of energy with no rest mass and no charge—just spin, and only a half-unit of spin, at that. We still have a lot more to learn about neutrinos, for they come in a number of different types of neutrino/antineu-trino pairs, and there is a suspicion that one or more of the pairs might have some rest mass. But we don't need to know every-thing about them to use them for talking to each other.

The biggest advantage and the biggest liability of neutrinos for communication is that, like gravitational waves, nothing stops them. It would take light-years of lead to stop the average neutrino, so if you build a communications system using a neutrino beam, you don't have to worry about intervening buildings or mountains blocking your path. To communicate with anyone, you just point your transmitter at the receiver (even straight down if the receiver is on the opposite side of the Earth) and the neutrino beam will pass right through any obstruction. But this penetrating power of neutrinos also makes it difficult to use them. Most matter is so transparent to neutrinos that it is difficult to make a receiver to detect the neutrino beam. The neutrinos pass right through the receiver without activating it.

In the past few years, however, some theoretical and exper-imental research carried out by Joseph Weber of the University of Maryland (the same Joseph Weber who pioneered the research into gravitational wave detectors) has given us some clues as to how one might make a future-magic neutrino telephone that would use neutrino beams to talk directly to any point in Earth and space. To understand how such a neutrinophone might work, we need to know a little more about neutrinos, especially how they are formed and how they interact with normal matter.

Normal matter is made up of atoms. There is a nucleus in the center of the atom that contains the protons and neutrons, which have most of the mass of the atom. A typical nucleus has approximately equal numbers of protons and neutrons, but as the mass of the atom increases, the number of neutrons needed in the nucleus to keep it stable increases. Finally we get to the very heavy atoms, such as radium and uranium, where there are many more neutrons than protons.

Unless the neutrons are tightly bound in the nucleus of an atom, they are not stable. If a neutron is left to itself, after about 15 minutes it will decay into a proton and an electron. In the lighter elements, the neutron is tightly bound in the nucleus so that this decay process is prevented. In the heavier elements, however, the binding of the neutrons is not as strong and occasionally a neutron inside a nucleus will decay. The electron will be ejected from the nucleus while the proton will stay. The reverse reaction also occurs occasionally, with a proton emitting an antielectron (positron) and turning into a neutron.

These processes cause the radioactive decay of the heavy elements like radium, transforming them ultimately into stable isotopes of lead. When the particles emitted from this kind of decay were first observed, the scientists didn't know what they were, so they called them "beta" particles. Later they found out the beta particles were sometimes negatively charged electrons and sometimes positively charged antielectrons.

When radioactive beta decay was first observed, there was a great deal of puzzlement. Since the neutron is rotating and has a half-unit of spin, and it decays into a proton and an electron, both of which have a half-unit of spin, it looked as though angular momentum was being created out of nowhere. Also, the electrons emitted during the decay process had a wide spectrum of energies. Some of the electrons had almost no energy and some had very high energies. The maximum energy of the electrons just equaled the energy due to the mass difference between the mass of the neutron in the nucleus and the combined masses of the proton plus electron, but most of the electrons had much less energy. Mass was being destroyed in the beta decay process, but only some of the missing mass was showing up as energy in the electrons. It looked as though mass or energy was disappearing.

To solve the problem, in 1931 Wolfgang Pauli hypothesized the existence of a new particle that would have no charge, so it would not be detected by charged particle detectors; spin one-half, so it would balance out the spins generated in beta decay; zero rest mass, so that the predicted range of electrons emitted from the beta decay process would fit the experimentally observed spectrum (which went from zero to maximum energy); and would interact so weakly with other matter that it would escape from any conceivable container without depositing any of its energy. Enrico Fermi named the particle *neutrino*, which is Italian for "little neutral one." There would be two types: the antineutrino, which would be emitted along with an electron in negative beta decay when a neutron in a nucleus turned into a proton; and the neutrino, which would be emitted along with a positron in positive beta decay when a proton turned into a neutron.

The postulated neutrino solved the case of the missing spin and energy in beta decay, but it would be two decades before one would be detected. In 1956 neutrinos were first experimentally observed when the flood of antineutrinos from a nuclear reactor was found to produce a few neutrons and positrons after reacting with the protons in water. Until that time, scientists had been assuming the existence of the neutrino on faith alone. They were so sure that the laws of conservation of angular momentum and mass/energy were obeyed, that they preferred to believe in an "unobservable" particle rather than give up their beliefs in the conservation laws. Later, the physicists even invented different neutrino/antineutrino pairs—the muon neutrinos and the tau neutrinos—to explain the decay spectrum of those more exotic particles.

Neutrinos are emitted in copious quantities by nuclear reactors and the sun (which is a large fusion nuclear reactor). It has been estimated that nearly 10 percent of the energy released by the sun is carried away by neutrinos and that 10^{14} solar neutrinos pass through the human body every second! The flux of solar neutrinos is being measured by a neutrino "telescope" consisting of a large tank containing 610 tons of dry cleaning fluid (carbon tetrachloride or C_2Cl_4) buried deep in a mine. About 25 percent of the chlorine atoms are the isotope chlorine 37. When a neutron in the nucleus of the chlorine atom captures a neutrino from the sun, it emits an electron and turns into a proton. The chlorine-37 atom with 17 protons has been transformed into an argon-37 atom containing 18 protons. Periodically the carbon tetrachloride liquid in the tank is flushed with helium, which collects the argon gas atoms generated by the capture of neutrinos. The argon atoms are counted in a mass spectrometer. The experiment has indeed been detecting solar neutrinos—but only one-third as many as what theory predicts. No one yet knows why.

Since it is relatively easy to make lots of neutrinos and they are not blocked by anything, they would seem to be the ideal medium for sending messages, if only we could find a way to detect them. The neutrino is only absorbed when it hits a proton or a neutron in a nucleus head-on, and even then the probability of actually interacting is extremely small. It is these extremely weak interactions that have limited speculations on neutrino communication systems.

Joseph Weber seems to have found an effect, however, that might make it possible to detect those elusive neutrinos in sufficient quantities to send messages back and forth through the

Earth. Some say it is an illusion, like a magic trick, while others say it is true magic, future magic, and it really does happen. The future will determine which is true.

The Weber Effect depends upon some very subtle aspects of crystal physics and quantum mechanics. A similar effect occurs in the radioactive decay of excited atoms that emit gamma rays (high-energy photons, or X rays). Rudolf Mössbauer won the Nobel Prize for discovering what is now known as the Mössbauer Effect, by predicting that if gamma-radioactive atoms were formed into a crystal before they decayed, then some of the gamma rays emitted by the decay of the atoms in the crystal would be emitted as though they came from the whole crystal, not just a single atom.

When an excited atom emits a gamma ray, the excitation energy is shared by the gamma ray and the atom. Most of the excitation energy goes into making the gamma ray, which shoots off in some random direction. When the gamma ray leaves, however, it gives a parting kick to the atom, which moves off in the opposite direction (to conserve momentum). This motion requires some energy, so the final gamma-ray energy is not quite equal to the excitation energy. If the excited atom is very light, then the kick from the gamma ray is strong and the atom ends up with a lot of energy. If the excited atom is very heavy, then its recoil velocity is less, and since the energy goes as the square of the velocity, the energy in the atom is less. If the atom could be made infinitely heavy, then it would recoil at an infinitesimally small velocity and nearly all the excitation energy would end up in the gamma ray. (This is the reason why a hunting rifle kicks less if you hold on to it tightly. By adding the mass of your body to the mass of the rifle, the amount of recoil velocity needed to conserve momentum is less.)

It turns out that when atoms are formed into crystalline solids, the atoms, being coupled together, no longer behave as single atoms, but react collectively. If the crystal structure is poor, an atom only "senses" a few of the atoms around it. If the crystal structure is good, then the motion of an atom is influenced by atoms many millimeters away (and there are a lot of them within a millimeter). In such crystals, only certain vibration levels are allowed by quantum mechanics, and it takes a certain amount of energy to excite those vibrations. If the crystal is made up of excited atoms with low excitation energy that emit low-energy gamma rays, then the amount of recoil energy given to the atom would be low. If this recoil energy is less than the amount needed to excite one quantum of vibration in the crystal, then the vibrational excitation will not occur. The gamma ray will leave the atom with all of the excitation energy. In effect, the gamma ray has "pushed off" from the entire crystal, not just one atom, because the atoms in the crystal acted collectively as one heavy atom.

It is important to note that the "size" of the emitted gamma ray is quite tiny. Its typical wavelength is less than the size of an atom, so it is not the gamma ray that "senses" the other atoms in the crystal. Instead, it is the collective coupling of the atoms themselves that allows one atom to "sense" and respond to the presence of atoms many centimeters away in the crystal.

The gamma rays emitted by a crystal of excited atoms can be stopped by a similar crystal of unexcited atoms. In a typical Mössbauer Effect experiment, a transmitter crystal of excited atoms is placed on one part of an apparatus and a blocking crystal of unexcited atoms is placed on another part. Behind the blocking crystal is placed a detector of gamma rays. When the blocking crystal is standing absolutely still with respect to the transmitter crystal, most of the gamma rays are reabsorbed by the unexcited atoms in the blocking crystal and the number of counts detected in the gamma ray detector drops dramatically. When either the transmitting or blocking crystal moves, however, the motion causes the gamma ray frequency to be shifted by the Doppler effect. The gamma rays are no longer "tuned" to the absorption line of the atom and they go through the blocking crystal into the detector. Velocities as small as a few millimeters per hour have been measured using the Mössbauer Effect.

Joseph Weber has taken the collective atom picture that has been experimentally verified by the Mössbauer Effect and applied it to the detection of neutrinos. He has calculated that a crystal containing N atoms has a cross section for the stopping of neutrinos that is N^2 times the cross section of an individual atom. For a crystal the size of a pea weighing a gram, the number of atoms is about 10^{24}, so according to his theory, the cross section of the crystal should be increased by a factor of 10^{48} over that of a single atom. Thus, if properly made, a few grams of crystal should be able to scatter most of the low-energy neutrinos striking it.

The crystal has to be stiff and pure and cold. If the crystal is not stiff, then only the very low energy neutrinos will be stopped. If the crystal is not pure, but has dislocations or regions where the crystallinity is not perfect, then it cannot be considered a single crystal, but is a bunch of smaller crystals. Since the cross section goes as the square of the number of scatterers, one large crystal will have ten times the cross section of ten small crystals with the same total mass. If the crystal is not cold, then there are vibrations in it that, in effect, "decouple" the atoms from one another, lowering the effective size of the crystal.

We don't have a highly efficient neutrino detector to place in back of the neutrino-blocking crystal as was done to detect the gamma rays in the Mössbauer Effect experiments. Thus, to detect the Weber Effect scattering of the neutrinos by a crystal, we must measure the action of the neutrinos on the crystal itself. Although one low-energy neutrino bouncing off a gram-sized crystal doesn't push it very much, the 10^{14} neutrinos per second coming from the sun or a nuclear reactor can give a measurable "shove" to a crystal. Joseph Weber has reported that he has used a sensitive torsion balance to detect the difference in force on a scattering crystal when another crystal was used to block the neutrinos from a reactor or the sun. He is continuing his experiments and soon others will repeat them in an attempt to confirm his results.

If it turns out that Joseph Weber is correct and his experiments are really detecting the highly efficient scattering of neutrinos by crystals a few centimeters in size, rather than light-years in size, then it isn't hard to imagine a future magic breakthrough in communications that would make obsolete our present point-to-point long-distance communication systems such as microwave links, undersea cables, and communication satellites, and perhaps even our multipoint and broadcasting systems such as telephone, radio, and television.

Large fixed point-to-point neutrino communication systems might want to use sources of neutrinos such as nuclear reactors. The reactors would be surrounded by a crystal shield with a hole in it. The neutrinos would leave the reactor, bounce around inside the shield until they found the hole, then leave in a collimated beam. If the shield were highly reflective and the hole were small, then the number of neutrinos inside the shield would build up in intensity until the number of neutrinos per second exiting in a beam from the small hole equaled the total number of neutrinos emitted per second from the whole reactor.

Portable communication systems could be powered by the neutrinos emitted from sealed vials of radioactive wastes with walls so thick that the only radiation that could get out would be heat and neutrinos. It may be that someday people will be paying high prices for radioactive waste and mining the nuclear waste dumps in order to get neutrino emitters to power their communication systems.

Then again, we already have a bright source of neutrinos in the sun. It might be possible to collect the neutrino light from the sun (even if it were on the other side of the Earth) and use that flux to power our neutrino communication system. Such a system would not need a power source, provided it had a method of tracking the position of the sun. This should not be too hard, since we would have to have the capability of detecting neutrinos to make the communication system work, and we could just use those detectors to find the brightest spot in the sky (or ground).

The receivers for the neutrino communication system would again be highly reflective crystals with sensitive force or energy detectors built into them to sense the recoil of the crystal as the flood of neutrinos in the transmitted beam bounce off it. One obvious sensing element is a piezoelectric crystal that generates electricity when a force is applied to it. Weber, Zipoy, and I used these in Weber's detectors for gravitational radiation to sense the tiny forces induced in the detector as the gravitational wave passed through it. Other obvious detectors are the super-conducting accelerometers currently favored for gravitational radiation antennas.

There are many problems left in implementing a neutrino communication system, such as devising a method for modulating the neutrino beam at high rates. Waving a blocking crystal back and forth in front of the hole in the transmitter is not going to be fast enough to allow the transmission of televi-sion-type pictures. But if the present research of Joseph Weber on highly efficient neutrino reflectors proves his theory correct, then in the not-too-distant future we may find ourselves talking from one point on the globe to another, using a neutrinophone that is as magical to us today as the telephone would have been to the people in the Middle Ages.

* * *

Another future-magic possibility for a communication system would be the use of tachyons to send messages. Tachyons are particles hypothesized by Gerald Feinberg and others that are postulated to travel *faster* than the speed of light. Tachyons are allowed to exist by the present theories of physics, but although they have been looked for, they have yet to be found. That is fortunate, since they would cause major philosophical problems if they were found. Since tachyons travel faster than the speed of light, they could be used to send messages not only back and forth through space, but back and forth through time. A black box that used tachyons for communication would indeed be future magic.

The Einstein Special Theory of Relativity is Einstein's theory for the behavior of matter and energy at high speeds. His theory predicts many strange things. As an object moves at velocities approaching that of the speed of light it gets heavier, it shrinks in the direction of travel, and time runs slower for it than for the rest of the universe. Because the object gets heavier as its velocity increases, it gets harder to push. As the speed of the object approaches the speed of light, the mass of the object approaches infinity, so according to the Einstein Special Theory of Relativity it is impossible for an object with mass to be pushed up to the speed of light. If a particle has no mass to begin with, just energy (some examples are photons, gravitons, and neutrinos), then the Einstein Special Theory of Relativity requires that the object travel *at* the speed of light to exist.

The Einstein Special Theory of Relativity is one of the best-tested theories known. We now have huge particle accelerators that can increase the velocity of particles until they exceed 99.99 percent of the speed of light. If they are particles that normally decay in billionths of a second, we can keep them alive a thousand times longer than their normal lifetimes by keeping them moving at high speed. The change in lifetime is exactly as Einstein predicted it. As we accelerate them to higher and higher velocities, we find that they become thousands of times heavier than normal and we have to keep adjusting our bending magnets to compensate for the increased mass and we find they get harder to push—just as Einstein predicted. The Einstein Special Theory of Relativity is well tested and anything it predicts should be taken seriously.

The Einstein Special Theory of Relativity has been invoked

in the past to say that it is impossible for anything to travel *faster* than the speed of light. Since, according to the theory, anything that had no rest mass had to travel *at* the speed of light and anything with rest mass had to travel *below* the speed of light, that seemed a reasonable conclusion. Then Gerald Feinberg noticed that the equations of the Einstein Special Theory of Relativity allowed a particle to travel *faster* than the speed of light if the particle had an "imaginary" rest mass. He called these hypothetical particles *tachyons,* from the Greek word *tachys,* for "swift." Particles that travel slower than the speed of light are then called *bradyons,* from the Greek word *brady,* for "slow," while objects that travel *at* the speed of light are called *luxons.*

The Einstein Special Theory of Relativity requires that the tachyons *always* travel *faster* than the speed of light. There is no problem with the tachyons having to get across the light barrier. Just as photons are created traveling *at* the speed of light, tachyons would be created traveling *faster* than the speed of light. Once the tachyons are made, you have to put energy into them to make them travel slower. As they are slowed down to approach the speed of light, they get heavier and the amount of energy needed to slow them down increases to infinity. Conversely, as they lose energy they move faster and faster with no upper limit to their velocity.

The fact that theoretically the tachyons have an imaginary rest mass is also not a problem. Since the tachyons always have to travel faster than the speed of light, they will never be at rest. Thus, their "rest mass" is not an observable quantity, just something for the theorists to put into their equations to make the numbers work out right. The observable quantities of a tachyon are its energy, momentum, charge, and lifetime. All of these are ordinary real quantities that can be measured.

One of the major objections to the possible existence of tachyons is that since they travel faster than the speed of light, some observers will see them traveling backward in time. Thus, it looks as though it would be possible to arrange a situation where tachyons could be observed in a detector *before* they were emitted by the transmitter; in effect, the messages carried by the tachyons would be sent backward in time. This would seem to allow a violation of the principle of causality, in that an effect would appear in time before the cause.

If the transmitter and receiver are not moving with respect to each other (or moving very slowly compared to the speed of light), then neither the operator of the transmitter nor the operator of the receiver will notice any violation of causality. A transmitter on Mars emits a message using tachyons traveling at one million times the speed of light and it is received on Earth a fraction of a second later, whereas a radio message from Mars takes a good part of an hour to reach Earth. To the receiver of the message, the tachyons always arrive *after* they are sent (although sooner than if they had been sent by radio).

But if someone were flying by the solar system in a rapidly moving spaceship in just the right direction at a high enough speed, and could somehow observe (using flashing lights on the transmitter and receiver perhaps) the instants of transmission and reception of the tachyons containing the message, then he would calculate (using the Einstein Special Theory of Relativity) that the tachyon message was received on Earth *before* it was transmitted from Mars. This observer would complain that causality is being violated, but those involved in the communication would not see any causality violation. Thus, although the existence of tachyons would raise some problems with causality, they are not major ones. Our present ideas of causality (which, by the way, are only based on "common sense," not any law of physics) would not be violated, only slightly disheveled.

There have been many attempts to find evidence for the existence of tachyons in various experiments, though most of them have reported negative results. One that did report the probable detection of tachyons occurred in 1974. Roger Clay and Philip Crouch were doing some cosmic ray experiments in South Australia using large arrays of particle detectors sitting out in the Australian desert. These detector arrays were designed to detect showers of ordinary particles produced when high-energy cosmic rays strike the upper atmosphere. An incoming high-energy cosmic ray will strike an air atom at about 20 to 40 kilometers altitude, producing a large shower of different kinds of particles all traveling at nearly the speed of light. The shower reaches the ground some 60 to 120 microseconds later.

To search for tachyons, they added a high-speed data recorder to their arrays of detectors and kept the recorder running all the time. When a shower of particles was observed, they then looked to see if there were any responses in the detector *before* the main shower arrived. Combining the results of over 1000 showers, they found a significant excess of events in the interval between 15 and 60 microseconds prior to the arrival of the main shower (which presumably was traveling at nearly light speed). They attribute these events to tachyons generated by the cosmic ray, but other scientists prefer to look for more mundane solutions.

Whether tachyons can be generated and detected is still an open question. If it turns out they can, then their existence will not only revolutionize physics and cosmology, but will drastically alter our perception of space, time, and causality. It will also, incidentally, present us with a future magic telephone that will cut the solar system, and even the universe, down to size. For with the tachyphone a call to Arcturus tomorrow will be no more difficult than a call to the Arctic today.

As a closing note, there are in progress today a number of efforts to search for radio signals possibly being sent by intelligent beings on planets around other stars. This Search for Extra-Terrestrial Intelligence (SETI) program has listened to many stars and has yet heard nothing. The search continues, but as time goes on, the lack of success may lead some to conclude that either intelligent, garrulous, radio-transmitting species are rare or that everybody is listening and no one is transmitting.

Instead, it could be that there are plenty of signals passing back and forth between stars, but the alien civilizations don't use such a primitive method of communication as radio waves, which get distorted and attenuated by the interstellar plasma. Instead, they might be using a much more efficient future-magic means of communication that we are not even aware of.

Jungle natives on Earth take pride in their ability to send messages from one tribe to another with drums, while over their heads and through their bodies are passing the electromagnetic signals from our broadcasting stations and communication satellites. We could be the technological equivalent of those jungle natives, sending our insignificant messages from one national tribe to another with our electronic tom-toms, while all the while passing through us are extraterrestrial signals of some more exotic kind.

What kind of carrier would this more efficient method of communication use to send messages? It could use the neutrinos, gravitons, and tachyons I have talked about here. It could use even more exotic particles that have been postulated by various theorists such as axions, majorons, gravitinos, or arions. Or it could use . . . (since we don't know what it is, or how it works, or what *they* call it) . . . magic. Future magic.

Magic Matter

You watch the screen as the aging executive ponders the stocks you suggested: Rotavator, Ltd., or MirrorMat, Inc., the new subsidiary of General Energy. Both are equally good investments. Your eyes wander to the clock at the top of the screen. It is near quitting time.

"Thank God it's Thursday," you mutter as the image on the screen finally decides to invest 35,000 international accounting units in MirrorMat, Inc. You politely inquire about the weather in Paris, then switch back to local. With relief you place the buy order, make your weekly sales report to the home office in Australia, and initiate shutdown as the clock reaches 16:00:00.

A hard day's work done, and you deserve the long holiday weekend coming up. With the Fourth of July falling on Monday, you are going to enjoy four days at the glamorous Sahara Copernicus in Las Lunas, with its fabulous casinos and nonstop entertainment. What you want to see is the new "Holiday in Flight" show, with swooping chorus lines of aerobats flying about in shimmering white wings in the low lunar gravity.

You open the door to the office, step out into the Arizona sunshine, and walk over to your Chevy Astro-Cruiser. Checking to make sure that the propellant tanks are topped off with water and there is plenty of magic matter in the storage bottle, you take off. Under controlled power, the 'Cruiser mutters off into the deep desert, heading for the greenly glaring pillar of fire that streaks upward into the sky. As you approach, you see others riding up on that green beam, boosted into low Earth orbit by laser tugs that collect the light from a battery of lasers surrounding the launch site, then use the energy to heat water into a blazing plasma exhaust that is too hot to be called steam.

The waiting line is too long. This is your vacation, so hang

31

the expense. You shoot your 'Cruiser into orbit using magic matter, despite the price per milligram of the stuff. Once up in orbit, you set the computer for the nearest space station and the jet spouts a flare of incandescent hydrogen and oxygen as invisible particles of magic matter are mixed with buckets of water. At the orbital space station, you refill the tank with water and replace the magic matter capsule with a new one from the MirrorMat filling station. It has a full load of 30 milligrams of magic matter. You then take off on the long trip across the black desert between the workaday Earth and the glamorous oasis above you in space, jets booming as you start a holiday away from the dreary reality of the work-screen.

Fiction? Or Future Magic?

What is magic matter? How can it let us escape the dreary bounds of Earth and let us shoot upward into the skies?

To travel you must move. To move you must have energy. To get energy you must convert mass. Every time you burn a tankful of gasoline to take you and your automobile farther down the highway on a long weekend trip to Las Vegas, mass has disappeared. In the process of burning gasoline, some of the mass of the gasoline has been converted into energy.

With chemical fuels, like gasoline and rocket fuels, the amount of mass that gets converted is parts in a thousand million. With fission energy, using uranium or plutonium as fuels, the amount of mass converted becomes parts in a thousand. With fission fuels like hydrogen and deuterium, the mass conversion ratio reaches almost 1 percent. Yet all of these fuels are eclipsed by magic matter, for when magic matter meets normal matter *all* of the mass in both the magic matter and the normal matter gets converted into energy. (Since normal matter is easy to come by, one could say that magic matter is the only fuel that is 200 percent efficient!) Magic matter has had many names, such as *contraterrene* and *antimatter*, but perhaps the most descriptive term is *mirror matter*, for it is a new form of stable matter that is the "mirror image" of normal matter.

The world is made of normal matter. The matter is in the form of atoms. The atoms have a heavy nucleus at the center, made up of particles called protons and neutrons. Surrounding the nucleus of each atom is a cloud of electrons. Everything we normally experience is made up of these three stable particles: protons, neutrons, and electrons.

Each of these three particles consists of a bundle of raw energy, wrapped up by nature into a compact, stable ball that we call matter. We don't really know why the proton and neutron weigh about the same, and yet are 1,800 times heavier than the electron. We don't really know why the charge on the electron is *exactly* equal and opposite in sign to the proton. We don't really know why all the other characteristics of each particle are what they are. That is still a mystery. It is as if each of the particles has some special kind of quantum-mechanical "glue" to hold it together. The type of glue defines both the amount of energy that can be bundled up into a particular kind of particle, and the properties that the resulting bundle would have.

For a long time after the electron and proton were discovered in the atom, scientists were puzzled at the asymmetry of nature. Why did the carrier of the positive electric charge weigh so much more than the carrier of the negative electric charge? Then, in the mid 1900s, the scientists solved the puzzle by finding that each particle had a "mirror" twin. The mirror particle for the electron was a particle that had exactly the same mass as the electron, but the sign of its electric charge was reversed. Like the electron, the positron also acted as if it were spinning like a top, generating a detectable magnetic field. Since the positron had a positive charge, while the electron had a negative charge, the magnetic fields were oppositely directed to the spin axis in the two particles. Thus the positron is the mirror image of the electron (see Figure 2).

The mirror particle for the proton is called the *antiproton*. It has the same mass as the proton, but its charge and magnetic moment are reversed. There is also a mirror twin for the neutron called the *antineutron*. Since both the neutron and antineutron have no charge, it is hard to tell them apart. The neutron spins about its axis, however, and even though it is electrically neutral, it does have a magnetic field (indicating it is not a simple object, but is made up of a proton and electron). The mirror neutron also has a magnetic field, but its spin is in the opposite direction.

Since normal matter is made up of atoms built from electrons, protons, and neutrons, then it should be possible to make mirror matter out of atoms built up from positrons, antiprotons, and antineutrons. Mirror matter is just like normal matter but with the properties reversed. For example, normal hydrogen is made

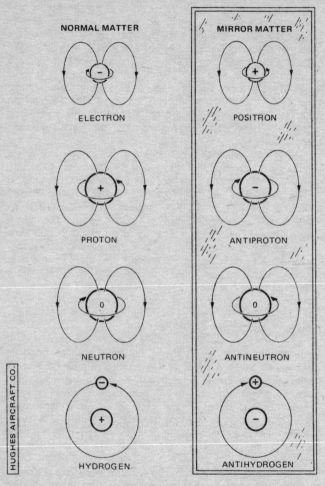

Figure 2. Normal matter and mirror matter.

of a single electron orbiting a proton, while mirror hydrogen is made of a positron orbiting an antiproton.

There is an important difference between the two forms of matter. Whereas a particle made of normal matter is a bundle of energy held together with quantum-mechanical "glue," the mirror particle is a similar bundle of energy held together with "antiglue." Each "glue" turns out to be a solvent for the other!

Thus, when a mirror particle meets a normal particle, the two glues dissolve each other, and the energy contained in the two particles is released in a micro-explosion. The mass of both particles is *completely* converted into energy. The amount of energy that is released is given by the famous Einstein equation $E = mc^2$ (one of the few equations you will ever find in a newspaper). This complete conversion of mass to energy makes mirror matter a highly efficient, compact, lightweight, almost magical source of energy. One milligram of mirror matter combined with one milligram of normal matter produces the same energy as 20 tons of the most energetic chemical fuel in use today, liquid oxygen and liquid hydrogen.

Where can we get this magic matter? As far as scientists have been able to determine, it seems that the Universe is made up of only one kind of matter, the normal kind that you, and I, and the Earth, moon, sun, stars, and galaxy are made of. Some theorists have speculated that this is just a local anomaly and that many of the galaxies that we see far from us in the deep skies could be mirror galaxies. We might be able to communicate with the mirror beings in them someday, but we could visit them only at our peril! Whatever the reason, the experimental fact is that only regular matter occurs in nature. If we want magic matter, we will have to make it.

It is at this point you might think, "This is nothing but science fiction." But mirror matter no longer belongs in the never-never land of science fiction. Instead, it has graduated to the dimly perceived realm of future magic. Recent advances in a number of seemingly unrelated sciences have combined to show that it is now physically feasible to make, capture, store, and utilize mirror matter in useful quantities. Whether it can ever be done at reasonable cost is a task for future technologists to determine.

You may have heard that mixing mirror matter with normal matter produces gamma rays. The first mirror matter that was produced was the positron, the mirror particle of the electron.

When positrons are mixed with electrons they *do* produce all of their energy as gamma rays, which are very difficult to cope with. When antiprotons are mixed with normal protons, however, the resulting energy does *not* come out as gamma rays. Instead, the proton and its mirror twin turn into a collection of particles called pions. On the average there will be three charged pions and two neutral pions. The neutral pions almost instantly produce gamma rays. These gamma rays can be stopped by a shield to produce heat to run the auxiliary systems.

The other 60 percent of the energy released, however, is in the form of highly energetic charged pions. The charged pions have a short life, but since they are traveling at 94 percent of the speed of light they cover a distance of 21 meters (60 feet) during their lifetime, which is more than enough to extract the kinetic energy from them (see Figure 3). After they decay, they turn into other charged particles called muons. The muons will travel 1.85 kilometers (over a mile) before they decay, turning into positrons and electrons. Since all these particles are electrically charged and moving near the speed of light, they act like a heavy, high-speed electrical current. This current can be directed by magnetic fields and perhaps used to drive power generators. The charged pions can also be used to heat normal matter, like water or hydrogen, to produce a hot plasma. The hot plasma can be ejected out a rocket nozzle to provide thrust or used to power electric generators.

Because the mixing of protons and antiprotons produces easily used charged particles, the key to the utilization of mirror matter for space power and propulsion is the generation, capture, storage, and use of the mirror twin of the proton, the antiproton. Most people are not aware of it, but antiprotons are being made, collected, and stored today. Thus, the production of mirror matter is no longer a question of technical feasibility, but a question of economic feasibility.

The only known major producer of antiprotons is the European Center for Nuclear Research (CERN) in Geneva, Switzerland. In 1980, it was reported that the U.S.S.R. Institute for High Energy Physics in Novosibirsk was constructing an antiproton production facility, but there have been no further reports since that date. The United States Fermi National Accelerator Laboratory in Batavia, Illinois, started the operation of their antiproton facility in late 1985.

In these mirror-matter factories, antiprotons are made with the

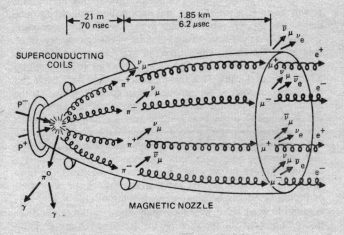

Figure 3. Thrust from proton–antiproton annihilation.

aid of huge "atom smashers." These machines use combinations of electric, magnetic, and radio fields to push against the electric charge on an electron or proton to accelerate them up to velocities close to that of light. The unit of energy that is used in particle accelerators is called the electron-volt or eV. If a metal plate has a positive voltage of one volt (a regular flashlight battery produces 1.5 volts), then an electron will be attracted to that plate. Just before the electron reaches the plate, it will have an energy of one electron-volt (1 eV).

Your television set produces about 20,000 volts inside (that is why there is a message on the back telling you not to open the back of the set). The electrons in the TV tube therefore reach 20 keV (20 kilo-electron-volts) and have enough energy when they strike the back of the screen to make the phosphor glow. A million-volt machine can accelerate electrons (or protons) up to energies of 1 MeV (1 million electron-volts). At 1 MeV, an electron is moving at 94 percent the speed of light, while the heavier proton is only moving at $\frac{1}{20}$ the speed of light. (The proton is 1,800 times heavier than the electron, so it doesn't have to move as fast to have the same energy as the electron.)

To get energies greater than a few million electron volts with just an electric field is difficult, because high voltages have a tendency to leak off into the air or emit corona discharge from sharp points, even in a good vacuum. However, once an electron or proton beam has been set moving using electric fields, it is possible to send radio waves traveling along in the same direction as the beam of particles. If the radio waves are properly tuned, the charged particles can gain energy from the moving radio waves, just as a surfboard gains energy from a water wave. By this technique, energies of thousands of millions of volts, or giga-electron-volts (GeV) have been reached. Fermilab has completed construction of a superconducting proton accelerator that is designed to produce protons with an energy of a million-million electron-volts or a tera-electron-volt (TeV) machine. The Fermilab machine is aptly called the Tevatron.

The amount of energy bound up into the mass of a proton is 0.938 GeV. Thus, any proton with a kinetic energy greater than 1 GeV has more energy in its motion than it has in its internal mass. A proton with a total energy of 100 GeV has within itself enough energy to make 99 more protons (or antiprotons!).

When the scientists in Geneva, Batavia, or Novosibirsk want some antiprotons to play with, they take the proton beam that is circling around in their multi-kilometer circumference machine, add more radio energy, boost the energy until the protons are moving at nearly light speed, then dump the high energy protons into a tungsten target. As the rapidly moving protons strike the heavy tungsten nuclei, their kinetic energy is converted into a spray of elementary particles, including antiprotons, antielectrons, and antineutrons, moving at speeds close to that of light.

You would think that the task of capturing the rapidly moving antiprotons from the cloud of debris emanating from the tungsten target would be as impossible as trying to catch the queen bee in the swarm of bees emanating from a kicked-over hive. But with the aid of a lens made of magnetic fields and a magnetic particle selector, the negatively charged antiprotons can be separated from the remainder of the debris, which consists of particles that have a different charge and mass than the antiproton. The antiprotons that are collected are then directed into a magnetic storage ring where they are accumulated.

The antiproton accumulator consists of a long vacuum tube made of stainless steel bent into a large ring many hundreds of meters in circumference. Spaced at intervals along the ring, like beads on a wire, are dozens of various kinds of magnets. They are huge, one to three meters long, full of iron and heavy wire, and weigh over a ton each.

Some of the magnets are used for "bending" the beam of antiprotons. As the negatively charged antiproton passes through the magnetic field penetrating the vacuum tube from top to bottom, the charge on the antiproton experiences a sidewards force that is at right angles to both the direction of the magnetic field and the direction of travel of the antiproton. This sidewards force causes the path of the antiproton to be bent slightly so the antiproton follows the curvature of the vacuum pipe. If everything is lined up properly, the antiprotons circle endlessly around and around inside the storage ring. The scientists at CERN in Switzerland have stored antiprotons in this manner for days.

Other magnets in the storage ring use more complex magnetic field shapes to keep the beam focused in the center of the tube so none of the antiprotons strike the walls and are lost. There are also smaller, stronger, magnets that can be pulsed to move the beam around inside the vacuum pipe, or to switch the beam into an extraction vacuum line when it is time to do experiments with the antiprotons.

When the antiprotons are generated in the tungsten target, they have a wide spread of energies. Before they can be used further, it is necessary to "cool" the antiproton beam so that all the antiprotons have the same velocity. Two techniques for reducing the spread in velocity have been demonstrated and both have been found to work well.

One technique, invented by Carlo Rubbia at CERN in Switzerland, is called *stochastic cooling. Stochastic* is a scientific word meaning "random" (even though the Greek root means "skillful in aiming"). With the wide spread in velocities, some of the antiprotons are moving faster than the average and some are moving slower. Thus, as they move around inside the vacuum tube at different velocities, they will pass each other and "clumps" of charged antiprotons will temporarily form. These clumps of charge are detected by a current sensor.

The signal from the sensor is amplified, switched in sign, and then quickly sent by cable from one side of the ring to the other. Since the cable cuts across the center of the ring, while the antiprotons have to circle around the circumference of the ring, the signal arrives before the clump of antiprotons, even through the antiprotons are moving at nearly the speed of ligh`. The signal then drives a "kicker" that accelerates or decelerates the "clump" of current, smoothing it out. By using hundreds of sensors and kickers, the scientists and engineers at CERN can decrease the randomness in the antiproton energies by an order of magnitude in less than two seconds. They also use other sensors to detect antiprotons that are not moving straight down the vacuum pipe, but which snake from side to side. Signals from those sensors are then sent to transverse kickers that straighten out the antiproton paths.

Stochastic cooling works well on the high-speed antiprotons that are initially collected from the tungsten target. After this preliminary cooling process using stochastic cooling, the antiprotons are then switched out of the capture and stochastic-cooling ring into a particle decelerator. At CERN, the antiproton *decelerator* is just a proton *accelerator* run backwards. The antiprotons enter the decelerator with an energy of 3500 MeV and leave the decelerator with an energy of 200 MeV. This seventeenfold decrease in energy means that the antiprotons, which used to be moving at relativistic velocities, are now moving at speeds well below the speed of light.

In Switzerland, the decelerated antiprotons are then sent to another storage ring called the Low Energy Antiproton Ring (LEAR). Actually, it is not a ring, but a square. For various reasons, the scientists wanted some long straight sections to do experiments with, so LEAR is a square with sides of about 20 meters and rounded corners. At each corner is a set of bending magnets that take the antiproton beam, turn it through an angle of 90 degrees and send it shooting down the next straight section of vacuum pipe to the bending magnets at the next corner.

The antiprotons had a low spread of energies after they were stochastically cooled in the Antiproton Accumulator. After stochastic cooling, but before deceleration, the spread in energy had been reduced from 1.5 percent to 0.17 percent of the average energy of 3500 MeV, or 6 MeV. After the antiprotons are decelerated to 200 MeV, however, that 6 MeV spread is now 3 percent of the average antiproton energy. Thus, after deceleration, it is necessary to cool the beam of antiprotons some more. It is possible to continue to use stochastic cooling, and at CERN in Switzerland, the scientists have decided to continue to use that technique in the Low Energy Antiproton Ring, even though stochastic cooling is not as efficient at low energies as it is at high energies.

At Novosibirsk, in Russia, the Soviet scientists are using another cooling technique (invented by Soviet scientists) called electron cooling. To carry out electron cooling, a carefully designed electron gun is used to make a beam of electrons that all have the same energy. The average velocity of the electrons is chosen to be exactly the average velocity of the antiprotons. Having very little variation around their average velocity, these electrons can be called "cold" electrons, since there is little relative motion between them.

This cold stream of electrons is then inserted into one of the straight sections of a low-energy antiproton storage ring to travel along with the beam of "hot" antiprotons. The negatively charged antiprotons will interact with the much lighter negatively charged electrons through their mutually repulsive electric fields. Those antiprotons that are moving faster than the electrons will bump into the electrons and be decelerated, while those antiprotons that are moving slower than the electrons will be bumped by the electrons and be accelerated. The much smaller electrons will be "heated" during the process, so the electron beam is removed further on down the straight section and new "cold" electrons reinserted until all the antiprotons are moving at the same speed as the electrons.

The electron-cooling technique works equally well on those antiprotons that have the right average speed, but have a direction that is at an angle to the average direction. The best way to see how electron cooling works on the antiprotons is to adopt a point of view that is moving along at the average speed of the electrons. From that viewpoint, we would see a cloud of slowly moving electrons and rapidly moving antiprotons. The antiprotons that are moving too slowly or too rapidly are coming toward us or going away, while those antiprotons that are at the wrong angle are weaving from side to side through the nearly stationary cloud of electrons. The moving antiprotons bump into the electrons and "heat" them up, but are themselves "cooled" in the process.

The scientists at CERN have stored up to a trillion (10^{12}) antiprotons in their Antiproton Accumulator. To give some scale to what has already been accomplished, a trillion antiprotons has a mass of about two-trillionths of a gram. When this infinitesimal amount of mirror matter is mixed with an equivalent amount of normal matter, it will release 300 watt-seconds (70 calories), an engineeringly significant quantity of energy. To obtain this "firecracker" amount of energy required the use of multimillion-dollar machines that used an enormous amount of electric energy. Still, it is important to recognize that scientists, working in basic physics, using research tools not designed for the job, have produced and continue to produce significant quantities of mirror matter.

The production efficiency of the present machines is abysmally low. They range from parts in a thousand million in Switzerland, to parts in a million in the U.S.S.R. Fortunately, the low efficiency is not due to any fundamental limitation, and can be improved by orders of magnitude. The reason for the low efficiencies is that all of the mirror-matter production facilities built to date have been built as crash projects under limited budgets. Production efficiency has been sacrificed to such considerations as speed, cost, scientific requirements, and national pride.

The motives of the scientists building the mirror-matter machines are interesting and have a significant impact on the present low efficiencies. The ordinary layman might think that the making of this magical form of matter would be enough motive. The real motive of the scientists, however, is to win Nobel prizes. Since the Nobel prize for the discovery of the positron was awarded in 1936 and for the antiproton in 1959, to elementary particle physicists, the study of mirror matter is no longer science—it is engineering. To win a Nobel prize in physics today, you have to discover a new "elementary" particle. To discover these new particles, you have to be the first one to build a machine that slams normal particles together with a collision energy greater than anyone else has achieved and hope you are lucky enough to find a new particle in the resulting debris.

The European scientists in Switzerland knew that the U.S. scientists at Fermilab were building a new machine that would be the first to explore the next highest energy range. They then realized that they might be able to beat the Americans if they used their old machine to collide two beams of protons head-on instead of colliding a beam of protons with a stationary target.

They came up with two possible design approaches. One approach was to build a copy of the machine that they already had in the same tunnel as the first one. (A major cost factor in the building of a new machine is digging the tunnel to put it in.) One machine would accelerate protons clockwise and the other counterclockwise. There would be a crossover point where the two beams would interact. The alternative approach was to use the old machine just by itself, but have it accelerate positively charged protons clockwise while it simultaneously accelerated negatively charged antiprotons counterclockwise. To carry out the second approach meant the scientists had to construct a separate antiproton production, capture, and storage facility.

Amazingly enough, their cost studies showed it was faster and *cheaper* to build an antiproton factory than to build a new accelerator ring. The Europeans hurriedly threw together a facility with limited funds, made enough antiprotons to do the job, found two new elementary particles, and two European scientists, Carlo Rubbia and Simon van der Meer, won the 1984 Nobel prize in physics. The prize was not awarded for the study of mirror matter, but for using mirror matter as an engineering tool to do physics. Fermilab, having been beat, belatedly started their own antiproton factory so that they could use their recently completed machine to explore the next highest range of energies and hopefully win the next batch of Nobel prizes.

Because of this race to be first and the limited budgets, many shortcuts are being taken in the designs of the mirror-matter factories. For example, in Switzerland, they had to use the proton accelerator machine they had available, even though they knew it generated protons with marginal energy for producing antiprotons. With a machine of the right energy, they could have produced 20 times the number of antiprotons per proton. Then, of the antiprotons coming out of the target, they manage to collect only one out of a thousand in the collector ring. The rest are allowed to get away because the scientists could afford only one focusing lens and one capture ring. An array of magnetic lenses would allow the capture of antiprotons coming from the target area at many different angles, while the ring tunnel could hold many capture rings, each designed to capture antiprotons at a different energy.

Another factor limiting the research groups is that their proton accelerators are designed for precision, not production. The proton current in these machines is designed to be low so that the machines can produce protons of extremely high and quite precise energy. Thus, when the protons strike a target, the scientists know their exact energy and can make precise measurements on the new particles that are produced so they can compare the measurements with the predictions from the latest version of elementary particle theory. As a result, these research tools have proton currents that are too low for optimum antiproton production. The machines are also not very efficient: typically, only 5 percent of the electrical energy from the power lines ends up as energy in the proton beam.

There are designs for proton accelerators that are much more energy efficient. They are called linear accelerators. As the name implies, instead of being built in a large circle, they are built in a straight line. In the circular proton accelerator rings, the protons circle around and around the ring, each time getting a kick from the single section of radio energy kickers. In a linear accelerator, there are many more radio energy accelerating sections and the protons only pass through once. Such linear accelerators would have an energy efficiency of 50 percent from the "wall plug" to energy in the proton beam. You can't do much better! A linear accelerator needed to produce protons with the optimum energy to make antiprotons, however, would be very long—40 to 100 kilometers (25 to 60 miles). But there is plenty of room in the deserts in Texas and New Mexico, and there is even more room in space.

In a recent study I carried out for the Air Force Rocket Propulsion Laboratory, I showed that if an antiproton factory were designed properly by engineers, instead of by scientists in a hurry to win a Nobel prize, the present energy efficiency (electrical energy in, compared to mirror-matter recombination energy out) could be raised from a part in a billion to a part in 10,000 or 0.01 percent. At this energy efficiency, mirror matter would cost about 10 million dollars per milligram.

This low production efficiency and the resulting high cost estimate have two significant implications. First, mirror matter cannot be used to make an ''antimatter bomb.'' A single antimatter bomb of the size of the small Hiroshima nuclear bomb (20 kilotons) would require a *gram* of mirror matter costing ten billion dollars. (This amount of money is about 1 percent of the national budget of the United States.) Any country trying to make antimatter bombs would go broke in the attempt.

Second, it is unlikely that mirror matter will be a cost-effective fuel for power and propulsion except in space, where any fuel is expensive because it must be lifted into space first. Even at ten million dollars per milligram, however, mirror matter is already cost effective for space propulsion and power. At the present subsidized price of a Space Shuttle launch, it costs about five million dollars to put a ton of *anything* into low Earth orbit. Since a milligram of mirror matter produces the same amount of energy as 20 tons of the most energetic chemical fuel available, then ten million dollars of mirror matter would be a more cost-effective fuel in space than 100 million dollars of chemical fuel.

How do you ''hold on'' to this magical mirror matter that disappears in a burst of energy the instant it touches normal matter? The scientists in Switzerland have demonstrated one solution to this problem. Their ''bottle'' is an evacuated tube about two inches in diameter and bent into a ring about 300 feet in circumference. As it goes around, the beam of antiprotons is directed and focused by magnetic fields to keep it from hitting the walls of the tube.

Scientists working in atomic physics and plasma physics have come up with a very compact trap for mirror matter. The trap's side walls consist of a carefully machined solid metal ring about two inches (five centimeters) in diameter. Above and below the hole in the ring are two domed metal end caps. This trap is placed in a vacuum chamber inside the bore of a superconducting magnet in a thermos jug containing liquid helium. The magnetic field from the superconducting magnet runs along the axis of the trap from one end cap to the other.

To capture an antiproton once it has been inserted into the trap, the end caps are given a negative charge and the ring a positive charge. The negative charge on the caps repels the negatively charged antiproton, keeping it from going in the axial direction. The antiproton will attempt to move out toward the positively charged ring electrode, but the magnetic field will keep the antiproton moving in a circle and it will never get to the ring.

These compact traps have already demonstrated their ability to store mirror matter. At the University of Washington in Seattle, one of these traps has held a positron for over a month. Gerald Gabrielse of Harvard University recently demonstrated that these Penning traps can also hold antiprotons. In July 1986, CERN gave Gabrielse's group one day on the LEAR machine. They slowed down the antiprotons coming from LEAR in a metal foil placed at the entrance to their relatively crude Penning trap. The slow antiprotons emerging from the other side of the foil were captured in flight by suddenly applying 1000 volts to the trap electrodes. In a typical run, from 100 to 1000 antiprotons were trapped, held for a number of minutes, then the trap voltages were turned off. The antiprotons annihilated on the walls and were counted by detectors outside the trap. Gabrielse and colleagues will return to CERN in the near future with a precision Penning trap to measure the mass of the antiproton to a part in 100 billion. Since the experiment is more accurate with only one antiproton in the trap, if they trap more than one, they will let the rest escape. Everyone expects that the antiproton mass should be the same as the normal proton mass, but if it isn't, then there is a Nobel prize waiting for the person who first finds out.

The simplest mirror atom is antihydrogen. It consists of a single positron orbiting an antiproton. Since the Europeans have had antiprotons in abundance for a number of years, and it is relatively easy to make positrons, you would think that they would have made antihydrogen long ago. In fact, four European scientists made such a proposal right after the first antiprotons became available. They proposed to produce a beam of positrons and run them side by side with the beam of antiprotons going around in the low-energy antiproton storage ring. They would then use a laser to stimulate the attachment of the positively charged positron onto the negatively charged antiproton to produce a beam of neutral antihydrogen. When their proposal came up before the experiment selection committee it got a very low priority rating. The reason? Everyone knows that when you put an electron next to a proton, it will react to form hydrogen. Demonstrating this experiment with mirror matter is not only not particle physics, it is not even *physics*. It is a trivial *chemistry* experiment. Thus, unless someone in the U.S. or U.S.S.R. does it sooner, the first manufacture of antihydrogen will have to wait until all the other possible "physics" experiments that can be done with the beam of antiprotons at CERN have been done.

Once mirror hydrogen has been made, it can be slowed, cooled, trapped, and stored, using a combination of electric fields, magnetic fields, and laser beams. If a laser beam is tuned to exactly the right wavelength, the laser photons will be absorbed by an atom. The energy in the photon causes the electron around the atom to jump into a higher orbit, while the momentum in the photon pushes the atom slightly in a direction away from the laser. The electron soon jumps down into its old orbit, emitting a photon. That photon goes off in some random direction, in the process kicking the atom in the opposite direction. The process is repeated thousands of times per second. The laser photons always push the atom in the same direction so their little pushes add up, while the reemitted photons go in all directions and their kicks average out. Thus, if a laser beam is tuned to the right wavelength, it can push on atoms without touching them.

Atomic scientists at the National Bureau of Standards, AT&T Bell Labs, and elsewhere have used six lasers coming from six different directions to form a region of "optical molasses." When a beam of atoms is injected into that region, the atoms pile up in a cold cloud. The scientists then turn on two other lasers that alternate between cooling and trapping the atoms. The optical trap is 0.5 millimeters across and holds as many as 10^8 sodium atoms for minutes at a time at an effective temperature less then a millidegree centigrade above absolute zero.

The atoms the scientists are currently attempting to trap are atoms of metals like sodium that absorb visible laser light. Soon other scientists will be demonstrating the same cooling and trapping techniques on hydrogen, first on atoms of hydrogen, then on molecules of hydrogen consisting of two hydrogen atoms combined together. This has required them to develop sources of tunable narrow-band ultraviolet laser light, since hydrogen atoms and molecules only respond well to laser light in the short ultraviolet wavelengths.

Molecular antihydrogen, like its mirror cousin, molecular hydrogen, is nearly magnetically neutral when it is in its lowest energy state. The two antiprotons and the two positrons each have a magnetic moment, but in the ground state of the molecule, the two antiprotons have their spins pointing in the opposite direction and the two magnetic fields cancel out, while the same thing is true for the two positrons. The only magnetic response that is left is called the "diamagnetic" response. When there is no magnetic field applied to a hydrogen molecule, it has zero net magnetic moment. When an external magnetic field is applied, however, the orbits of the positrons about the antiprotons are changed. The changed orbital motion is equivalent to an additional current. This induced current causes an induced magnetic field of opposite sign to the applied field. This induced magnetic field property is called diamagnetism.

A diamagnetic molecule has the tendency to move toward a region with low magnetic field and stay there. We can use this property to make a magnetic "bottle" for antihydrogen. The bottle will consist of a vacuum chamber kept at very low temperature, with two superconducting metal rings built into the walls. In the superconducting rings will flow a persistent super-current that will generate a magnetic field that is strong near the walls of the vacuum chamber and weak at the center of the chamber. Any antihydrogen put into this container will avoid the strong magnetic fields near the walls and collect in the center as a ball of antihydrogen ice. The ice ball would be so cold that only a few mirror atoms per day would evaporate from the surface.

Electric fields can also be used to store and manipulate antimatter. If a ball of antihydrogen ice has a slight excess electric charge, electric fields can be used to move it around. A weak beam of ultraviolet light can be used to drive positrons off the antihydrogen ice ball to keep it charged. Experimenters at the Jet Propulsion Laboratory have been experimenting with such traps for use in zero-gee laboratories on Spacelab and the Space

Station. They have already used such traps to stably levitate balls of water ice.

The JPL traps consist of two large curved metal plates about four inches (ten centimeters) apart in a vacuum chamber. Between the two plates is a ball of ice that is kept charged by ultraviolet light that kicks electrons off the ice, leaving the ice ball positively charged. The top plate of the trap is charged negatively and the bottom plate is charged positively, so the ice ball is levitated in the Earth's field by the electric fields from the charged plates. The curvature of the two plates keeps the ice ball centered radially.

The vertical position of the ice ball is not stable. If the ice ball approaches the upper plate, the attraction of the charges on the plate becomes stronger. Thus, unless prevented, the ice ball will quickly slam into the upper plate. In the JPL trap, the voltage between the plates is varied by a fast-acting voltage generator that is controlled by a television camera watching the position of the charged ice ball, so that the ball stays levitated in the center of the chamber.

It will be many years before mirror matter becomes a product that is bought and sold like gasoline or diesel fuel. There are many, many, many difficult problems left to solve in the production, capture, cooling, storage, transport, and use of this extremely potent, extremely expensive, nearly magic source of raw energy. But as one skeptic after another takes a look at the problems that have been overcome and the problems still left to be solved, it begins to look as if there are no "showstoppers." There is no physical reason why mirror matter, in some form, cannot be made and stored in enough quantity to produce the kilowatts and megawatts of prime power and propulsion power needed for rapid space travel.

The scientific and engineering interest in mirror matter is broad and growing. The particle physicists at the European Center for Nuclear Research in Switzerland, the Institute for High Energy Physics in the U.S.S.R., and Fermilab in the U.S. are all upgrading their antiproton production facilities to aid in their quest for Nobel prizes, while at the same time allowing some preliminary engineering experiments critical to the understanding of the problems of storing antiprotons and the generation of mirror matter. Scientists at the University of Washington will shortly be taking their cryogenic traps across the ocean and one day may be returning carrying mirror matter through

Customs. Scientists and engineers at Los Alamos National Laboratory are busy with a number of interlinked studies to generate antiprotons with an upgraded particle accelerator, collect them in magnetic traps, study their interaction with normal matter atoms, and design magnetic chambers and nozzles to extract energy from the high-temperature plasmas produced by the interaction of mirror matter with normal matter. Engineers at the RAND Corporation are looking at the space-system implications of the availability of mirror matter.

The Air Force Rocket Propulsion Laboratory has been supporting studies of advanced propulsion using mirror matter at Lawrence Livermore Laboratories and the Hughes Aircraft Company. They are also initiating an in-house program to study the slowing and cooling of molecular hydrogen with laser light sources. The Air Force Rocket Propulsion Lab interest in propulsion is augmented by studies of mirror matter–powered missions to the planets by engineers and mission analysts at the NASA Jet Propulsion Laboratory. Similar mission studies and preliminary design studies of mirror matter–powered rocket engines are under way at Boeing Aerospace and United Technology Research Center.

This "mirror matter underground" primarily consists of optimists. But they are intelligent optimists that have better things to do than to waste professional time on something that will not work. They are convinced that making mirror matter is feasible. The real question is cost.

Mirror matter, at the present cost of $100 billion per milligram, has already been proven cost-effective for scientific experiments to win Nobel prizes. Mirror matter at $100 million per milligram would definitely be cost-effective for unmanned probe missions to the rings of Saturn. When the cost of mirror matter starts to drop below $10 million per milligram, many new applications come to the fore, for mirror matter then becomes cheaper in energy delivered to orbit than any chemical fuel, and possibly even cheaper than nuclear fuel.

Where will we get the energy to run these magic-matter factories? Some of the prototype factories will be built on Earth, but for large-scale production we certainly don't want to power these machines by burning fossil fuels on Earth. There is plenty of energy in space. At the distance of the Earth from the sun, the sun delivers over a kilowatt of energy for each square meter of collector, or a gigawatt (1,000,000,000 watts) per square kilometer. A collector array of 100 kilometers on a side would provide a power input of 10 terawatts (10,000,000,000,000 watts), enough to run a number of antimatter factories at full power, producing a gram of antimatter a day.

Once we have learned how to make and store antimatter, then we can start using it for propulsion. In science-fiction stories in the past, the usual assumption has been that antimatter rockets would use equal parts of matter and antimatter. Instead, it is now recognized that for any trip speed less than one-third the speed of light, you do not want to use equal parts of matter and antimatter. Instead, you use a small amount of antimatter to heat a much larger amount of matter (either hydrogen, water, or anything else convenient). What is most remarkable is that when the engineers calculated the optimum mix of matter and antimatter for a given payload and a given mission, they found that the amount of normal matter that you need is practically independent of the journey planned.

For any journey, whether it is from one orbit to another, a trip to the moon, to Mars, or to the nearest stars, the optimum ratio is about two tons of water for one ton of spaceship. The only thing that varies is the amount of antimatter needed, but in all cases, the amount of magic matter fuel needed is so small that its mass can be neglected in the calculations.

To give some examples: If we wish to go to the moon in four hours, we will want to travel the 384,000 kilometer distance at a speed of better than 30 kilometers per second. For a 2033 Chevy Astro-Cruiser weighing one ton, this will require 30 milligrams of antimatter mixed with two tons of water.

If we want to take longer journeys in larger vehicles, then ten grams of antimatter heating 20 tons of water can propel a ten-ton space vehicle to Mars in a week. Similarly, a kilogram of antimatter will send the same ten tons to Pluto in a month, while 100 kilograms could send a ten-ton deep-space probe to the nearest stars at a speed of 10 percent that of light, reaching Alpha Centauri in less than 50 years.

We know how to make antimatter. We know how to store antimatter. With a fully developed magic-matter technology, the solar system and the nearby stars can be ours. There is no question about the feasibility of the technology, it is only a matter of scaling and cost. The question is not "Can we do it?" It is "Do we *want* to do it?"

The long trip to Las Lunas is over. The autopilot beeps and you tear your gaze from the retreating blue marble. You monitor the Chevy Astro-Cruiser's rendezvous with the outer end of the Lunar Rotavator as it cartwheels about the moon, its ends touching down to the surface once every hour. There are a hundred cables splayed out from the upper end in a seeming rat's nest of threads, each one designed to lower a passenger ship down to the lunar surface on their next long slow swing. There are no empty cables. You are not about to wait. This is your vacation. You go down on jets.

You touch the controls, and deep inside a zero-cold bottle, a tease of laser light extracts another microgram of magic matter from the frozen ball that rests in darkness there, suspended in an invisible cat's cradle of magnetic lines of force. The speck of magic matter is carried off by controlled pulses of electric and magnetic fields to the roaring hot hell of the rocket chamber, where the still icy speck of ultrapure magic meets a glob of dirty water. The two explode in a blaze of purifying fire as the lunar dust rises to hide the glittering casino signs towering in the distance.

Magic Beanstalks

The concept of a stairway to heaven is a constant theme throughout mythology. In the Old Testament we have two examples. In Genesis 11:4, early mankind used bricks mortared with bitumen in an attempt to build themselves a tower with its top in the heavens. Then later, in Genesis 28:12, Jacob dreamed that there was a ladder set up on the Earth, and the top of it reached to heaven, and the angels of God were ascending and descending on it. From the Far East came tales of magicians who could toss the end of a rope into the air, where it would stay, hanging from seemingly nothing. In the ancient children's story "Jack and the Beanstalk," the beanstalk grows up into the clouds and Jack climbs up the beanstalk to find adventure and riches in the clouds.

Today we know that one sure way to get to the heavens is to use rocket power. In fact, rockets have been so successful that other methods to reach the heavens have been nearly forgotten. How about those other ancient techniques? Can we build a tower or magic beanstalk and climb up to the stars? Or can we hang a rope ladder onto the nearest star and lower the ladder down to the ground? The answer is yes.

Although it may be hard to believe, it may not be too long from now that one form or another of future-magic beanstalk technology will become future reality. Instead of leaving Earth using rockets, we will emulate Jack and climb up a magic beanstalk to find our own adventure and riches in space. There is not one, but many ways to make a stairway to heaven, and since the germ of the beanstalk concept has been in our culture since before recorded history it is not surprising that newer and "more practical" versions of these various ideas are independently invented and reinvented again and again by different people. There are literally dozens of people (including myself) who claim to be the first to think of one or more of the beanstalk ideas we will discuss here. But (to coin a phrase), ideas are a dime a dozen. Any mere genius can dream up an idea, but the true genii of future magic are those well-trained, hardworking, carefully thinking persons that can come up with an idea that is backed with solid, engineeringly useful equations. Not too long from now these future magic genii will be able to duplicate those ancient magic tricks in reality, and grow beanstalks and hang ropes from the sky that will open up the adventure and riches of space to us all.

How about building a modern version of the Tower of Babel? Is it possible to build a tower up into space? Some engineers at the Convair Division of General Dynamics once carried out a feasibility study to see if very high towers could be built as platforms to aid in launching rockets into space. It turns out that under reasonable engineering limits, such as cost and adequate safety margins, steel towers could be built up to 6 kilometers high and aluminum ones to almost 10 kilometers high. For comparison, Mount Everest is 8.8 kilometers above sea level (but on a very broad base). A tower built using currently available graphite composite materials could reach a height of 40 kilometers from a 6-kilometer base. This is some 100 times taller than the tallest building, but still not at the 50-kilometer altitude that officially designates the boundary of space. It seems like the limits of the compressive strength of materials will prevent us from ever raising a tower up into space.

How about a modern version of the Hindu rope trick? Out at the very special distance of 36,000 kilometers from the surface of the Earth (about six Earth radii), there now exist dozens of satellites in geostationary orbit. Here the rotation of the satellite in its orbit is 24 hours, exactly equal to the rotation of the Earth below. Thus, as you stand on the Earth and look up into the sky, the geostationary satellites stay fixed in one position above you while the stars slowly rotate from east to west.

Suppose some friendly giant in the satellite were to let down a long cable—36,000 kilometers long. If the cable were strong enough to hold its own weight, then the cable could reach down to the surface of the Earth. It would be a Skyhook, a magic beanstalk in reverse. Given adequate supplies stashed along the way, a lightweight spacesuit, and enough time, a person would be able to emulate Jack and climb up into space (resting along the way occasionally to enjoy the scenery), instead of having to use a rocket.

One of the first persons to think of the concept of a cable hanging down from a geostationary orbit was a Soviet engineer and popular science writer named Yuri Artsutanov. In 1957 a fellow graduate of the Leningrad Technological Institute told him about a tiny whisker of material that was so strong that it could support a 400-kilometer length of itself in the Earth's gravity field. Artsutanov realized that a cable that long would extend out away from the Earth where the gravity field of the Earth would be weaker and consequently the length could be even longer. Also, if the cable were tapered it could be made even longer still. He worked out the relatively simple equations, but he never published them in an engineering journal where they could be found. Instead, he published the idea as a popular article in the Sunday supplement section of *Komsomolskaya Pravda* (Young Communist Pravda) in 1960.

The Skyhook was independently reinvented in 1966 by John Isaacs, Allyn Vine, Hugh Bradner, and George Bachus, who were oceanographers. It is not surprising that they thought of the idea since they deal often with long cables hanging downward for long distances to the surface of the Earth below. The only difference is that the bottom of the Marianas Trench is a mere 11 kilometers down from a vehicle on the geopotential sea surface, while the tallest mountain is 36,000 kilometers down from a vehicle in the geostationary orbital arc. The Skyhook was reinvented again in 1975 by the aerospace engineer Jerome Pearson, who published some detailed engineering studies.

The Pearson design for a Skyhook starts with a cable-making machine at a central station in geostationary orbit. For balance, the machine would extrude two cables, one upward and one downward. The cables would be thin at first, then, when the length of the cable hanging down becomes longer, the thickness of the cable would be increased to provide enough strength to support the increasing weight below. The thickness of the upward-growing cable would also have to increase as the cable became longer, but for a different reason. Instead of the Earth's gravity pulling on the cable, the pull is due to the centrifugal force from the once per day rotation of the central station and cable about the Earth.

If the extrusion rates of the two cables are carefully

controlled, then the net pull on the central station in geostationary orbit would be zero, and the cable-laying machine would remain in geostationary orbit. Eventually, the lower end of the cable would reach the ground (or the top of some convenient near-equatorial mountain) 36,000 kilometers below. At that time, the outgoing cable would be 110,000 kilometers long. The outgoing cable has to be longer than the Earth-reaching cable because of the way the gravity forces and centrifugal forces vary with distance.

If everything were done smoothly and slowly, there would be no horizontal motion to the cables. In fact, the gravity and the centrifugal forces combine to produce a force that helps to maintain the cable exactly vertical. The bottom end of the long cable could now be anchored to the ground so it doesn't blow about in the winds, and a large counterweight (a small asteroid) would be attached to the outer tip. The counterweight, like a stone in a giant sling, would keep the cable under moderate tension to help keep it straight.

A future-magic material would be needed to construct a Skyhook for the Earth. What is needed is a material that is both strong and light. The best would be a Skyhook made from a tapered fiber of perfect diamond crystal. Unfortunately, making tapered diamond fiber will require the use of some yet uninvented future-magic technology and we will have to wait awhile for that. In the meantime, crystalline graphite fiber is the best candidate material. Theoretically it is twenty times stronger than conventional steel and four times less dense, making it potentially 80 times better than steel for Skyhook cables. It is because of this high strength-to-weight ratio that you find graphite fibers used in tennis rackets, fishing rods, golf clubs, and other sports equipment. Weaving large cables of graphite fibers with strengths near that of the present tiny whiskers is the major technical hurdle that must be overcome if terrestrial Skyhooks are to become a reality. In the coming years we can expect the strength of the graphite cables to improve until they are adequate for terrestrial Skyhooks. Interestingly enough, they are already more than strong enough for constructing Skyhooks on the Moon and Mars.

Actual measurement of tiny graphite whiskers shows a tensile strength of 2.1 million newtons per square centimeter or three million pounds per square inch. With that strength, a one-square-centimeter cable of crystalline graphite could lift 210 tons in the gravity field of the Earth. A one-centimeter cross-section crystalline-graphite cable weighs about 220 kilograms per kilometer of length, so with a 210-ton lifting capability, a graphite cable could support almost a 1,000-kilometer length of itself in the gravity field of the Earth. By building the cable with a taper to it, it can be made even longer. Fortunately, the gravity field of the Earth decreases with altitude, so that less taper is needed at the higher altitudes. With a taper of ten-to-one, a graphite cable could be built to go all the way out to synchronous orbit, some 36,000 kilometers above the Earth's surface—and beyond.

The first cable to be lowered down would have a total mass of about 900 tons. It would have a diameter of about one millimeter at the Earth's surface and would be able to lift only two tons. The initial cable, however, could be used in a bootstrap operation to lift more cable up from Earth until it was strengthened a thousand times. Once the Skyhook is in place, then it could be climbed like the proverbial magic beanstalk. For smaller diameter cables, special electrically powered cars would be built to climb up on the outside. If the Skyhook design used a number of cables arranged in a hollow structure, the electrified tracks could be built inside the structure. As each car climbs the beanstalk from the Earth's surface into geostationary orbit, it would consume an appreciable amount of electrical energy. The cost of the electricity, two dollars per kilogram, would be much less, however, than the present cost of using rockets, which is five thousand dollars per kilogram.

As the cable cars climb up the Skyhook, they always stay fixed above their anchor point on the Earth below. Like a stone in a sling, they have a higher absolute velocity through space than the anchor point. An object dropped from a cable car during the first few kilometers of travel would fall nearly straight down to the surface below. As the car climbs higher, the point of impact would move toward the east, since the object would leave the cable car at a higher horizontal velocity than the more slowly moving anchor point on the surface of the Earth below. At the 25,000-kilometer point on the cable, an object dropped from the car would have so much horizontal velocity that it would sail over the horizon of the Earth and go into a highly elliptical orbit. At altitudes higher than 25,000 kilometers, objects dropped out of the cable cars would all go into orbit around the Earth, with the orbits becoming more circular and closer to a 24-hour period as the cable car approached 36,000 kilometers.

The turnover point for the cable cars would be the central station at 36,000 kilometers up. Here the gravity and centrifugal forces balance. If you drop something out of the cable car (or step out yourself), there will be no motion relative to the cable car. At this point the cable car is traveling horizontally at geostationary orbit velocity. Communication satellite payloads brought up on the cable cars would be simply floated out to become synchronous satellites.

Cars continuing beyond the central station would be pulled along the cable by the ever-increasing centrifugal force, like a skater at the end of a "crack-the-whip" chain. The cable cars would have to brake to keep from flying out too fast. If the braking were done by an electric motor, the braking energy could be turned into electricity instead of heat and used to raise the next cable car on its way up.

On reaching the ballast stone, the cable car would be 150,000 kilometers from the center of the Earth and moving with a horizontal velocity of 11 kilometers a second. If the cable car were to let go of the cable at just the right time, the car (now turned spacecraft) would be able to coast slowly to Saturn on a minimum energy orbit or travel rapidly to all the other planets nearer than Saturn.

By reversing the process, returning payloads can be brought back to Earth without the use of heat shields, braking rockets, or atmospheric braking. Also, a Skyhook is a conservative system. If electric motors are used to lift payloads up the elevator and brake payloads going down the elevator, and the mass flow is the same in both directions, incoming traffic would provide all the energy needed to power outgoing traffic.

An Earth Skyhook would be a future-magic engineering marvel. The job of building the 36,000-kilometer section down to the Earth would be equivalent in difficulty to building a suspension bridge completely around the Earth. In order to lift appreciable loads, say 100 tons at a time, the Skyhook would have to weigh about 600,000 tons. Fortunately, the carbon needed for the graphite fibers can be found in special kinds of asteroids called carbonaceous chondrites. After the carbon was extracted from the asteroid, the remaining slag could be used as the counterweight.

The construction job would be staggering in scope. To build

the 36,000-kilometer Earth-going section of the Skyhook in five years would require an average construction rate of cable and track of 20 kilometers a day. After the Skyhook was built, the cable cars would have to travel at more than 6,000 kilometers per hour (ten times faster than a jet airplane) in order to make the trip up to the central station in less than six hours. Some kind of magnetic levitation design for the track and cars would be needed, for no rubbing or rolling contact can be tolerated at those speeds.

For protection against space debris, the Skyhook would probably be constructed of many interconnected cables in a large open structure. Thus, orbiting debris smaller than a meter in size would cut only one cable at a time and the slack would be taken up by the others until repairs could be made. Even if cut completely through, the Skyhooks would be quite safe since the entire structure is in orbit. If a large object like an out-of-control airplane or satellite accidentally cut the cable, the portion below the cut would fall to the ground, but the portion above would stay almost in the same place, rising only slightly because of the reduced load. After things had quieted down, a new starter cable could be dropped down from the cutoff end, and contact reestablished with the Earth's surface.

Mars is the best planet in the solar system for a Skyhook, having both a shallow gravity well and a high rotation rate. Since the 24.5-hour rotation rate for Mars is nearly the same as that of Earth, while its gravity field is only 38 percent of that of Earth, a Mars Skyhook using graphite would have to mass only 42 times what it could lift. Mars also has a 21-kilometer-high mountain on the equator, Mons Pavonis, that can be used as an anchor point, and a small moon, Deimos, that is available at almost just the right orbit to act as the counterweight. As Arthur Clarke showed in his novel, *The Fountains of Paradise*, the problem of a possible collision between the Martian Skyhook and the moon Phobos can be avoided by deliberately exciting the first vibrational bending mode of the Skyhook so that the cable *twangs* to one side just as Phobos passes by. Similar techniques could be used on Earth to avoid the 1,000 or so larger satellites that orbit the globe.

It won't be long before the first precursors of these magic Skyhooks will be flying in space. Although the Space Shuttle is a remarkable vehicle that can haul large payloads into orbit, it has one major problem. The volume of space that the Space

Shuttle can reach is limited to the small region just outside the atmosphere of Earth. The Shuttle cannot fly up to higher orbits. In fact, nearly all satellites launched by the Shuttle have to have a booster rocket to put them into their final orbits.

It turns out that there is a way for the Space Shuttle to put spacecraft into their proper orbits without using rockets. The Shuttle can use a long cable or tether to "fly" the spacecraft into another orbit. But what makes the spacecraft on the end of the tether "fly" to different altitudes is not the pressure of air, but the tides of gravity.

Because of the way that gravity and centrifugal forces work at orbital altitudes, it is just as easy to send a tether up to a higher altitude as down. The Shuttle, in its orbit about the Earth, has the pull of the Earth's gravity exactly canceled by the centrifugal force due to its orbital motion. It is in free-fall. If the Shuttle sends a mass down on the end of a tether, the mass will experience a stronger gravity pull, but its motion will be that of the Shuttle, so the centrifugal force is smaller than the gravity force and it is pulled downward. If the Shuttle sends a mass up on the end of a tether, the Earth gravity pull will be weaker, but the mass, moving at the same speed as the Shuttle, experiences a centrifugal force that is stronger than the gravity, so the mass flies outward.

For the past decade, NASA and the Italian government have funded studies for a long-tether experiment to fly in the late 1980s. The NASA-built tether will be used to "troll" an Italian scientific satellite 100 kilometers down from the normal Space Shuttle altitudes into the upper reaches of the atmosphere at 150 kilometers.

The Italian satellite weighs half a ton. It is basically spherical in shape with a tail to keep its aerodynamic instruments always pointing in the forward direction. It is designed to sample the atmosphere at that altitude and make other measurements. This half-ton satellite will be supported by a very thin, very flexible metallic or synthetic line one to two millimeters in diameter and 100 kilometers or longer in length. Although the satellite has a mass of 500 kilograms, or half a ton, the tension in the cable is only 200 Newtons or 40 pounds.

Launching the tethered satellite is quite easy. A collapsible boom takes the satellite out about 20 meters and gives it a push vertically downward. Since the satellite is closer to the Earth than the Space Shuttle, the gravity force on it is slightly larger, so it is pulled away from the Shuttle, pulling out the tether even farther. As the satellite moves downward away from the Shuttle, it starts to move ahead of the Shuttle, down toward the Earth. As the satellite moves away, the tether runs from the reel. The three-kilowatt (four-horsepower) drive motor on the reel operates as a brake, causing the satellite to be deorbited from its position, moving it farther downward. A slow deployment will be nearly vertical. A fast deployment can excite back-and-forth librations of the satellite on the end of the tether. These can be brought under control by varying the length of the tether just the way that a fly fisherman brings a large brook trout under control. The reel lets out tether when the tension is more than usual and winds it in when the tension is less than usual.

Once the NASA engineers have flown one or more of these systems without incident, then perhaps some of the more risky tether experiments can be attempted. A payload can be sent upward hundreds of kilometers from the shuttle on the end of the tether. Normally, a satellite at this altitude will be moving slowly, but the Space Shuttle will be pulling it along with a velocity appropriate to its much lower orbit. Since the upward-deployed satellite is moving faster than normal, if it is released from the end of the tether it will fly up into a higher elliptical orbit. The peak of this orbit could be high enough to catch onto a tether hanging down from a space station in geostationary orbit. Longer tethers could even launch a payload into an Earth escape trajectory.

Simple tethers may also be useful in planetary exploration. In one proposed approach, a surface sampling payload is sent out ahead of a spacecraft in low orbit around one of the airless bodies of the solar system, like Mercury, the asteroids, or one of the smaller moons of the outer planets. The main spacecraft would then pull on the tether, slowing the payload down so it is shifted into an elliptical orbit that intersects the surface of the planet ahead of it. The payload drops like a fisherman's well-walked wet fly and touches down for five to ten seconds on the surface of the planetoid. As the main spacecraft passes by, it pulls up the sampling package payload containing surface analyses and the valuable core sample extracted during its brief sojourn on the surface.

Once we have a permanent station on Mars, it may be possible that these short tethers can be used to make a very inexpensive Earth–Mars transportation system. Paul Penzo of the

Jet Propulsion Lab has shown in a study for NASA that for the price of a launch into low Martian orbit, a payload can be sent all the way to Earth. After the payload is lifted up out of the Martian atmosphere into low Martian orbit, it is sent upward from the launch vehicle on a 375-kilometer tether. Released at that point, it has enough energy to fly out to 8,000 kilometers from Mars, where it can rendezvous with a 1,000-kilometer-long down-going tether from the Martian moon Phobos. Using electrical power supplied by a solar power station on Phobos in its 9,400-kilometer orbit, the payload is brought up to Phobos and sent on out at the end of an outgoing 1,000-kilometer-long tether. It releases from there and now has enough energy to rendezvous with a 3,000-kilometer-long tether hanging down from Deimos out at 23,500 kilometers distance. It climbs that tether to Deimos, then continues on out the 6,000-kilometer tether hanging outward from Deimos. Out here the payload now has enough velocity to go into an escape orbit from Mars back to the Earth.

There is another version of the Skyhook I call the Rotavator. It uses a cable that is much shorter than the geostationary-orbit Skyhook. The Rotavator rotates as it orbits about the Earth, the ends of the cable touching down near the surface. This concept was the brainchild of Yuri Artsutanov, the same person who also first thought of the Skyhook. In 1969 Artsutanov published the idea of synchronously rotating cables as a popular article in the magazine *Znanije-Sila* (Knowledge-Is-Force). The magazine illustrator's title drawing for the article shows a huge wheel rolling over the surface of a small Earth—an apt illustration of the concept since the rotating cable acts like a pair of spokes rotating inside an invisible wheel. It was Hans Moravec, however, who published the first technical paper on the concept.

The Moravec design for a Rotavator uses a cable that is 8,500 kilometers long. This is two-thirds the diameter of the Earth, but only one-quarter the length of a 36,000-kilometer geostationary Skyhook. The central portion of the cable would be put into an orbit that is 4,250 kilometers high with a period of 183 minutes. The cable would be set to spinning at one revolution every 122 minutes. Three times each orbit, once every 61 minutes, one of the ends of the cable would touch down into the upper portions of the Earth's atmosphere. These entry points would be the three ports of embarkation from the Rotavator

Transportation System. Because of the large dimensions of the bodies involved, the ends of the cable would seem to come down into the upper atmosphere nearly vertically, with almost no horizontal motion. The cable, although made of one of the stiffest materials known, would still have some stretch to it. This means that a coupling vehicle at the end of the cable could use jets and aerodynamic forces to "fly" the elevator car at the end of the cable to a rendezvous point. This could allow the elevator car to arrive ahead of its nominal touchdown time and delay its return to orbit. There would be almost a full minute available for dropping off and picking up cargo and passengers.

A 8,500-kilometer-long Rotavator designed to touch down three times per orbit would have a taper of about twelve to one. To be able to lift a 100-ton cargo into space, it would have to have a total mass of about 7,500 tons. At touchdown the end of the cable would approach and leave the Earth with an acceleration of 1.4 Earth gravities. Counting the one Earth gravity field of the Earth itself, there will be a total acceleration at liftoff of only 2.4 Earth gravities, less than that experienced by the Space Shuttle astronauts.

A future-magic scenario for a Rotavator Transportation System would probably work like this: You check in at any one of the major hypersonic airports around the world, clear Earth Customs, and board a small capsule six meters in diameter and twenty meters long. The capsule will look like a section cut out of a modern wide-bodied jet aircraft. There are seats for about 30 passengers, with cargo space below. There is a diminutive cockpit/control center in a bubble topside, containing an alert capsule crew. The crew checks on the sealing of the capsule as it is carried away on the bed of a truck to the corner of the field, where automatic rollers move the capsule onto the flatbed spine of a hyperlift cargo airplane. Fairings slide out to merge the body of the capsule into the midsection of the plane. Now aerodynamically restored, the aircraft taxis down the field and takes off. It reaches altitude over the nearby ocean and accelerates to Mach 3. The capsule crew has little to do except monitor the radar displays while the crew of the hyperlift plane takes it higher in altitude and speed, heading southward for a rendezvous in space and time with the Rotavator. The rate of climb of the aircraft slows as the atmosphere becomes thinner. The plane passes through the 50-kilometer altitude that used to mark the difference between a pilot and an astronaut, but there is no pause as it climbs higher on its powerful oxygen-augmented jets.

There is crackling conversation between the aircraft crew, the capsule crew, and the space beings still hundreds of kilometers overhead, diving downward on the rapidly dropping grapple-craft at the end of the Rotavator cable. The aircraft crew unlatches the capsule and dives down and away, leaving the wingless egg to soar on through the nearly empty upper atmosphere in a long arcing trajectory that will end in a parachute recovery if something goes wrong. The capsule sails upward toward the rendezvous point, its crew busy. Looking out the sides through the heavily tinted windows, you can see attitude-control jets flash as the crew keeps the capsule in proper position and orientation for the pickup. You then look up through the ceiling ports to see a similar flaring of jets from the grapple-craft streaking vertically downward, trailing a long thin thread. The grapple-craft comes to a hovering stop a little way above the capsule, then slowly drifts downward.

Carefully, taking their time, the grapple-crew attaches the four grapple hooks to the lifting lugs at the top of the capsule. The capsule crew confirms attachment, then the grapple-craft adds its jets to those of the capsule to match speed with the cable. The free-fall environment of the dropping capsule is slowly replaced with an upward acceleration. In ten seconds, the acceleration reaches 2.4 gravities, and you are glad that you are strapped into the comfortable seat beneath you. Having started at 80 kilometers altitude, in five minutes the capsule reaches 260 kilometers altitude and a velocity of 1.2 kilometers per second. The acceleration slowly drops as you continue your ride into outer space, traveling on the whip end of a fine thread. After 30 minutes the capsule is at the high point in its giant swing through space and you look down on the blue-white globe 8,500 kilometers below. There is a warning klaxon and an announcement from the capsule pilot. You strap in securely, there is a multiple click as the grapples release, and then you and the capsule are in free-fall, heading for the moon with a velocity of nine kilometers per second. You settle down with a good book. It will be 12 hours before you get there.

After two books, two meals, and a nap (disturbed by the unfamiliarity of free-fall), the capsule arrives in the vicinity of the moon. Here it is again met by a grapple-craft crew on the

Lunar Rotavator and is lowered almost to the lunar surface. There the capsule is handed over to a jet-tug, which takes you to Copernicus Base. You are home once again, in familiar surroundings, and glad to get away from the oppressive gravity, air, and crowds of Earth.

A Rotavator on the moon would have an enormous advantage over rockets for providing the resupply and crew rotation needed for space industrialization. A lunar Rotavator could be made with currently available materials, like the superfiber Kevlar™ made by DuPont. With a density of only 1.44 times that of water and a tensile strength of 280,000 newtons per square centimeter (400,000 psi), it has about 5 times the strength-to-weight of steel. Kevlar is currently being used in large quantities for bulletproof clothing, radial tires, and parachutes. A 3,700-ton Kevlar Rotavator around the moon would be able to lift and deposit 100 tons every 20 minutes. Rotavators could also be used on any of the other moons in the solar system. Jupiter's Ganymede and Saturn's Titan are larger than the Earth's Luna, but a Kevlar Rotavator with a taper of six-to-one would suffice for these bodies.

A variant of the Rotavator concept is the Bolo satellite. The Bolo is a more modest version that is shorter in length, but rotates faster. It has been studied in detail by Philip Chapman as a possible near-term addition to a more general space transportation system. His basic design is a rotating cable with relatively large end-mass stations. Some versions have a central station at the center of mass of the system.

In the Chapman design for a Bolo Space Transportation System, one Bolo would be in low Earth orbit and the other would be in geostationary orbit. A payload would be launched from the Earth using either a rocket, the Space Shuttle, or some new hypervelocity single-stage-to-orbit vehicle. The payload would go into a low-energy arcing trajectory that would rendezvous with the lower tip of the Bolo in low Earth orbit. The payload is attached to the Bolo and the launch vehicle returns to Earth. The payload is released from the Bolo at the highest point of its swing. This puts it into a transfer ellipse orbit with the apogee near geostationary orbit. At the top of the transfer orbit the payload would rendezvous with the second Bolo, whose center of mass is in geostationary orbit. If the payload is going on to the moon or elsewhere, it waits until the direction is right and is slung by the Bolo into an escape orbit. If its destination is geostationary orbit, it is hauled up the cable of the Bolo to the central station and floated off to join the rest of the satellites ringing the Earth at 36,000 kilometers altitude. While awaiting the next payload, the angular momentum and energy of the Bolos would be replenished by means of on-board, high-efficiency solar-powered thrusters.

A big advantage of the Bolo Space Transportation System is that the payload would not have to be launched with the normal full orbital velocity of almost 8 kilometers a second that is needed to get into low Earth orbit. Instead, the payload only needs to reach 6.3 kilometers a second. This relatively small change in required launch velocity capability translates into a 50 percent increase in payload mass delivered to a Bolo rendezvous, compared to insertion into low Earth orbit. More important, the reduced velocity requirement greatly increases the feasibility of constructing a single-stage-to-orbit aerospace plane than can take off from a normal runway and deliver payloads into space.

At maximum throughput, this system is capable of transferring over 4,000 payloads of 25 tons each or 100,000 tons to geostationary orbit each year. This is 30 times the mass of the Bolos in the system. For a while, as we build space stations and solar-power satellites, the mass flow outward will be greater than the mass flow inward. The energy and momentum in the payloads comes from the Bolos and it will be necessary to haul up propellant to keep the Bolos spinning and orbiting at the proper altitudes. To minimize the amount of propellant needed, it would be desirable for the mass flow down through the Bolo system to equal the mass flow up.

To supply energy to a Bolo system, a new breed of wildcatter might spring into being. It might be profitable for some entrepreneur to haul back an iron-nickel asteroid and sell chunks of it to the Bolo Space Transportation System operators—not for raw materials to build things, but as a source of energy to power the Bolos. Blocks of asteroid would be sent swinging down the Bolo system as payloads came swinging up. A simple drag brake, made from asteroidal material, might be sufficient to reduce the terrestrial-impact velocity below the speed of sound and the asteroidal material would pile up into a mountain of nickel–iron ore that could be sold for scrap (by the same entrepreneur) after all the valuable gravitational potential energy had been extracted from it.

Similar spinning Bolo cables in solar orbits between the planets could act as transfer points or "velocity banks" to cut the travel time between the planets in the solar system. Instead of heading off on a low-velocity trajectory toward a distant planet that may be in a bad position on the other side of the sun at that time of year, the capsules would head at high speed for the nearest momentum transfer Bolo. As they approach the spinning cable, they would chose the point along the spinning thread that matches their approach velocity. Once attached, the capsule would then move along the cable, climbing up or down in the centrifugal field, until the capsule reached the point on the Bolo that had the velocity needed for the next leg in the journey. There would be a short waiting period until the direction was correct; then, with a command to the attachment hooks, the capsule would be freed from the Bolo to go flying off into space toward its distant objective. As long as more mass is dropped inward down the gravity well of the sun than is going out, no energy source would be needed to operate this interplanetary space transportation system once it was set into motion.

Hanging a cable down from the sky using the tensile strength of materials is just one way of making a magic beanstalk. There is another way. Like Jack's magic beanstalk, this beanstalk grows from the ground up, but unlike a tower or a Skyhook, it does not depend upon either the compressive or tensile strength of materials. I call it the Space Fountain, for it holds objects up in space in the same way that a water fountain supports a ball bobbing at the top of its vertical jet of water.

The Space Fountain concept originated in early 1980 in the etheric depths of a computer net. Some scientists who usually work in artificial intelligence, Marvin Minsky of MIT and John McCarthy and Hans Moravec of Stanford, were speculating back and forth over the net about variations on the Skyhook concept with some scientists who usually work on laser fusion, Roderick Hyde and Lowell Wood. One of the ideas was a method of supporting the upper ends of a Skyhook at altitudes that were much less than geostationary-orbit altitudes. This would be done with a stream of pellets that would be shot from a space platform hovering motionless up at 2,000 kilometers altitude to another platform partway around the Earth. The pellets would be deflected by that platform to the next platform until the polygonal pellet stream made its way around the Earth back to the original station. The deflection of the pellets at each station would be sufficient to support that station in the gravity field of the Earth at that altitude. Since the stations would be only 2,000 kilometers from the surface of the Earth, instead of 36,000 kilometers, it would be more feasible to find materials strong enough to hang Skyhooks from the stations down to the surface of the Earth.

Instead of the "dynamic tension" concept as advertised by Charles Atlas on the back of the pulp magazines, this system would be supported by "dynamic compression." The pellet streams, although they consist of disconnected components, are functionally equivalent to a solid beam under compression since they apply repulsive forces to the pellet deflector stations at each end. There was still some concern expressed by the computer-net debaters whether strong enough material could be found to make a cable even 2,000 kilometers long.

I joined the discussion on the net at about that time and suggested that instead of a dynamic compression hexagonal pellet stream held together with Skyhooks under tension, that a pellet stream be shot straight up from the surface of the Earth to support a pellet deflector station at the upper end that would reflect the pellet stream back down to the surface again. There was initially some skepticism by the others on the net link, because of the Earth's atmosphere at the lower altitudes and the Coriolis forces due to the rotation of the Earth. Further hard work and detailed engineering calculations by Rod Hyde, however, showed that the concept was valid. Hyde has now worked out all the engineering design details for a Space Fountain right down to the design of the transistors to switch the currents in the projectile accelerators and decelerators.

In the Hyde design for a Space Fountain, a stream of projectiles is shot up the bore of a hollow tower. As the projectiles travel along the tower they are slowed down by electromagnetic drag devices that extract energy from the upgoing stream and turn it into electricity. As the projectiles are braked, they exert a lifting force on the tower, which supports the weight of the tower. When the projectiles reach the top of the tower, they are turned around by a large bending magnet. In the turnaround process, they exert an upward force on the station at the top of the tower, keeping it levitated above the launch point.

As the projectiles travel back down the tower, they are accelerated by electromagnetic drivers that use the electrical energy extracted from the upgoing stream of projectiles. The push exerted by the tower drivers also acts to support the weight of the tower. The projectiles reach the bottom of the tower with almost the same velocity they had when they were launched. The stream of high-speed projectiles is bent through 90 degrees by a bending magnet so that it is traveling horizontally to the surface in an underground tunnel. The projectile stream is then turned in a large circle by more bending magnets and energy is added by electromagnetic drivers to bring the projectiles back up to the original launch velocity. The beam of projectiles is then bent one more time by 90 degrees to send it back up the tower again to repeat the cycle. Thus, the Space Fountain acts as a continuous mass driver with captive projectiles. The various parts of the external structure are stressed by the transfer of momentum from the pellet stream. The stressed structure and flowing-projectile stream together form a rigid, stable structure that is not limited in height by the strength of materials.

Since the projectiles are slowed down or speeded up just enough to balance the gravitational force on the tower at every point, there is no requirement anywhere for ultrastrong materials. In actuality, the braking and driving motors will be placed some distance apart in deflector stations spaced along the length of the tower. The tensile strength of the tower materials will be used to support the tower components between deflector stations. In the lower parts of the tower, there will have to be an airtight pipe supported between the deflector stations to keep out the atmosphere so that the drag on the projectiles is negligible. But after the first 100 kilometers, the only structure that would be needed is a minimal framework to hold communication and power lines and the guide tracks for the elevator cars.

The Space Fountain is not bothered by the sideways Coriolis force due to the rotation of the Earth. At each motor station, the direction of the upgoing stream is deflected slightly to one side to keep it going straight upward from the launch point. The tower structure responds by experiencing a force in the other direction, of course. But this sideways force is canceled by an opposing force from the driver motors on the same platform as they deflect the down-going stream a small amount in the opposite direction to keep it going straight. Thus, there is no net transverse force applied to the Space Fountain due to the Coriolis acceleration of the projectile streams.

Note that to first order, no energy is needed to support the Space Fountain. When the projectiles return to the base of the tower, they have essentially the same speed and energy they started with. Their momentum has been changed, but not their energy. As a result, the input power required to support the Space Fountain is determined by the inefficiency in the electro-magnetic motors and the air drag on the projectiles.

One of the major advantages to the Space Fountain concept is that it can be built slowly from the ground up. The driver loop and the bending magnets in the base station are constructed first; then the top station with its turnaround magnets is constructed right above it. The system is loaded with rings and tested at full power with the top station sitting safely just above the Earth's surface. Once these major components have been thoroughly tested, the power is increased, and the projectile velocity rises until the top station starts to lift off the ground. More projectiles are added and the top station rises a few hundred meters, pulling up out of the ground a section of vacuum pipe, along with the first deflector station. The next deflector station and section of pipe are assembled around the exit and entrance tubes to the driver, power is increased, and the Space Fountain rises into the air as fast as the additional sections can be attached.

A Space Fountain should be built with a good deal of redundancy in it. Instead of just one double projectile stream, there should be two, three, or six, each with a separate power supply. Each stream by itself should be able to support the basic Space Fountain structure with a small amount of safety margin. All of them working together would have sufficient power to haul heavy loads up into space while providing adequate safety margin for minor failures and other problems like heavy transverse wind loads at the surface.

If all the power systems fail, the Space Fountain will fall apart. The top station and the upper portions of the tower will go into orbit around the Earth. These can perhaps be salvaged and used again. The intermediate portions will go into elliptical orbits that intersect the atmosphere of the Earth. They can be designed in small enough portions that they will all burn up and be of no danger to those on the ground. The lower portions will pile up on the ground to the east of the launching point, so base sites should be chosen with lots of empty ocean or jungle off in the easterly direction for a few hundred kilometers.

Rod Hyde carried out a detailed design study of the Space Fountain concept for a fountain that rose to 80 percent of geostationary orbit. To maximize their electromagnetic interaction, the projectiles to be used in his version of the Space Fountain are elliptical rings of beryllium or aluminum metal. The dimensions depend upon the exact design, but they are about the size of a hula hoop and weigh about nine kilograms or 20 pounds apiece. There are over a million rings circulating in the system, with a total mass of 9,000 tons.

The rings are driven by a large superconducting electromagnetic mass driver built in tunnels under the ground. The driver is two kilometers in radius, which gives twelve kilometers of distance to turn the high-speed ring stream around, accelerate it back up to proper speed and send it back up the Space Fountain. The magnetic field used in the turnaround magnets is 150,000 gauss, which is easily produced by a vanadium-gallium superconducting alloy.

The rings are launched from the exit to the mass driver at a speed of 24 kilometers per second, slowly losing speed as they travel up the tower. The momentum loss is sufficient to support a tower with an average weight of ten kilograms per meter of length. The speed of the rings at the top of the tower has dropped to three kilometers per second. The turnaround momentum from this "low-speed" ring stream is sufficient to support a top station mass of two million tons. The rings have bunched up as the speed decreases, but they are still ten diameters apart from one another.

The total circulating power in the Space Fountain is a staggering 7 terrawatts (7,000,000,000,000 watts), but because the motors that Rod Hyde designed are so efficient, the total wall-plug electric power required to overcome the losses in the tower will only be about 14 gigawatts (14,000,000,000 watts). This is about two Grand Coulee Dams or about half the power output of the Space Shuttle when it takes off. Of this lost energy, less than one gigawatt shows up as heat in the rings, which rise in temperature by only 38 degrees during the acceleration phase and have over three hours to cool off during their round-trip up and down the Space Fountain.

Because the circulating power is so much greater than the driving power, and the round-trip time for the rings is over three hours, the tower will continue to operate for many hours, even if the main-drive power fails, as long the control circuits are still operating (they can be powered by electricity extracted from the energy in the ring stream).

There are 8,000 deflector stations weighing about five tons each, spaced at roughly four-kilometer intervals along the Space Fountain. They would be closer together in the atmosphere, where the deflector stations must support an evacuated tube to keep the atmosphere away from the flowing rings, and farther apart at higher altitudes, where the gravity force pulling on the tower structure is lower.

The elevators that would take payloads up the Space Fountain could conceivably ride up tracks on the tower structure using electrical power supplied by the tower, treating the Space Fountain solely as a mechanical structure. A more attractive option would be to design the tower structure, the deflector stations, and the elevator cars so that the cars can interact directly with the ring streams themselves rather than coupling to the tower structure at all. In this manner, both the momentum needed to hold the elevator car up in Earth gravity and the energy needed to raise it to a higher level will come directly from the ring stream.

One straightforward design, which I used in my science-fiction novel *Starquake*, had a Space Fountain with six separate pairs of ring streams in a hexagonal pattern. Each deflector station was hexagonal with two triangular cutouts to let the triangularly shaped upgoing and down-going elevators pass through. Each elevator rode on three pairs of ring streams, dragging on the upgoing streams and pushing on the down-going streams. Their couplers were strong enough that they could decouple from one or more ring streams and ride on the rest. By doing this sequentially, they could pass over the stream couplers to the deflector stations.

What is most amazing about the design studies that Rod Hyde has done for the Space Fountain is that none of the design parameters requires the use of future-magic materials. As Rod Hyde likes to point out, this is a Skyhook that we can build now. Yes, the structure is immense in mass and length compared to anything that we build now. Yes, it will take years to power it up and push it into the sky. Yes, it will take a city's worth of power to keep it running. But the payoff is enormous. The Space Fountain can carry a payload at any one time that is 2 percent of its total mass. If that payload moves at a reasonable speed of 1 kilometer per second once it gets out in vacuum, it can make the 30,000-kilometer trip up the Space Fountain in eight hours. At that rate, the amount of mass transmitted into space by just one Space Fountain is six million tons per year, just for the cost of the electrical power to run it. This is indeed a magic beanstalk that will open up space for exploration, industrialization, and finally colonization.

A Space Fountain does not have to go straight up. The projectiles from the base station could be sent off at an angle in a large partial-orbital arc that intersects the ground some distance away. A second base station could then receive the stream of projectiles, turn them around and send them back to the first base station, completing the loop. This concept has been studied in detail by Paul Birch and Keith Lofstrom. The Keith Lofstrom design is called a Launch Loop. It has a long straight section on top that is used to launch payloads into low Earth orbit. The projectiles used in the Launch Loop are bars of iron 2.5 millimeters thick, 5 centimeters wide, and 1 meter long. The ends of the bars are interleaved like tongue and groove boards into a continuous ribbon of iron moving at 12 kilometers a second.

Surrounding the two high-speed projectile streams is a nonmoving hollow double-track system that shields the moving projectile stream from the atmosphere. The track contains sensors, cables, control electronics, permanent magnets, electromagnets, and parachutes in case of catastrophic system failure. The track supports itself by hanging one centimeter below the ribbon of iron, using the attractive forces from permanent magnets augmented by active electromagnetic control forces to maintain the spacing. The track is also designed to support vehicles that ride on the outside of the stationary track, using electromagnetic levitation, while extracting kinetic energy by coupling magnetically to the high-speed iron ribbon inside the track. The ribbon of iron bars is launched from the west turnaround terminal by a mass driver at about a 15-degree angle to the surface. The ribbon climbs to about 120 kilometers altitude, where it is deflected by the west deflector station into a trajectory that follows the Earth's surface below.

The path of the iron ribbon is that of the orbit of a satellite at 120 kilometers altitude modified slightly by the weight of the track that it must support. The 12 kilometers per second "orbital speed" of the iron ribbon is much greater than the true orbital speed of 7.8 kilometers per second at this altitude, so the ribbon has a tendency to fly outward. This net upward force on the

ribbon means it can support a weight of over a kilogram per
meter of length of nonmoving track while remaining parallel to
the Earth's surface. This "straight" portion of the Launch Loop
continues for 2,000 kilometers to the east deflector station,
where the ribbon is deflected downward to the east turnaround
terminal. There the ribbon of iron bars is turned around, brought
up to speed with the mass driver, and launched on the return
path.

The vehicles are hauled up on 120-kilometer-long elevator
cables to the west deflector station and placed on the acceleration track. They are launched from there to the east, in order to
utilize the rotation of the Earth to aid in reaching the desired
terminal velocity. The vehicles slip-couple to the rapidly moving
iron ribbon with magnetic fields and accelerate at three Earth
gravities. Depending upon their desired final destination, the
vehicles can be launched with any velocity up to Earth-escape
velocity of 11 kilometers per second. The Launch Loop can be
used for landing by simply reversing the process, with the
kinetic energy of the returning vehicle being put back into the
iron ribbon instead of being dissipated as heat. The excess
energy can be used to launch another vehicle or turned back into
electricity by using the electromagnetic mass drivers as electromagnetic brakes. A single Launch Loop could easily launch a
five-ton vehicle to escape velocity every hour with an input of
200 megawatts of electrical power. At five cents per electrical
kilowatt-hour, that amounts to two dollars per kilogram for
launching payloads into space.

A Launch Loop can be assembled and started up on the
ground. The east and west deflector stations start out near and
just above the deflection magnets at the east and west turnaround terminals. Between the deflector stations is a temporary
sheath containing a magnetic support system that operates in an
inverted fashion to hold up and stabilize the stationary iron
ribbon in the middle of the vacuum tubing. The mass-driver
motors are then started. The ribbon weighs 6,000 tons, so to get
it moving at 12 kilometers per second requires a lot of energy.
If the energy is put in at a one gigawatt (1,000,000,000 watt)
rate, it will take 120 hours to pump the ribbon up to speed while
the loop is flat on the ground. After the ribbon is up to speed,
the east and west deflector stations are slowly allowed to rise
diagonally so they approach each other. The heavy temporary
sheath sections between the stations are replaced with light-

weight sheaths for the inclined portions and acceleration track between the stations. Unlike the Space Fountain, the Launch Loop structure does not extract energy from the projectile stream to hold itself up on the inclined portions. Instead, it depends upon the tensile strength of the structural materials to support the weight of the structure over the 120-kilometer distance between the stations and the ground.

Because the iron bars are not connected, they can be easily replaced if they develop cracks or other problems. The mass-driver motor is directed to accelerate those iron bars ahead of the designated bar and decelerate those behind the designated bar until the overlap of the sliding joints is exceeded and a gap appears at both ends. Then a deflector magnet can switch out the bad bar and insert a good one. This technique can also be used during the erection phase to add or subtract to the length of the iron bar stream.

An ultimate extension of the Launch Loop concept would be an orbital ring of projectiles. Like many magic beanstalk concepts, the idea was independently invented by a lot of people, but the person who has done most of the hard engineering studies is Paul Birch. In the Paul Birch design of an Orbital Ring system, a ring of massive projectiles is placed in a low Earth orbit. Riding on this ring, supported electromagnetically, are ring stations that stay in one place above some designated point on Earth. Hanging down from these ring stations are Skyhooks made from cables with high tensile-strength-to-mass ratio. Since these Skyhook cables are much shorter than a cable out to geostationary orbit, it can be made with currently available cable materials. A Kevlar™ cable can support a 230-kilometer length of itself, so it only takes a small amount of taper to make a 300- or 600-kilometer-long Skyhook. These can safely support payloads that mass a good fraction of the cable mass.

Paul Birch has found that since the ring stations can be used to deflect the projectiles in the Orbital Ring sideways as well as vertically, it is possible to deliberately cause the Orbital Ring to precess around the Earth instead of staying fixed in inertial space while the Earth rotates beneath it. By making the precession rate large enough, the Orbital Ring can be made to precess at the once-per-day rotation rate of the Earth. The orbit is now "geostationary," without having to be either at the normal geostationary altitude or even in the equatorial plane.

This means that using the Orbital Ring concept, a ring station can be positioned above any desired point on Earth, so that anywhere on the globe can be served by a Skyhook, instead of just the poles and the equator. A network of Orbital Ring systems crossing, for example, at the poles, could cover the whole planet with an array of Skyhooks and geostationary ring stations.

If one of these short Skyhooks fall, the debris will land in a relatively small, easily predictable area. For a 300-kilometer-high Skyhook, all the debris will land in a strip to the east that is only 1.8 kilometers long and a few hundred meters wide, while a 600-kilometer-high Skyhook will require a safety zone to the east that is 5 kilometers long.

Once a payload has climbed up the Skyhook and reached the Orbital Ring, it can then accelerate horizontally by coupling to the moving projectiles in the Orbital Ring. If there were Orbital Rings around each moon and planet, transport around the solar system would be fast, easy, and inexpensive.

Skyhooks, Rotavators, Bolos, Orbital Rings, Launch Loops, and Space Fountains are definitely future-magic forms of space transportation. Yet soon we will see the first experiments with tethers hanging both upward and downward from the Space Shuttle. If those experiments are successful, then the NASA engineers will become more comfortable with these strange new rocketless forms of space propulsion. They will start to pay attention to their own studies, which show the great benefits to be obtained from the use of long tethers for inexpensively hauling large quantities of mass into and around in space.

Newer materials with higher strength-to-weight ratios are already coming out of the organic and inorganic materials laboratories, driven by the trend toward composite materials in aircraft, automobiles, and sports equipment. These newer materials will make Skyhooks, Rotavators, and Bolos technically feasible and perhaps even commercially viable if good engineering solutions can be found for the space-debris problem.

Even the projectile-stream concepts might come into fruition within the foreseeable future. Work on mass-driver accelerators, tracks, and methods of controlling hypervelocity projectiles is undergoing intensive development as part of the Strategic Defense Initiative. This weapons work will provide the engineering data needed to design closed-loop projectile energy-storage systems with high electrical efficiency.

The first closed-loop projectile systems would be used for energy storage. They would be completely underground and used to provide load leveling in an electrical power grid or surge power for large defense installations. Next will come long underground kinetic-energy power-transmission lines; then perhaps a completely enclosed, nonelectric replacement for the overhead line or third rail in subways and electric-train systems. We will then be ready to consider Launch Loops, Orbital Rings, and Space Fountains.

One use for the Space Fountain concept will be in constructing tall antenna masts for news events and military operations. Perhaps after a few years of experience with the Fountain Masts, the braver camera crews might be willing to ride up on the top station for better overhead shots. Once experience has been gained with smaller Fountain Masts, larger Fountain Towers, perhaps 10 to 20 kilometers high, might prove to be commercially viable for radio and television broadcasting in the Plains states. The real test of confidence in the Fountain Tower concept will be when buildings many kilometers in height are constructed using Fountain Towers as support beams to hold up the building. There would naturally be multiple redundancy in the number of Fountain Beams in each corner of the building. Each Fountain Beam would have an independent control power supply and there would be enough inertia in the flowing streams of projectiles to stay up for hours even in the event of a main power failure. Fountain Towers might also prove to be an economical alternative to communication satellites for point-to-point television and FM radio communication between the various islands of some of the smaller nations in the Pacific Ocean. Finally the Fountain Towers would rise higher and higher until they went into space. We would then have a true Space Fountain, reaching upward into the heavens.

The arched fountain structures can start small. The first ones may be demonstrations for Congress. Fountain Bridges made using subsonic cables inside steel tubing will arc across the Potomac, following the path of George Washington's silver dollar. With the development of superconducting magnets and accelerators, projectile-supported Fountain Bridges can be made across the Channel, the Sahara, the Alps, the Bering Strait, and the waters that separate the Third World islands in the Pacific. Finally the Fountain Bridges will arc so high they will reach into space and become Space Bridges.

There the Space Fountains and the Space Bridges will connect to a system of Orbital Rings running from pole to pole and around the equator in a globe-encircling interlinked network. Built and maintained by the larger nations, the EarthLink net would allow rapid transportation anywhere on Earth and easy access to the solar system. For access to space, all a Third World nation would have to do is build its own Space Bridge or Space Fountain. One end would be firmly embedded in its own soil while the other would be attached to the EarthLink that unites all the nations of the world into one. Once off the Earth, the vehicles of each nation could then couple to the high-speed projectiles inside the EarthLink rings to withdraw enough of the energy to send the vehicle on its way into Earth orbit, or on to the moon and the planets. The projectile stream inside EarthLink would slow slightly as some of its energy is lost, taken away by the disappearing vehicle, but it will regain it when the vehicle returns with its massive cargo and passengers, and its equally important, but massless, cargo of knowledge.

Magic Starships

It was only a few centuries ago that the human race realized those bright lights in the night sky were suns, like our sun. We then realized that those other suns probably had worlds orbiting around them, some hopefully like our world. Since that time, one of the dreams of the human race has been to visit those other worlds in ships that travel between the stars. But as we began to realize the immensity of the vast distances that separate our star from the other stars, we began to despair of ever building a starship using the puny technology that the human race controls.

Science-fiction writers, in an attempt to get their storybook heroes to the stars before the readers got bored, evoked magic starships with faster-than-light drives, space warps, and other forms of future magic. At the same time, the general public evoked fantasy starships in the form of flying saucers flown *to* the Earth *from* other stars. These starships were propelled by antigravity or magnetism, and were piloted by benevolent little green men that would save the world from its folly.

If little green men can cross the great gulf—can we?

Yes. It is difficult to go to the stars, but it is not impossible. The stars are far away, and the speed of light limits us to a slow crawl along the star lanes. To travel to the stars will take years of time, gigawatts of power, kilograms of energy, and billions (if not trillions) of dollars. Yet it can be done—if we wish to.

And if we decide to go, what kind of future magic can we see coming that will get us to the stars? What kind of starships can we build?

It turns out there are many types of starships possible, each using a different technology. There are some starships that we can build now. For these technologies, we know the basic physical principles and have demonstrated the ability to achieve the desired reactions on a laboratory scale. All that is needed for the design, engineering, and construction of the starship is the application of large amounts of money, material, and man power.

There are also some promising starship designs that use future magic. Here we know the basic physical principles, but we have not yet controlled the future-magic technology in the laboratory. Once we have turned future magic into future reality, we can then proceed with starship designs based on those technologies.

It is not easy to comprehend the distances involved in interstellar travel. Of the billions of people living today on this globe, many have never traveled more than 40 kilometers from their place of birth. Of these billions, a few dozen have traveled to the moon, which, at a distance of almost 400,000 kilometers, is 10,000 times 40 kilometers away. Soon, one of our interplanetary space probes will be passing the orbit of Neptune, 10,000 times farther out, at 4,000,000,000 kilometers. However, the nearest star, at 40,000,000,000,000 kilometers, is 10,000 times farther than that.

The spacing between stars is so large that there is no standard unit of measurement that gives any sense of the immensity of those distances. Even in terms of the distance between the Earth and the Sun (1 AU or one astronomical unit), the nearest star is 270,000 AU away. To cut interstellar distances down to size, we use the unit of distance that has the name of a unit of time in it, the light-year.

A light-year is the distance that light, traveling at 186,000 miles per second, or 300,000 kilometers per second, travels in one year (which is 365.2422 days, or 8766 hours, or 525,949 minutes, or 31,556,926 seconds). It takes light 1.3 seconds to reach the moon, 8.3 minutes to reach the sun, 4.2 hours to reach Neptune, and 4.3 years to reach the nearest star system.

The nearest star system is called Alpha Centauri. Also known as "Rigil Kent," it is the brightest star in the southern constellation Centarus, and the third-brightest star in the sky after Sirius and Canopus. Alpha Centauri is not a single star, but a collection of three stars. The nearest of those stars is a small red dwarf called Proxima Centauri. The other two stars are one-tenth of a light-year farther and are called Alpha Centauri A and B. Alpha

Centauri A is similar to our sun, while B is slightly redder. These two stars orbit around each other every 80 years, while Proxima circles the pair with a period of millions of years.

To carry out a one-way robotic probe mission to this nearest star system in the lifetime of the humans who launch the probe will require a minimum speed of 10 percent of the speed of light. At that speed, it will take 43 years to get to Proxima Centauri and 4.3 years for the radio information to get back to tell us what the probe found as it zoomed through the three-star system at a sizable fraction of light speed.

Much farther away in the heavens are some single-star systems with stars that are also similar to our sun. These are felt to be our best candidates for finding an Earth-like planet. They are Epsilon Eridani at 11 light-years and Tau Ceti at 12 light-years. To reach these stars in a reasonable time will require starship velocities of 30 percent of the speed of light. At this velocity it will take nearly 40 years for the starship to get there, plus another 11 or 12 years for the information to return to Earth.

Yet, although we need to exceed 10 percent of light speed to get to *any* star in a reasonable time, if we can attain a cruise velocity of 30 percent of the speed of light, then there are 17 star systems with 25 visible stars and hundreds of planets within 12 light-years. This many stars and planets that are reachable with starships limited to less than 30 percent of the speed of light should keep us busy exploring while our future engineers are working on even faster starship designs.

No matter how fast we can make a starship go, we must resign ourselves to the fact that interstellar travel will always take a long time. Even if we had a starship that traveled at the speed of light, it would take over 4.3 years to travel to the nearest star system, then another 4.3 years before a message (or the starship) returned. We don't have speed-of-light starships yet, and won't for a long time. Although time will pass quickly for the crews on relativistic starships, decades and centuries will pass before the stay-at-homes learn what the explorers have found.

The energies required to launch a manned interstellar starship are enormous, for the mass to be accelerated is large and the speed must be high. Yet even these energies are not out of the question once we move our technology out into space, where the constantly flowing sunlight is a never-ending source of energy—over a kilowatt per square meter, a gigawatt per square kilometer.

Why should we bother going to the stars if it is so difficult? There is one reason that should be obvious to us all. It is built into our genes. We cannot ignore it. But it is so selfish, so intuitive, so *animal* . . . that we often try to ignore it. We must go to the stars to spawn.

For survival of the human race it is necessary that the human race leave the Earth. Homo sapiens has survived quite nicely on the Earth for tens of thousands and perhaps millions of years. So did the dinosaurs. But the dinosaurs are now extinct. If the human race is to survive, some small portion of it must leave this big blue egg and travel somewhere else to start a new branch of the human race.

For a while, we can escape extinction by nuclear or biological warfare by having some of our population in space stations. Over longer periods, we can escape the death of the Earth by ice ages, meteorite strikes, or other catastrophes by colonizing the other planets around our sun. But to escape the ultimate death of the sun, it will be necessary for the human race to establish viable colonies on planets that are around other, younger suns.

Another major reason for interstellar travel would be to find other intelligent life-forms. Some argue that if the life that forms on planets around other stars were intelligent, we could communicate with them by radio signals. Not all intelligent life-forms will have radio, however. It is easy to dream up alien civilizations that are intelligent, have information and technology that are of value to us, and yet, because of their environment, cannot and will not have radio technology. For example, life could evolve on an ocean-covered world to produce intelligent whalelike or octopuslike creatures. These beings could be highly advanced in music, mathematics, philosophy, hydrodynamics, acoustics, and biology, but they would have no technology based on fire or electricity.

If there are beings with radio out there, and *if* they are willing to transmit gigawatts of radio power instead of just listening like we are, and *if* we listen in the right direction at the right time at the right frequency with the right bandwidth and the right detection scheme, then a radio search for intelligent extraterrestrials will make a significant contribution to our knowledge. However, interstellar exploration with automated probes, although still decades in the future, is definitely more likely to produce a contribution of equivalent value. In my opinion, interstellar exploration with automated probes is complementary to a program to search for extraterrestrial radio signals, rather than competitive with it.

As Arthur Clarke said in his book, *The Promise of Space,* "This proxy exploration of the Universe is certainly one way in which it would be possible to gain knowledge of star systems which lack garrulous, radio-equipped inhabitants."

Also, a life-form does not have to be intelligent to be important. All life on Earth is made of the same stuff: carbon, hydrogen, oxygen, nitrogen, and trace elements organized into specific chemical compounds such as amino acids, sugars, proteins, enzymes, and other standard building blocks of life-as-we-know-it. The discovery of a different form of life would be extremely important.

A different form of life could have a drastically different chemistry, such as compounds based on the element silicon, instead of carbon. This would be useful on planets where temperatures are too high for carbon-based life-forms.

A different form of life might use a different kind of replicating mechanism, such as a tri-string form of DNA that uses two-out-of-three voting when making the new tri-string to block the effects of mutation. This would require three sexes for procreation and would be useful on planets with high radiation environments.

A different form of life might have almost the same biology as Earth life, except one or two of the amino acids used in the DNA genetic code would be different. Or it might be that the compounds are almost exactly the same as those used in Earth life-forms, except that all the compounds are left-handed. (All the organic compounds produced by living organisms on Earth rotate the polarization of light passing through them to the right.)

It could be that the life found on other planets is *exactly* like ours in chemical structure, indicating a common origin. (That would *not* mean the alien animals would look anything like any animals on Earth. A mosquito, sequoia, human, octopus, whale, and duck-billed platypus are quite different in form, yet we all use the same genetic code.) Our search would then turn to find that common origin. The common origin could be due to the inexorable laws of biology, which only allows one type of life to form. The common origin could be due to a version of the panspermania theory, where life travels between stars as spores pushed by light pressure. Or the common origin could even be due to the "garbage" theory, that life on Earth formed from picnic garbage left by long-ago alien visitors to our barren planet. Once we have found a different form of life, our biologists and medical researchers will have their understanding of "life" stretched. They will then hopefully see new ways to understand, control, and repair our form of life.

What kind of starships can we build now? There are many. The ones we can build now use nuclear propulsion and beamed power propulsion. In the coming decades we will see more advanced starship designs that use other forms of future magic.

The first travelers to the stars will be our robotic probes. They will be small and won't require all the amenities like food, air, and water, which humans seem to find necessary. The power levels to send the first squadron of robotic probes out to the stars are within the present reach of the human race. If we wanted to, we could have the first interstellar probe on the way to the nearest star system before the present millennium is out.

The design of the first interstellar probe is the critical driving item in any program for interstellar exploration. The rigors and length of a journey involving high accelerations with high-energy-density engines, the years of bombardment against interstellar matter at high velocities, and the decades of operation with no means for repair, or even diagnostic help from Earth, means that advanced designs for a self-diagnostic, self-repairing probe must be developed. Ultimately, the computer in the interstellar probe will have to exhibit semi-intelligent behavior when presented with new and unforeseen circumstances.

The requirement of multiple planetary exploration at each stellar system will limit the number and weight of the lander probes available and will put a premium on long-range sensor capabilities to gather the same data from orbit. Yet, despite these needs for sensor performance, the energy requirements for achieving flight velocities of a few tenths of the speed of light are so large that the weight of the interstellar probe should be kept to a minimum.

What is desired in an interstellar probe is a large physical size (to give the transmitting and receiving apertures desired), and high power (for active sounders and data transmission), all combined with light weight. The design of such a future-magic interstellar robot probe is an important challenge, for the mass of the interstellar probe determines the size and power of the propulsion system.

The most advanced form of flight-tested propulsion system we have today is electric propulsion. In this type of propulsion system, some source of energy is used to produce electricity and the electricity is used to expel the reaction mass at high speed to provide thrust. In most electric propulsion systems, the electrical energy is obtained from solar cells that convert sunlight into electricity. Unfortunately for interstellar missions, the sunlight rapidly becomes weaker as the spacecraft leaves the solar system, so that solar electric propulsion will not get us to the stars.

One possible method for overcoming the problem of the spreading of sunlight with distance is to consider laser electric propulsion. In this propulsion system, the incoherent sunlight is turned into coherent beams of laser light by using the sunlight to pump the laser. The laser energy is then used to illuminate specially designed solar cells that are optimized to absorb that particular color of laser light with high efficiency. The size of the collector arrays could then be made smaller, resulting in a compact, lightweight, efficient energy power conversion system.

Comparative studies were carried out by engineers of the NASA Jet Propulsion Laboratory on the various forms of electric propulsion that might be used for extrasolar space missions to be launched around the year 2000. These studies indicated that a nuclear fission reactor was a better choice than a laser beam collector for the energy source for an electric propulsion system. A nuclear electric propulsion system would be capable of reaching an escape velocity of 150 kilometers per second or $\frac{1}{2000}$ of the speed of light in 12 years after using up all the fuel in the nuclear reactor. Such a spacecraft would be useful for exploring extrasolar space to search for trans-Plutonian planets and nearby "brown dwarf" stars. However, as the JPL engineers pointed out, at this speed it would take the nuclear fission–powered electric propulsion system 10,000 years to reach the nearer stars. Long before it got there, it probably would be passed by a vehicle using a faster propulsion system. Thus, although fission reactors are a currently available source of controlled nuclear energy, because of the large masses needed in the fission reactor and the heat-to-electricity converters, nuclear fission–powered electric propulsion systems do not seem to be an adequate form of interstellar propulsion.

A very old design for a nuclear-powered interstellar vehicle is one that is propelled by nuclear bombs. Called the "Orion" spacecraft, it was invented in the late fifties at the Los Alamos National Laboratory by an inventor of the hydrogen bomb, Stanislaw Ulam. The original goal of the Orion Project was to send manned spacecraft to Mars and Venus by 1968. Because nuclear fuel is so much more powerful than chemical fuel, an Orion mission to Mars would have cost only a small fraction of the Apollo project, which took us only to the moon.

The Orion vehicle works by ejecting a small nuclear bomb out the rear where the bomblet explodes. The debris from the nuclear explosion strikes a "pusher plate," which absorbs the impulse from the explosion and transfers it through large "shock absorbers" to the main spacecraft. Although it seems amazing that anything could survive a few dozen meters away from a nuclear explosion, a properly designed pusher plate with an ablative surface can stand not one, but many thousands of such nuclear explosions.

Freeman Dyson took these well-engineered ideas for an interplanetary spacecraft and extrapolated them to an interstellar spacecraft. The ship would necessarily be large, with a payload of some 20,000 metric tons (enough to support a small town of many hundred crew members). The total mass would be 400,000 tons, including a fuel supply of 300,000 nuclear bombs weighing about one ton each. (This is approximately the world's supply of nuclear bombs. What an excellent way of disposing of them!) The bombs would be exploded once every three seconds, accelerating the spacecraft at one Earth gravity for ten days to reach a velocity of $\frac{1}{30}$ of the speed of light.

At this speed, the Orion spacecraft would reach Alpha Centauri in 140 years. To give this ship a deceleration capability at the target star, it would need to be redesigned to have two stages. Although the Orion spacecraft has minimal performance for a starship, it is one form of interstellar transport that could have been built and sent on its way in the last decade.

In addition to nuclear bomb–propelled starships, we can envision future magic in nuclear technology that could make possible new kinds of nuclear-powered starships. This future magic technology is called controlled fusion. Although our scientists are sure of the basic physical laws behind controlled fusion, our technologists have yet to demonstrate it in the laboratory. This is one form of future magic that is almost certain to turn into future reality within a few decades since the Department of Energy is spending a large portion of its budget on a number of techniques for achieving a controlled fusion reaction on a scale suitable for use in power plants.

One technique, called magnetic containment fusion, involves the use of magnetic "bottles" to confine a high-temperature plasma gas of deuterium (a hydrogen atom with an extra neutron in the nucleus) and tritium (a hydrogen atom with two extra neutrons in the nucleus) until the two forms of heavy hydrogen fuse together to make a helium nucleus and a high energy neutron.

Another technique, called inertial implosion fusion, attempts to compress tiny pellets of deuterium and tritium by hitting the pellet from all sides with either laser beams, electron beams, ion beams, or beams of high-speed BBs. In inertial fusion, the energy and pressure from the incoming beams is supposed to compress the fusion fuel in the pellet, heat it up, and get it to fuse into helium before it has time to expand. It is the "inertia" of the fuel, pellet, and beams that keeps it contained long enough for the reaction to take place.

Once we have achieved controlled fusion in the laboratory, then we can start designing a starship based on those types of fusion techniques that turn out to be feasible. If we achieve controlled fusion by compression and heating of a plasma in a magnetic bottle, then perhaps all we need to do to convert the fusion reactor into a starship rocket engine is to allow the magnetic bottle to "leak" a little bit, and the hot plasma exhaust will produce thrust.

If we achieve controlled fusion by implosion of micropellets with beams of laser light, electrons, ions, or high-speed shot, then the same technique can be used to implode the pellets in the throat of a rocket nozzle made of magnetic fields, which will turn the isotropically exploding plasma into directed thrust. Scientists at Lawrence Livermore National Laboratory have already anticipated the success of their laser imploded fusion program. They have used their fusion plasma computer codes to design a magnetic nozzle for a laser fusion–powered rocket for travel in the solar system.

The deuterium–tritium reaction currently being used in both the magnetic containment and inertial implosion fusion research projects involves the use of tritium. Since tritium is a radioactive material with a lifetime of 12.3 years, any interstellar rocket system using this reaction must have a method of generating the tritium on board. This can be done by capturing the high energy neutrons emitted by the fusion reaction in a blanket of lithium. The neutron causes the lithium to fission into a helium atom and a tritium atom, which can be extracted and used to make more fusion pellets. The weight and efficiency of this auxiliary system, while not a serious problem for an interplanetary spacecraft, could limit the final velocity achievable by a starship.

Alternatively, research on magnetic containment and implosion fusion techniques could produce the higher pressures, temperatures, and densities needed to achieve fusion with other fuel mixtures that don't involve radioactive tritium. These reactors would fuse together fuels such as deuterium and helium-three (a helium nucleus that is missing a neutron), deuterium and deuterium, and protons with protons.

Thus, given some future-magic advances in nuclear technology, we can already envision some propulsion technologies that will get a starship to the stars, although they only travel at 1–3 percent of the speed of light. At 3 percent of the speed of light, it would take over 300 years to get to the interesting star systems like Tau Seti and Epsilon Eridani. These slow travel times for nuclear-powered starships are longer than the present lifetime of a human being, so it looks like the travelers on our slow nuclear starships will have to be long-lasting robots rather than ephemeral humans, unless we can come up with some new type of future magic that will allow a human crew to live longer than our currently allotted three-score-and-ten-year lifetimes. Biologists are currently studying the aging process in cells and multicellular organisms. They are finding that our cells seem to be programmed to stop replicating after a given number of cycles. If they can find the right genetic switch, perhaps they can turn off the aging process and allow us to live the centuries that will be necessary to explore the stars using slow nuclear rockets. With death dead, our only enemies would be accidents and boredom.

Other biologists are studying the process of suspended animation, by either freezing or hibernation. Sperm cells have been kept frozen for decades and are viable enough to produce thoroughbreds and beef cattle when thawed. Even fish and small mammals have been frozen and rethawed. Larger animals, such as people, will be significantly more difficult to freeze because of the need for rapid cooling and thawing to prevent the formation of damaging ice crystals. However, some future magic breakthrough may make possible crews of "corpsicles" who experience the thrilling adventure of exploring one stellar system after another without having to endure the boring drive through the dark between those adventures.

Scientists studying hibernating animals have found the hormone that initiates hibernation and have used the drug to induce hibernation in other animals. Whether this drug will induce hibernation in humans without causing serious side effects is unknown. Also, it is unknown whether hibernation actually increases life span, or just makes living possible when there is insufficient food. Still, there is enough biological research on suspended animation that one of these days we may use that method of keeping a crew alive long enough to carry out century-long exploration missions.

Even if these particular biological forms of future magic do not turn into a real suspended animation capability, there is another method for carrying out a slow-ship mission without invoking future magic. We will let the people die, but allow their children to carry on. A slow-ship journey to the stars will send a colony of people off in a generation starship. Although only the first generation would be true volunteers, with enough thought and planning, we could turn the slow-moving starship into a truly acceptable worldship, with all the amenities and few of the problems of living on Earth.

Living on a worldship would be like living in a space colony, except that the colony would have some sort of fusion rocket to push it up to speed and bring it to a halt again at each target star. At each stop, it would refuel its tanks with hydrogen and helium isotopes from a gaseous giant planet like Jupiter. After a few decades of experience in space stations around the Earth, we may have enough confidence in the environmental support systems for a worldship that we would risk a colony on an interstellar mission.

The important thing to realize is that our present technology can take us to the stars. To be sure, our first robotic interstellar probes will be slow, consume a lot of power and money, and will return sparse amounts of data. If we find an interesting planetary system, it will take even more power, and more money, plus biological breakthroughs and crew dedication to take the slow-ships to the stars. It would be no different in principle from the *Mayflower* or the ships that colonized the

Dutch East Indies. But no matter how difficult, interstellar travel by slow starships can be done with reasonable extensions of our present technology.

There is, however, a fundamental problem with any interstellar mission that travels at speeds less than 10 percent the speed of light. The fundamental problem with slow starships is magic. Future magic, to be exact. For even as a worldship is launched onto its centuries-long journey, propulsion engineers back on Earth will be dreaming about more advanced propulsion systems that can make starships that travel faster than the ship that is leaving. Within 20 or 30 years, those advanced propulsion systems will no longer be future magic, but future reality. In another 10 to 20 years, a faster starship will zip past the lumbering worldship, explore the new star system first, then set up a welcoming party for the worldship colonists as they are picked up and brought in by a second wave of fast starships.

Thus, until we run out of ideas for new propulsion systems, it seems to me that no interstellar mission should be launched if it takes more than 100 years. Instead, the money for the mission should be spent on research to build a faster propulsion system or to find a new propulsion energy source.

In our near future is a magical propulsion energy source that is a thousand times more powerful than nuclear energy. This magical source of energy is mirror matter, or antimatter. Antimatter represents a highly concentrated form of energy with the ability to release "200 percent" of its mass as energy. When a particle of mirror matter, such as an antiproton, is put near a particle of normal matter, such as a proton, the two attract each other and almost instantly annihilate to completely convert all of the mass of both particles into energy. A spacecraft using antimatter as its source of propulsion energy could "drive" anywhere in the solar system with mission times ranging from days to weeks. A starship using antimatter could travel to the nearest stars in a human lifetime.

Although an antimatter rocket is the ultimate in rockets, it is not necessary to use the rocket principle to build a starship. A rocket consists of a payload, some structure, an energy source, some reaction mass (in most rockets the reaction mass and energy source are combined together into the "fuel"), and an engine that combines the energy with the reaction mass and expels it to provide thrust to the spacecraft. Because a standard rocket has to carry its fuel along with it, its performance is significantly limited. For missions where the final vehicle velocity V is much greater than the exhaust velocity v, the amount of fuel needed rises exponentially as the ratio V/v. Thus, as a practical matter, the final velocity of a rocket is limited to about two or three times the exhaust velocity.

It is possible to conceive of space-vehicle designs that do not use the rocket principle and thereby avoid the exponential mass growth implicit in the design of a standard rocket. These are excellent candidates for starships. One example, and a favorite of science-fiction writers, is the interstellar ramjet invented in 1960 by Robert Bussard.

The interstellar ramjet starship consists of a payload, a fusion reactor engine, and a large scoop. The interstellar ramjet carries no fuel because it uses the scoop to collect the hydrogen atoms that are known to exist in space. The hydrogen atoms are used as fuel in the fusion reactor, where the fusion energy is released and the energy fed back in some manner into the reaction products (usually helium atoms), which provides the thrust for the vehicle.

Bussard originally estimated that a 1,000-ton vehicle would require a scoop with frontal intake diameter of about 100 kilometers to achieve a one Earth gravity acceleration through interstellar space with a density of 1,000 hydrogen atoms per cubic centimeter. The speed needed for the ramjet to start working is extremely low, so that conventional chemical rockets would suffice to get it started. As the vehicle increases its speed so that it approaches the speed of light, the interstellar fuel flow appears to increase in density due to its relativistic contraction in the space–time reference frame of the vehicle.

If an interstellar ramjet could ever be built, it would have many advantages over other possible starships. Since it never runs out of fuel like fuel-carrying rockets, and never runs away from its source of power like a beamed-power propulsion system, it can accelerate indefinitely. It is the only known starship design that can reach the ultrarelativistic velocities where ship-time becomes orders of magnitude longer than Earth-time. This would allow human crews to travel throughout the galaxy or even between galaxies in a single human lifetime.

A lot of invention and research is needed, however, before the future-magic technology of a Bussard interstellar ramjet becomes future reality. We must first achieve controlled fusion. The fusion reactor must not only be lightweight and long-lived, it must be able to fuse protons, not the easier-to-ignite mixture of deuterium and tritium. The reactor must be able to fuse the incoming protons without slowing them down; otherwise, the frictional loss of bringing the fuel to a halt, fusing it, and reaccelerating the reaction products will put an undesirable upper limit on the maximum velocity attainable. All of this needed technology is still future magic.

Other versions of the interstellar ramjet concept do not require that the starship carry a fusion reactor. In these concepts, the ramjet scoop is used to scoop up the hydrogen in space. Instead of fusing the hydrogen into helium atoms, however, the hydrogen is heated either by antimatter carried on board, or by antimatter beams or laser beams sent from the solar system.

The major difficulty with any ramjet starship is the design of the scoop, which must be ultra-large and ultra-light. If the interstellar hydrogen were ionized, then a large, super-strong magnet might be sufficient to scoop up the charged protons. Although some stars have clouds of ionized hydrogen near them, most of the hydrogen near the solar system is neutral. Schemes that use laser beams or electron beams to ionize the hydrogen ahead of the ship have been proposed, but they are not light in weight nor low in power consumption.

The present scientific consensus for the composition of the local interstellar medium is that the solar system is embedded not far from the edge of a warm (10,000-degree), mostly neutral gas cloud with a radius of a few 10s of light-years and a relatively low density of 0.1 atoms per cubic centimeter. This is 10,000 times less dense than the 1,000 atoms per cubic centimeter that would be preferred for an interstellar ramjet. That means that a scoop for an interstellar ramjet, instead of being 100 kilometers in diameter, would have to be 10,000 kilometers across to scoop up the same amount of fuel per second.

It gets even worse as we travel farther from the sun, for this warm cloud we are in, is surrounded by a larger, hot (million-degree), ionized plasma with a density of only 0.001 ions per cubic centimeter that extends some 150 light-years or more in all directions observed. This ubiquitous, low-density, hot-gas "bubble" is most likely the result of past supernova events.

Thus, for now, in regions near the solar system, the interstellar ramjet remains in the category of science fiction. The concept of picking up your fuel along the way as you journey through "empty" space is too valuable to be discarded lightly, however, and I hope that future scientists and engineers will keep working on the remaining problems until this vision of future-magic technology turns into a real starship.

There is another whole class of spacecraft that do not have to carry along any energy source or reaction mass, or even an engine. These spacecraft consist only of payload and structure. They work by beamed-power propulsion.

In a beamed-power propulsion system, the heavy parts of a rocket (the reaction mass, the energy source, and the engine) are all kept at home in the solar system. Here, around the sun, there is an unlimited amount of reaction mass readily available. In addition, the energy source and the engine can be maintained and even upgraded as the mission proceeds. Three examples of such beamed-power propulsion systems have been published in the engineering literature. All of these versions can be built with "reasonable" extrapolations of present-day technology. The examples are pellet-stream-pushed, microwave-beam-pushed, and laser-beam-pushed vehicles.

In the pellet-pushed-probe concept proposed by Clifford Singer, small pellets are used to push a starship. The pellets would be launched by a very long linear electromagnetic mass driver that would stretch across the planetary orbits of the solar system and be accurately aimed at the target star. The accelerator would be powered by energy sources using nuclear or solar power. The high-speed pellets would be intercepted by the starship and reflected back in the opposite direction, resulting in an increase in velocity of the starship.

The absolute pointing accuracy of the mass launcher is not a serious limitation. The starship would detect the incoming pellet stream and adjust its position to stay in the stream. A series of course-correction stations could be located downrange from the launcher along the pellet stream. Each station, for example, would be three times farther downrange and would produce one-third as much velocity adjustment. The coarser adjustments could be made electromagnetically or electrostatically, and the finest adjustments could be made remotely by light pressure from a laser or by interaction with a plasma gun or neutral atom stream.

One readily feasible method for accomplishing the interception of the high-speed pellets at the vehicle is to vaporize them into a plasma with a pulse of photons or particles. The high-speed ionized plasma would then be reflected from a magnetic field on the starship in a manner somewhat analogous to the expulsion of plasma from a magnetic "nozzle" in a pulsed fusion rocket system.

Extensions of the pellet-stream concept include changing the pellet composition and velocity so that the pellets are fusion fuel that is captured at a low relative velocity, then used in a fusion engine for acceleration and deceleration. Deceleration could also be accomplished by rebounding the pellets from an expendable unmanned lead ship to decelerate the manned vessel at the target system. Of course, once the "interstellar highway" has been traversed once, then a pellet-stream launcher can be constructed at the other end for relatively easy two-way travel.

Another form of beamed power propulsion uses beams of microwaves to drive the starship. Microwave energy has the great advantage that it can be made and transmitted at extremely high efficiencies, although it is difficult to make narrow beams that extend over long distances. Because of the short transmission range, the starship being pushed by the microwave beam must accelerate at a high rate to reach the high velocities needed for interstellar travel before the starship gets too far from the transmitting system. The accelerations required are larger than a human being can stand, so microwave-pushed starships seem to be limited to use by robotic probes. There is one design that looks quite promising. I call it Starwisp, because of its extremely small mass.

Starwisp is a lightweight, high-speed, interstellar flyby probe pushed by beamed microwaves (see Figure 4). The basic structure of the Starwisp robotic starship is a wire-mesh sail with microcircuits at the intersection of the wires. The microwave energy to power the starship is generated by a solar-powered station orbiting Earth. The microwaves are formed into a beam by a large Fresnel-zone-plate lens made of sparse metal mesh rings and empty rings. A configuration of rings that form circular zones where the microwaves are allowed to pass through or are reflected back will act as a crude but effective lens for a microwave beam. It has very low total mass and is easy to construct.

The microwaves in the beam have a wavelength that is much larger than the openings in the wire mesh of the Starwisp starship, so the very lightweight perforated wire mesh looks like a solid sheet of metal to the microwave beam. When the microwave beam strikes the wire mesh, the beam is reflected back in

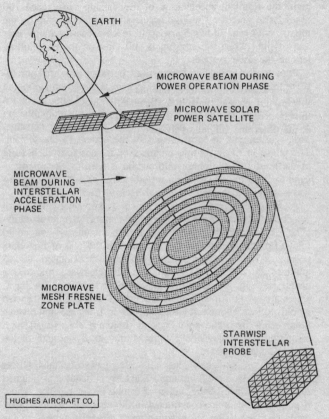

Figure 4. Starwisp—microwave pushed
          interstellar probe.

the opposite direction. In turn, the microwave energy gives a push to the wire mesh sail. The amount of push is not large, but if the sail is light and the power in the microwave beam is high, the resultant acceleration of the starship can exceed 100 times Earth gravity. The high acceleration of the starship by the microwave beam allows Starwisp to reach a coast velocity near that of light while the starship is still close to the transmitting lens in the solar system.

Prior to the arrival of Starwisp at the target star, the microwave transmitter back in the solar system is turned on again and floods the star system with microwave energy. Using the wires in the mesh as microwave antennas, the microcircuits on Starwisp collect enough energy to power their optical detectors and logic circuits to form images of the planets in the system. The phase of the incoming microwaves is sensed at each point of the mesh and the phase information is used by the microcircuits to form the mesh into a retrodirective phased array microwave antenna that beams a signal back to Earth.

A minimal Starwisp would be a 1 kilometer mesh sail weighing only 16 grams and carrying 4 grams of microcircuits. (The whole spacecraft weighs less than an ounce—you could fold it up and send it through the mail for the cost of first-class postage.) This 20-gram starship would be accelerated at 115 gravities by a 10,000,000,000 watt (10 gigawatt) microwave beam, reaching 20 percent of the speed of light in a few days. Upon arrival at Alpha Centauri some 21 years later, Starwisp would collect enough microwave power from the microwave flood beam from the solar system to return a series of high resolution color television pictures during its fly-through of the Alpha Centauri system.

Because of its small mass, the 10-gigawatt-beamed power level needed to drive a minimal Starwisp is about that planned for the microwave power output of a solar-power satellite. Thus, if power satellites are constructed in the next few decades, they could be used to launch a squadron of Starwisp probes to the nearer stars during their "checkout" phase.

Once the Starwisp probes have found interesting planets, then we can use another form of beamed-power propulsion to visit those planets, called laser sail propulsion. Although microwave beams can only be used to "push" a robotic spacecraft away from the solar system, if we go to laser wavelengths, it is possible to design a beamed power propulsion system that can use laser beams from the solar system to send a starship to the nearer stars, and then bring the starship and its crew back home.

Of all the future-magic technologies for achieving star travel with human crews, the one concept that is closest to reality is laser sail propulsion. It will be some time before our engineering capabilities in space will be up to building the laser system needed, but there is no new physics involved, just a large-scale engineering extrapolation of known technologies.

In laser sail propulsion, light from a powerful laser is bounced off a large reflective sail surrounding the payload. The light pressure from the laser light pushes the sail and payload, providing the needed thrust. The laser sail starship is about as far from a rocket as is possible. The starship consists of nothing but the payload and the lightweight sail structure. The rocket engine of our starship is the laser, powered by an energy source such as the sun. The reaction mass is the laser light itself.

The sails that the laser craft would use would be advanced versions of the sun-pushed light sails that have been designed by the NASA Jet Propulsion Laboratory for comet missions and fast trips to the asteroid belt. The lasers would be advanced versions of the high-power laser arrays currently being studied for the Strategic Defense Initiative Office of the Department of Defense. The basic principles of the lasers and sail are known; all that is left to do is the engineering.

For interplanetary operation and interstellar flight, the lasers would be in space and powered by sunlight collected by large reflectors. For interplanetary operation the lasers could be in high Earth orbit, sending their beams out to push the sails of the interplanetary fleet with the light pressure from their powerful beams. For pushing an interstellar starship, the lasers might work better if they were in orbit around Mercury. There is more sunlight there and the gravity attraction of Mercury would keep them from being "blown" away by the reaction from their light beams. They would use the abundant sunlight at Mercury's orbit to produce coherent laser light, which would then be combined into a single coherent beam and sent out to a transmitter lens floating between Saturn and Uranus.

The transmitter lens would be a Fresnel-zone-plate lens with dimensions tuned to the laser frequency and consisting of wide rings of one-micrometer-thick plastic film alternating with empty rings. The transmitter lens would not be in orbit, but would either be freely falling (very slowly at that distance from the sun), or "levitated" in place by rockets or by the momentum push from a portion of the laser light passing through it. The lens would be 1,000 kilometers in diameter and mass about 560,000 tons. A lens this size can send a beam of laser light over 40 light-years before the beam starts to spread.

The first interstellar mission that could be performed with this laser and lens system would be a one-way flyby robotic probe mission to the nearest star system. The robotic probe would have a total mass of one metric ton, about one-third each of payload, support structure, and thin aluminum-film reflecting panels. The sail portion of the probe would have a diameter of 3.6 kilometers.

The probe would be pushed at an acceleration of $\frac{1}{30}$ of Earth gravity by an array of solar-pumped lasers with a total power of 65,000 megawatts or 65 gigawatts. While this is a great deal of laser power, it is well within our future capabilities. Power levels of this magnitude are generated by the Space Shuttle rocket engines during lift-off, and one of the ways to make a high-power laser is to put mirrors across the exhaust of a high-power rocket. If the acceleration is maintained for three years, the interstellar probe will reach the velocity of 11 percent of the speed of light at a distance of only 0.17 light-years. At this distance it is still within range of the transmitter lens and all of the laser power is still focused on the sail.

The laser is then turned off (or used to launch another robotic probe) and the robotic starship coasts to its target, flying through the Alpha Centauri system 40 years after launch. If the discoveries made by the flyby probe generate interest in further exploration of the target star system, the next phase of interstellar exploration would be to send a larger, unmanned starship to rendezvous at the target star and explore it in detail.

When I first invented laser-pushed lightsails back in 1962, I thought it was obvious that since all the laser can do is push the lightsail, it would not be possible to use a solar system laser to stop the lightsail at the target system. Thus, the idea seemed to be limited to flyby precursor probe missions. It wasn't until 20 years later, while trying to find a new way of traveling to the stars for a novel I was writing, I realized that if the lightsail were separated into two parts, then one part might be used as a mirror to reflect the laser light back toward the solar system. That retrodirected light might then be used to decelerate the other portion of the lightsail. When I worked out the equations and put numbers into it, I found that not only was it a good science-fiction idea, but it would really work. The concept has since been published as a scientific paper in the *Journal of Spacecraft and Rockets*, and one of the references to prior work in the paper is my novel, *The Flight of the Dragonfly*.

At launch, the lightsail for a rendezvous mission would have a diameter of 100 kilometers and a mass of 785 metric tons. This is a lot of mass and it will take a lot of laser power to push it. In order to minimize the amount of laser power needed, we would accelerate the vehicle at only 0.5 percent of Earth gravity. The amount of laser power needed is not trivial. It comes to 7,200,000,000,000 watts or 7.2 terrawatts. For comparison, the Earth now produces about 1 terrawatt of electrical power. We would certainly want to power the lasers by collecting sunlight from space with large reflectors rather than using Earth-based power sources.

All the laser power will be used to push the lightsail, since the spot size of a 1,000-kilometer lens at a distance of a mere 4.3 light-years is 98 kilometers, which is less than the diameter of the lightsail. Under a constant acceleration of 0.005 gravities, the time it takes the starship to travel a distance of 4.3 light-years is 40 years. At the end of this constant acceleration period, the lightsail has reached a velocity of 21 percent of the speed of light. The starship is now approaching Alpha Centauri and must decelerate.

The lightsail is built in two sections, an outer doughnut-shaped ring, and an inner circular section 30 kilometers in diameter. This 30-kilometer payload section of the sail has a mass of 71 tons, including a science payload of 26 tons. The remaining, ring-shaped "deceleration" stage has the mass of 714 tons, or 10 times the mass of the smaller payload stage. The 30-kilometer central payload section of the sail is detached from the larger stage and turned around so that its reflecting surface faces the reflecting surface of the ring-shaped stage. At a time 4.3 years earlier, the laser power from the solar system was upgraded to 26 terrawatts (there are 37 years to get ready for this increase in power). The slug of laser light from the solar system travels across the intervening space to the larger ring sail and bounces off, pushing the ring sail even faster. The light reflected from the ring sail is focused onto the smaller sail, now some distance behind. The light rebounds from the payload sail, giving it a push opposite to its velocity and slowing it down.

Since the smaller sail is one-tenth the mass of the larger sail, it decelerates at 20 percent of Earth gravity and comes to a halt in the Alpha Centauri system in only one year, giving a total trip time of 41 years. In the Alpha Centauri system, the robotic payload can use the laser sail as a "solar" sail to travel around the three-star system, carefully examining the planets that the initial flyby probe has found.

If the reports from the interstellar rendezvous probes are favorable, then the next phase would be to send a human crew on an interstellar exploration journey. More than just the nearest star system will ultimately need to be explored, so I designed the laser lightsail starship (see Figure 5) to allow a round-trip exploration capability out to 10 light-years, so Tau Ceti and Epsilon Eridani can be visited within a human lifetime. I assumed the diameter of the lightsail at launch to be 1,000 kilometers in diameter, the same size as the transmitting lens. The total weight would be 80,000 tons, including 3,000 tons for the crew, their habitat, their supplies, and their exploration vehicles. The lightsail would be accelerated at 30 percent of Earth gravity by 43,000 terrawatts of laser power. At this acceleration, the lightsail would reach a velocity of half the speed of light in 1.6 years. The expedition will reach Epsilon Eridani in 20 years Earth-time and 17 years crew-time, and it will be time to stop.

At 0.4 light-years from the target star, the 320-kilometer rendezvous portion of the sail would be detached from the center of the lightsail and turned to face the large ring sail that remains. The laser light coming from the solar system would reflect from the ring sail, acting as a retro-directive mirror. The reflected light decelerates the smaller rendezvous sail and brings it to a halt at Epsilon Eridani.

After the crew explores the system for a few years (using their lightsail as a solar sail), it will be time to bring them back. To do this, a 100-kilometer-diameter return sail is separated from the center of the 320-kilometer rendezvous sail. The laser light from the solar system hits the ring-shaped remainder of the rendezvous sail and is reflected back on the return sail. The laser light then accelerates the return sail and its payload back toward the solar system. As the return sail approaches the solar system 20 Earth-years later, it is brought to a halt by a final burst of laser power. The members of the crew have been away 51 years

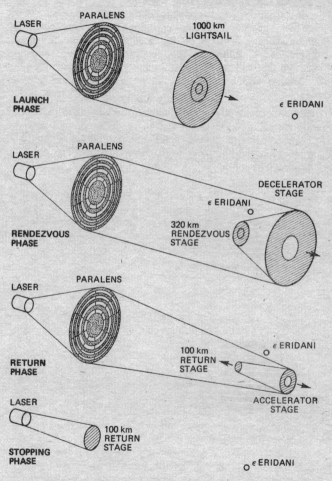

Figure 5.   Round-trip travel by laser-pushed lightsails.

(including 5 years of exploring), have aged 46 years, and are ready to retire and write their memoirs.

It is difficult to go to the stars. But it is not impossible. There are not one, but many, many future-magic technologies, all under intensive development for other purposes, that, if suitably modified and redirected, can give the human race a magic starship that will take us to the stars.

And go we will.

Magic Gravity

From birth to death, gravity pervades our life. Our every step, day in, day out, is a struggle against this relentless force. It cuts our baby knees when we fall. It pulls on our limbs so that every motion is burdened by its enervating presence. It sucks our bodies into the mud, preventing us from soaring into the skies like the birds.

Is there some future-magical method to control gravity? Can we somehow find a way to "turn off" or "nullify" the gravity field of the Earth? Could we possibly arrange for a mass to push us gently away into the skies instead of hugging us firmly to its crushing bosom?

The answers are: yes . . . maybe . . . someday.

But to control some force in nature, you need to know something about it. You need a theory of how it works; and the more detailed the theory, the better your chances of control. What do we know about gravity? What are the theories? How can we use those theories to nullify gravity?

The first theory of gravity, usually attributed to Ug the caveman, was simple:

"Things fall down."

This theory served Ug quite well in its time. Ug used his theory to make gravity his servant rather than his master. Instead of having to walk right up to a saber-toothed tiger to bash it in the head with a sharp rock (and getting all scratched in the process), Ug climbed a tree and, wisely using his theory of gravity, dropped the sharp rock down on the head of the saber-toothed tiger. This was the first use of gravity as a tool for the betterment of the human race.

It wasn't too much later that Ug found a way to use his new theory to nullify the effect of gravity. One day, while sitting high up on a slippery elm branch waiting for a saber-toothed tiger to walk beneath him, he tossed his favorite sharp rock back and forth from one palm to another. His newly developed and still-awkward opposed thumb missed a toss and the rock bounced away.

Not wanting to lose his favorite tool, Ug jumped after it. After his jump, Ug noticed a strange thing. The rock no longer fell down. Instead, it just hung there in the rapidly rushing air just an arm's length away. By his jump from the branch Ug had made one gigantic leap for mankind toward the conquest of gravity. As he reached out and plucked the floating rock from midair, he thought about all the admiration he would receive around the cave fire that night as he explained the secret of nullifying gravity.

"Just jump," he would tell them . . . At that point the uprushing ground terminated his thought processes.

Ug would be amazed to know that even today we use his simple yet effective technique to nullify gravity. Each flight of the Space Shuttle utilizes his marvelous invention to make multiton communication satellites float weightless so mere men and women can push them around like leaden pillows. To nullify gravity all the astronauts have to do is to use the Space Shuttle rockets to "jump" high enough that they can go into free-fall.

Unlike Ug, however, whose career as an astronaut ended in a second, the Space Shuttle astronauts can fall forever. That is because while the astronauts are falling vertically ten meters, their orbital velocity takes them horizontally eight kilometers. At this new point, the surface of the Earth below is now ten meters farther away than it was before, so the astronauts can fall another ten meters without getting any closer to the dangerous ground. Thus, by using the Ug theory of gravity and constantly falling as they move, our astronauts can nullify the effects of Earth gravity.

The Ug theory of gravity served the human race well until sailing ships were invented. Then reports began to trickle in from the sailors that the world was round and that there were people living on large island continents on the "other side" of the Earth. Amazingly enough, even though they were obviously upside down, they didn't have to hang on to trees or handles set into the ground, but instead walked around on their feet in just the same way that people did on the topside of the Earth. It was finally realized that the Ug theory of gravity, despite all its advantages, was not the correct theory of gravity and a new theory would have to be found.

Finally, in 1687 Isaac Newton discovered a better theory of gravity. The Newton theory of gravity is somewhat more complicated than the Ug theory of gravity, but the basic idea is quite simple:

"A mass attracts all other masses."

There is more to Newton's theory of gravity than that, but it consists mostly of details that are used for making accurate mathematical predictions.

In the Newton theory of gravity there is no shielding of the gravity attraction. The pull of the sun on the Earth does not suddenly stop during an eclipse when the moon interposes itself between the Earth and the sun. During an eclipse, the light from the sun gets blocked, but the motion of the Earth along its year-long orbit does not experience a "hiccup" when the "day side" of the Earth turns dark.

Using his theory of gravity, Newton was able to predict the motions of the moon and the planets in the sky to high accuracy. To carry out the calculations, he had to invent a new form of mathematics, called "calculus," that revolutionized both science and engineering.

The first use of this new gravitational technology was to predict the future motions of the moon through the starry background of the sky. Navigators on ships far out at sea could measure the position of the moon in the sky, compare it with the predictions made by the gravitational engineers using the Newton theory of gravity, and figure out where the ship was on the trackless sea surface.

Amazingly enough, using only Newton's theory of gravity, it is possible to design a simple antigravity machine that can "nullify" the gravity field of the Earth. As we shall see, although we know how to *design* the machine, it will be some time before our engineering technology is up to the task of actually *building* the machine. To design our Newtonian antigravity machine, we will need to look more closely at the details of the Newton theory of gravity.

The basic form of the Newton theory of gravity is that masses attract other masses. In a more detailed form, the Newton theory of gravity can be expressed as:

"A big mass will attract another mass. The bigger the attracting mass, the stronger the attraction. The closer the two masses, the stronger the attraction. (It goes as the square of the distance between the two masses.)''

How can we use this Newtonian theory of gravity to cancel the gravity field of the Earth?

Well, one way to use the Newton theory of gravity to keep the Earth from pulling you down would be to put another planet, with the same mass as Earth, above your head. The Newtonian antigravity field of the above-Earth will pull you up with the same force as the Newtonian progravity field of the below-Earth is pulling you down. The two forces would cancel each other out; over a broad region between the two ''Earths,'' there would be no gravity. Everyone and everything would be in free-fall.

There is no question, from a mathematical point of view, that this method of nullifying the gravity field of the Earth using Newton's theory of gravity would work. But it is also obvious that this is not a very practical solution. We do not have another Earth handy to use as the above-Earth, and besides, there is no practical way to keep two Earth-sized bodies that close to each other without their falling into each other from their mutual gravity attraction and spoiling all our free-fall fun. Notice, however, that the Newton theory of gravity says that the gravitational attraction gets stronger as the two masses get closer to each other. It turns out there is a way we can use that aspect of the Newton theory of gravity to create gravity magic.

Let us look at the gravity field of a large knob of rock about 100 meters (a football field) in diameter. (Single rocks of this size are often found in Sequoia or Yellowstone National Park and many other places around the country.) If it is a very dense rock, it will weigh about four million tons. Although it would admittedly be difficult, we could imagine that we could hire a team of gravitational engineers to lift that rock up on strong pillars and make a small room underneath it. We now have a small asteroid perched on man-made pillars sitting on the roof of our room. In that room, 50 meters from the center of the rock overhead, the gravity field of the Earth would be decreased by the gravity pull of the rock. The amount of gravity-decrease would be about ten microgravities. We have antigravity of a sort, but not very much.

Now, mindful of the admonition of Newton's theory of gravity, which says that the amount of attraction varies as the square of the distance between you and the attracting body, suppose we could get closer to the four-million-ton rock. If we could get ten times closer or about five meters away, then the gravity from the rock would increase to one-thousandth of Earth gravity. If we could get 100 times closer or 50 centimeters away, the attraction would increase to one-tenth of Earth gravity. The rock is now beginning to have a significant effect on the gravity of the Earth. If we could get 16 centimeters away from a four-million-ton mass, the gravity attraction would rise to one Earth gravity. The gravity field of the rock is now strong enough to cancel out the gravity field of the Earth, which is a trillion times more massive than the rock.

But how do you get very close to a rock? It doesn't work to dig a hole and crawl inside. You have to make the rock smaller while maintaining its mass, so you can get closer to the center while still staying outside. That means we have to find a way to make matter denser than it normally is.

An atom in normal matter contains a lot of nothing. In the center is the nucleus, containing the protons and neutrons, which comprise most of the mass of an atom. Surrounding the nucleus is a tenuous cloud of electrons. An oxygen atom, for example, has a nucleus with eight protons and eight neutrons, and is about a trillionth of a centimeter across.

The eight units of positive charge in the nucleus of an oxygen atom are balanced out by eight negatively charged electrons that orbit around the nucleus. It is this outer electron cloud that is the surface connecting the atom to the rest of the atoms in your body (and the outside world). This electron cloud is thousands of times larger than the size of the nucleus of an atom and weighs practically nothing. Thus, an atom is mostly made up of empty space between the nucleus and the outer electron shells.

We know that more dense forms of matter exist. We can see white-dwarf stars in the sky that have the mass of a sun condensed into a ball the size of the Earth. White-dwarf-star densities are about a million times greater than normal densities. In a white-dwarf star, the gravity field of the star is so strong that the electron shells about all the atoms have collapsed. The positively charged nuclei of the atoms remain separated because of their mutual electric repulsion, while the electrons flow freely between the nuclei like a liquid, instead of being stuck in orbits about a single nucleus as in normal matter.

We also know that neutron stars exist. Here the mass of a sun has been condensed into a sphere that is only 20 kilometers across! Neutron-star densities are a hundred trillion times greater than normal densities. Below the surface of a neutron star, the nuclei of the atoms have been forced so close to each other that the neutrons in the nuclei are free to wander from nucleus to nucleus. Near the center of a neutron star the pressures are so high that the electrons recombine with the protons to make neutrons and the crushed atomic nuclei turn into a sea of liquid neutrons with a sprinkling of protons and electrons.

Thus, one future-magic key to controlling gravity using Newton's theory of gravity is to find a method to collapse ordinary matter with its bloated electron orbits into matter with white-dwarf-star densities or greater. We can't do it now, but one of these days we may develop the technology. When we do, we can envision our four-million-ton rock condensed into a ball 32 centimeters or one foot in diameter, with a surface gravitational attraction of one Earth gravity. Even better would be to make it in the shape of a disc that is 45 centimeters in diameter and 10 centimeters thick.

This disc would have the property that the gravitational attraction would be the same on both sides of the disc and would be fairly uniform near the center of the disc. The strength of the gravitational attraction near the center of the disc would be one Earth gravity. If this disc were somehow supported in the one Earth gravity field of the real Earth, then on top of the disc there would be a gravity field of two Earth gravities: one Earth gravity from the gravitational attraction of the Earth, and one Earth gravity from the gravitational attraction of the dense mass in the disc. On the bottom of the disc, near the center, the one Earth gravity attraction of the mass of the disc would cancel the one Earth gravity attraction of the mass of the Earth. There would be a gravity-free region under the disc where we could carry out free-fall experiments.

But now we come to another problem. How do we hold the four-million-ton antigravity roof up over our heads? The roof loading works out to 3.5 million tons per square foot or 3.5 million atmospheres! It would take a remarkable material to stand that sort of pressure. The material exists, however, and it is remarkable. It is diamond. The highest pressure ever made in the laboratory to date has been 1.7 million atmospheres. It was achieved by pressing the flat surfaces of two diamond anvils together using a turnscrew. Believe it or not, since the total area under pressure between the two diamonds is so small, the turnscrew is turned by hand! At 1.7 million atmospheres, one of the two diamond anvils used in the high-pressure machine "flowed." The other diamond, however, being made of sterner stuff, did not.

How strong is a perfect diamond? Strong enough to help make antigravity possible? Dare we envision a future where one of the attractions at a Disney park is a Free-fall Pavilion, rising upward on massive swooping buttresses of pure diamond, which support a brilliantly reflecting roof of ultradense matter . . . and under that roof floats a crowd of fun seekers, swimming through the warm air with colorful feathered wings attached to their arms, living out the legend of Icarus for the price of an E coupon?

Because of the unfortunate coincidence that the Earth is massive and its surface gravity is strong, while the density of matter that we can make is small so that its surface gravity is weak, antigravity machines using the Newton theory of gravity are still future magic in practice, even though we know how to build them. As we shall see later, this will still hold true for antigravity machines built using the secrets of the Einstein theory of gravity. To make any antigravity machine capable of canceling out the gravity field of the Earth will require the use of ultradense matter, and the method of making ultradense matter is still a form of future magic practiced only by white-dwarf and neutron stars.

There is a form of gravity cancellation, however, that can be practiced right now. It uses a combination of Ug antigravity and Newtonian antigravity to create a large volume that is completely free of gravity forces even though the volume is embedded in the gravity field of the Earth and even when the volume has gravity-producing masses in it! This gravity-free volume could be built in a few years and profitably used to make exotic materials that cannot be made under the influence of gravity.

Many of the experiments currently carried out on Space Shuttle flights, especially those where the Spacelab is flown as cargo, are called "zero-gee" materials processing experiments. Some involve forming "perfect" spheres of metal or latex by squeezing out drops of liquid into free-fall. The surface tension forces form the drops into spheres and then the drops solidify into balls. Others involve mixing two metals with greatly differing density, such as lithium and lead (to make a bearing alloy). If you attempted to cast such an alloy on Earth, the bottom of the crucible would contain mostly lead and the top would contain mostly lithium. Another space manufacturing process, called electrophoresis, uses the flow of strong electrical currents through a liquid to collect dilute quantities of precious biological chemicals from blood samples or a watery mass of bacteria and their excretions. The purity of the end product depends strongly on the dominance of the electrochemical currents over the convection currents in the liquid caused by the heated water "rising" in any residual gravity forces.

At the present time, these "zero-gee" space manufacturing experiments are done using only the Ug form of antigravity. The Space Shuttle "jumps" into space and goes into a free-fall orbit around the Earth. This effectively cancels most of the gravity field of the Earth, but not all of it. The only part of the Space Shuttle that is under absolutely zero net gravity force is the center of mass of the spacecraft. The rest of the Space Shuttle, especially the nose, tail, and wingtips, is experiencing gravity forces due to the tides of the Earth. These residual gravity forces are not large, a few microgravities (millionths of Earth gravity), and do not cause any large effects in the present crude space manufacturing experiments. But as the manufacturing apparatus goes from the experimental stage on the Space Shuttle to the "making money" manufacturing phase on the Space Station, the apparatus will become larger, the residual gravity tidal forces will become larger, and they will begin to affect the quality of the manufactured product. I have invented a way to reduce these gravity effects by another factor of a million, so that the residual forces are less than a picogravity (a trillionth of Earth gravity). I do this by using various arrangements of massive dense spheres, disks, and rings to nullify the residual gravity effects inside the processing apparatus.

Suppose you were floating around in the bay of the Space Shuttle. The Shuttle has all of its control thrusters off and is floating in free-fall, its nose pointing to the ground below. If you were floating at the point in the middle of the bay that is the center of mass of the Shuttle, you would stay at that point, since both you and the Shuttle are in *exactly* the same orbit. If, however, you were up in the nose of the Shuttle, 15 meters away from the center of mass, you would find after two minutes of time that you would have drifted some 30 centimeters away from the center of mass of the Shuttle, closer to the nose. Your motion was caused by a residual tidal force of 4.5 microgravities. In two minutes under this intense gravity force you will have reached the tremendous velocity of five millimeters per second and will soon be smashed against the forward bulkhead, where you will be crushed by the intense 4.5 microgravity gravity force. Although you are perfectly capable of surviving this experience, a space manufacturing facility located in the nose of the Space Shuttle would be significantly affected by these residual gravity tidal forces. The "perfect" ball bearings would be elliptical, the "uniform" alloy would have density gradations, and the "pure" biological extract would be contaminated with impurities.

There are two ways to look at how these residual tidal forces occur. One picture uses the concept of orbital motion and the other uses the concept of gravity gradients. The two ways are equivalent as long as the region we are interested in (the inside of a Space Shuttle or a manufacturing facility on the Space Station) is much smaller than the distance to the center of the Earth.

In the orbital picture, the center of mass of the Space Shuttle is in orbit around the Earth, moving at a certain speed appropriate for that orbit. You are in the nose of the Space Shuttle, 15 meters closer to the Earth. However, at the start of the experiment you have arranged your velocity so that you are not moving with respect to the walls of the Shuttle. You are now moving with the velocity of the Space Shuttle, but you are in a lower orbit, which requires a *higher* velocity than the Space Shuttle velocity if it is to be a circular orbit. Since your velocity is too low for your altitude, you are *not* in a circular orbit, but at the peak of an elliptical orbit. As you and the Space Shuttle continue in orbit, the Space Shuttle remains at the same distance above the Earth, while you drop away in your elliptical orbit and soon smash against the front bulkhead. The same picture applies if you start out near the tail of the Space Shuttle, only now in your higher orbit you are going too fast for your altitude and rise up away from the Shuttle orbit.

Now suppose the Space Shuttle were in a perfect equatorial orbit, always following the equator of the Earth, with its wings pointing north and south. If you started your space-float at the end of one wingtip, you would be at the same altitude as the Space Shuttle, moving at the same speed as the Space Shuttle, but your orbit started out a wingtip's length north of the equator. Your orbit has to cross the equator after a quarter of an orbit, go south until it reaches a wingtip's length after a half orbit, cross back over the equator again and then return to the north after a full revolution. Since your orbit has to cross over the equatorial orbit of the Space Shuttle, you will find that after two minutes you will have floated 15 centimeters (one-half foot) from the wingtip "toward" the center of mass of the Space Shuttle.

A similar effect occurs if the wings of the Space Shuttle are oriented along the equator. Now, however, because the line from the wingtips through the center of mass is a straight line, while the Shuttle orbit is curved, if you start out on a wingtip, you are in a higher orbit than the Space Shuttle and going too fast. As you rise in your elliptical orbit, you slow down and the Space Shuttle overtakes you, bringing you closer to its center of mass, so that again you will have moved 15 centimeters after two minutes.

Thus, from the orbital picture, objects inside the Space Shuttle that are not right at the center of mass of the Shuttle move in their own orbits. From the viewpoint of those in the Shuttle, those objects that are above or below the Space Shuttle center of mass move outward with an acceleration of 0.3 microgravities per meter of distance away from the center of mass, while those objects in a plane tangent to the Earth move inward with an acceleration of 0.15 microgravities per meter of distance away from the center of mass.

There is an alternate way of looking at the same effect that uses the concept of gravity gradients, or the change of the gravity field of the Earth with distance. Imagine that the Space Shuttle is not in orbit. Instead it is just dropping nose-first toward the Earth. If you were floating in the nose of the Space Shuttle, dropping along with it, you would be 15 meters closer to the center of the Earth than the center of mass of the Shuttle. Since Newton's theory of gravity says that the gravity field of the Earth gets weaker with distance (as the inverse square of the distance), then the gravity field on you is *stronger* than the gravity field on the Space Shuttle and you fall faster than the center of mass of the Space Shuttle, pulling you toward the nose. If you were at the back of the Shuttle bay, you would be in a weaker gravity field, while the Shuttle is in a stronger field and is pulled away from you. Thus, because the gravity field of the Earth changes with vertical distance above the Earth, objects at different altitudes fall at different rates. The farther apart the objects are from each other, the greater the difference in their rates of fall.

This gravity gradient or differential acceleration effect is better known to you as the tidal force. The tides in the oceans of the Earth are caused mostly by the gravity gradient forces of the moon. The moon pulls on the oceans underneath it, and pulls them up away from the center of mass of the Earth, causing the below-moon tidal bulge. At the same time, the moon is pulling the Earth away from the ocean water on the far side, causing the opposite-moon tidal bulge. That is why the tides come about every 12 hours instead of every 24 hours.

There is also a horizontal gravity gradient. The reason for the horizontal accelerations is a little harder to understand, but the horizontal gradients are *always* just as important as the vertical gradient. For a spherical attracting mass like the Earth, the horizontal gradients are half the strength of the vertical gradients, but there are two of them. Going back (briefly) to our still-falling Space Shuttle, suppose you were out near one wingtip, falling along with the Shuttle. Both you and the Space Shuttle are falling directly toward the center of the Earth. But since the two trajectories ultimately meet at the center of the Earth, as you fall along your trajectory it gets closer to the trajectory of the center of mass of the Space Shuttle and you experience an inward gravity gradient force.

If we move our point of view to the center of the mass of the Space Shuttle, we see that the gravity tide pattern from the Earth consists of a tension in the vertical direction that is twice as strong as the uniform compression in the horizontal direction (see Figure 6). The amount of acceleration between two objects is directly proportional to the distance between them and inversely proportional to the cube of the distance to the Earth. For an object in free-fall (either dropping down or in orbit around the Earth), the amount of inward acceleration in the horizontal directions is about 0.15 microgravities per meter of separation, while the outward acceleration in the vertical direction is twice that.

To eliminate these residual gravity fields we can use my gravity gradient compensator consisting of six dense masses in a ring around the region to be protected. (A solid ring or any number of masses greater than three can be used instead, but six seems to be optimum.) The plane of the ring of masses is arranged to always be tangent to the surface of the Earth below. The tidal gravity pattern from the six compensator spheres in a ring is almost exactly the same as the tidal gravity pattern from

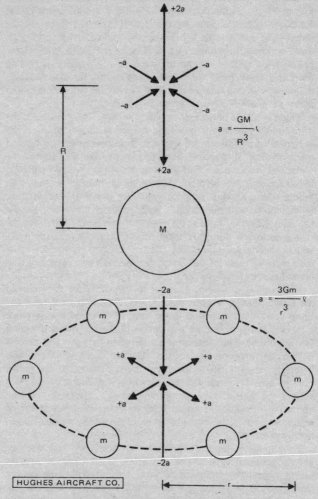

$$a = \frac{GM}{R^3}$$

$$a = \frac{3Gm}{r^3}$$

HUGHES AIRCRAFT CO.

Figure 6. Tidal patterns of Earth and six-mass compensator.

the Earth, except the accelerations are reversed in direction. This pattern of forces is easily understood if you imagine a small test object in the middle of the ring. If the test object is exactly in the center, the combined gravitational attraction of the six spheres cancels out. If the test object moves above or below the plane, the combined attractions of the spheres will pull it back. If the test object moves toward one of the spheres, the attraction of that sphere increases while the attraction of the sphere on the opposite side of the ring decreases, and the test object is pulled even farther away from the center. The amount of acceleration produced by the compensator spheres is proportional to their mass, inversely proportional to the cube of the radius of the ring, and increases linearly with the distance of the test object from the center of the ring. Thus, by merely adjusting the radius and tilt of the ring of compensator spheres we can ''fine-tune'' the gravity tidal pattern of the compensator to match the tidal pattern of the Earth at any altitude. Since we will not be trying to compensate for the whole gravity field of the Earth, but only for the differential tides, we will not need ultradense matter for the compensator spheres, but only normal density material like lead or tungsten.

Since the gravity gradient field patterns of the Earth and a compensator are opposite in sign, they will cancel each other out if the six spheres are placed in a ring tangent to the surface of the Earth and the radius of the ring is mechanically adjusted to the right value and held there. If we assume that the spheres in the compensator are 100-kilogram balls of tungsten, then the spheres will be 22 centimeters (9 inches) in diameter. To cancel the gravitational tides of the Earth at 500 kilometers, the diameter of the ring should be 51 centimeters (20 inches). Subtracting the finite size of the compensator spheres, this gives a working area inside the compensator that is 29 centimeters (11 inches) in diameter. Up in geostationary orbit at 36,000 kilometers altitude, the gravity field of the Earth is 300 times weaker, and the compensator spheres can be moved back to 156 centimeters from the center, giving a working volume free from gravity and gravity tides almost three meters in diameter.

The match of the compensating fields to the Earth fields is only perfect at the exact center of the ring. The match is fairly good, however, in a significant region about the central point. For an orbital altitude of 500 kilometers, the normal Earth tidal accelerations are about 0.25 microgravities per meter or about ten nanogravities at four centimeters from the center. (A nanogravity is a billionth of Earth gravity.) Calculations show that if the compensator ring were properly adjusted, the residual gravity forces inside a disk-shaped region about the size of a box of bath powder at the center of the compensator ring would be reduced by a factor of 100.

At geostationary orbit altitude, the size of the compensated region becomes bigger and the fields become smaller. The compensator ring can now lower the residual accelerations to less than a picogravity over a disk-shaped volume the size of a large hatbox, 24 centimeters high and 30 centimeters in diameter.

These large volumes of force-free space will certainly be valuable for scientific experiments that require a region free from Earth tides. They also will be useful, up to a point, for space manufacturing. The lower acceleration limit for space processing is set by the self-gravity of the molten metals or liquids being processed. A ball of water and bacteria one meter across will have a self-gravity field at its surface of 29 nanogravities, while a molten ball of steel only ten centimeters across has a self-gravity field of 22 nanogravities (greater than the accelerations due to the Earth tides). These self-gravity forces will cause convection currents to flow in the liquid, disturbing the desired equilibrium conditions.

It turns out that, with a little bit of Newtonian antigravity magic, we can not only cancel any Earth tides that might affect those materials-processing experiments, but we can also cancel the self-gravity field everywhere inside the sample! The shape for a space materials-processing experiment sample that gives the most volume with the lowest residual gravity is a thick disk. For a specific example, let us assume a disk of material with the density of water that is 30 centimeters in diameter and 10 centimeters thick (about the size of a large double-layer cake). The self-gravity field pattern of this thick disk is quite complicated. It is zero at the center and becomes stronger as you go toward the surface, reaching about three nanogravities at the top and bottom and around the rim.

I first smooth out the variations in the acceleration due to the "edge effects" by surrounding the sample volume with a "guard ring" consisting of a container in the shape of a ring filled with material that has the same density as the material in the sample chamber. The material in the sample volume and the guard ring are to be kept separated by a thin wall. The material in the guard ring will not be free from accelerations, and convection currents will be set up in it. The thin wall will keep the protected material in the sample volume from being disturbed by these currents. I then add ''guard caps'' to the top and bottom of the sample volume plus guard ring. With the guard ring and guard caps in place, we find that the original complicated self-gravity force pattern inside the sample has become very regular and increases linearly with distance from the center. How can we cancel these self-gravity accelerations? Let us take them one at a time.

To compensate for the inward vertical component of the self-gravity of the disk, we will use the outward vertical acceleration of the Earth tides. If the Earth tide at the altitude of our manufacturing facility is too strong for the self-gravity of the disk, we cancel a portion of it with our six-sphere tidal compensator. If the Earth tide at that altitude is too weak, we augment the Earth tidal forces using my two-sphere tidal augmentor.

A tidal augmentor consists of two 100-kilogram spheres placed above and below the sample disk. The gravity tidal pattern the augmentor produces at the point between the two spheres is identical to the tidal pattern of the Earth. Thus, by judicious use of either the compensator or augmentor, depending upon the orbital altitude and the density of the sample of material undergoing processing, we can adjust the Earth tides so they will compensate for the vertical component of the self-gravity of a properly guarded sample disk.

The horizontal component of acceleration is another matter. The horizontal self-gravity accelerations of the disk are inward-directed, as are the accelerations induced by the Earth tides. After we have used the Earth tides to null out the vertical self-gravity, we will find that the horizontal accelerations have been doubled. The combined self-gravity and Earth tide accelerations can now be canceled by a last bit of Newtonian magic. Instead of using the Newtonian theory of gravity, however, we will use Newton's theories of motion. I then cancel the horizontal accelerations by a slow rotation of the sample disk about its vertical axis.

The rotation of a disk causes an outward centrifugal acceleration that has no component along the vertical spin axis, just a horizontal acceleration that everywhere increases linearly with distance from the axis. A carefully chosen rotation of about one revolution every 2.7 hours will now cancel both the inward acceleration of the self-gravity of the sample and the inward acceleration of the Earth tides.

Thus, by a combination of guard rings and guard caps to make the self-gravity more uniform, the use of the Earth tides augmented or compensated by 100-kilogram masses, and a slight rotation of the sample volume, it is possible to cancel all the gravity inside a sample volume of material some 30 centimeters in diameter and 10 centimeters thick. The technique can be used at any orbital altitude, but the best results can be obtained in a space manufacturing facility in geostationary orbit. In one example that I calculated, our birthday-cake-sized sample disk of water had the gravity fields inside decreased by a factor of 1,000, so that the maximum gravity acceleration anywhere inside the disk was less than a picogravity. At this level of acceleration it would take an atom eight seconds to fall its own diameter!

One of these days there will be large space laboratories in orbit, with special isolated rooms where ultralow gravity experiments can be carried out. There will be no humans near those rooms, for the gravity of even the most petite experimenter would be enough to disturb the delicate experiments floating inside. From some of the laboratories will come exotic alloys, from others ultra-light, ultra-strong foamed metals. From still other laboratories the valuable extract will not be tangible products like pharmaceuticals and new materials, but that intangible yet infinitely more valuable product of scientific research—knowledge. Perhaps new knowledge about the innermost secrets of gravity.

Newton's theory of gravity served the human race well for over 200 years. As the followers of Newton carried out more and more detailed calculations of the motion of the moon and planets, the better the Newtonian theory of gravity looked. For example, the motion of Mars in its orbit is predominantly due to the gravitational attraction of the sun, but the mass of nearby Jupiter causes perturbations in that orbit, and the mass of Earth causes perturbations in that perturbed orbit, and the mass of Saturn causes perturbations in that perturbed, perturbed orbit, etc. Finally, perturbation calculations were carried out for the effect of every planet around the sun on every other planet. All the observations of the planets agreed with the predictions of the amazing Newtonian theory of gravity . . . almost. There were a few nagging problems left.

Using the Newton theory of gravity, astronomers could predict the motion of the four large moons of Jupiter about that massive body. When they looked through their telescopes at the pattern of the four moons as they orbited Jupiter, they noticed some slight timing discrepancies. When Jupiter was on the same side of the sun as the Earth and the distance between the two planets was at its minimum, the appearance of a moon from behind the limb of Jupiter seemed to come early. When Jupiter was on the other side of the sun and the Earth and Jupiter were far apart, the appearance of a moon from behind Jupiter seemed to come later than the predictions using the Newton theory of gravity. It wasn't long before the astronomers realized that the light from Jupiter and its moons had a finite velocity. When Jupiter was at its closest to the Earth, it took about 35 minutes before we would see the occultation of Ganymede by Jupiter. When the Earth–Jupiter distance was its greatest, the delay would be 52 minutes.

This bothered the astronomers a little. If light traveled at a finite velocity, did that mean that gravity traveled at a finite velocity? There was nothing in Newton's theory of gravity about the time it takes for gravity to travel. Some astronomers modified the Newton theory of gravity to include a finite propagation time and recalculated the orbit of the Earth around the sun. Because light takes about eight minutes to travel from the sun to the Earth, the position of the sun that we see in our sky is not its true position, but where it was eight minutes ago. Since a day is 1,440 minutes long, that means the "true" position of the sun is two degrees ahead of where it appears in the sky.

If this two-degree offset held for the Newtonian gravity attraction, the attraction of the gravity from the sun would be pulling backward on the Earth, slowing it down in its orbit, and causing it to spiral into the sun in a time very much shorter than the known lifetime of the solar system. Fortunately for us, the orbit of the Earth shows no measurable slowing down tendency, and the Newtonian theory of gravity, without any modification for the time of propagation of gravity, works perfectly in predicting the Earth orbit.

One conclusion that could be drawn from this agreement between Newton's theory of gravity and the measurements of the orbit of the Earth is that gravity travels at speeds much greater than the speed of light. As far as the Newton theory of gravity is concerned, the velocity of gravity is infinite. The second you create a ball of mass, the gravity field of that mass instantly starts attracting every other mass in the entire universe. This instantaneous "action-at-a-distance" aspect of the Newtonian theory bothered some astronomers, but the rest of them swept it under the rug and continued to use the very successful theory to refine their predictions of the motion of the planets and to start calculations on the motions of the myriad stars they were finding in globular clusters and spiral galaxies.

As the measuring instruments of the astronomers became better and the positions of the planets were measured with more and more accuracy, the calculating computers of the astronomers also became faster and the predictions of the Newton theory of gravity kept up with the measurements. But small discrepancies remained between the measured and predicted positions of two of the planets. One was the innermost planet, Mercury, and the other was the outermost planet known at that time, Uranus.

Uranus was not following a smooth elliptical orbit, but was wandering through the sky like a slightly tipsy pedestrian. It was finally guessed that the erratic behavior was due to some other planet still farther out. Having great faith in the validity of the Newton theory of gravity, the mathematicians successfully solved the problem of taking the measured position data for Uranus and predicting the mass, orbital radius, and position along the orbit of the mysterious Planet X that was perturbing the orbit of Uranus. With the approximate position in the sky known from the calculations, it was a simple matter for the observational astronomers to find the new planet—named Neptune—which till then had been overlooked. As soon as Neptune was discovered in 1846, the orbit of Uranus was recalculated and this time the observations agreed perfectly with Newton's theory of gravity . . . almost. There were still small differences between the predicted and the measured positions.

With Neptune found and its orbit pinned down more accurately, it was possible to go back to star maps made by previous observers and find the tiny starlike object that had been overlooked in the dense sprinkle of real stars. Thus Neptune's orbit could be reconstructed fairly accurately. But even it showed variations that could not be explained using the Newton theory of gravity.

Spurred by the success of the previous work, Percival Lowell thought that there might be another planet farther out than Neptune. He calculated that Planet P should be in an unusually elliptic orbit about 40 times larger than the orbit of Earth with a period of 260 years. To have caused the perturbations observed on the orbits of Uranus and Neptune, Planet P should have a mass of at least six times that of Earth.

An object this large should be easy to find, so in 1915, Lowell sat down at his moderate-sized but adequate telescope and started looking. He died without finding it. It was there, but it was much fainter than it had a right to be and he had missed it. To be that faint, a planet that large would have to be painted black! Later searches with photographic plates also missed it, although it was later found that it had been photographed twice. Once it was masked by a bright star and the other time the image fell on a flaw in the negative!

It wasn't until 1930 that Pluto was found. The radius, eccentricity, and period of the orbit were very close to what Lowell had predicted. Because the orbital calculations were so closely verified, there was no reason to doubt Lowell's prediction that Pluto had a mass of at least six times that of the Earth, except that the size of the image of Pluto was impossibly small. Later measurements showed that it was smaller than Mercury. To have that mass and that size, Pluto would have to be made of matter 600 times denser than water, and the heaviest known material, osmium, is only 22 times denser than water.

For a long time the astronomers, rather than saying there was something wrong with the Newtonian theory of gravity, continued to believe that Pluto was the missing planet of Lowell and tried to sweep under the rug the "inconvenient" density of the planet. Finally, in 1978, observers at the United States Naval Observatory reported the discovery of a moon about Pluto. With a moon in orbit, it is possible (using the Newtonian theory, of course) to calculate the mass of the planet. We now know that instead of Pluto having a mass greater than six times the mass of the Earth, the mass of Pluto is more like $\frac{1}{400}$ the mass of the Earth. Pluto is *not* the Planet P that is causing the perturbations of the orbits of Uranus and Neptune.

Others have attempted to find the real Planet P, through mathematics and observations, but to date the search has proven futile and the discrepancy in the orbit of Neptune remains. The astronomers are continuing to sweep the discrepancy under the rug. It is probably true that Newton's theory of gravity (and its later replacements) is still correct for accurately predicting the motions of the planets, but it could be that these annoying discrepancies are trying to give us a clue as to a different theory of gravity that may hold for very large distances, distances greater than the size of the solar system.

It was just such a minor but annoying clue that led to the replacement of the Newtonian theory of gravity with the present favorite, Einstein's theory of gravity. For it was the ''slight inaccuracies'' in the prediction of the orbit of Mercury that led to the discovery that the Newton's theory of gravity is not a correct description of gravity when one of the masses is very large and you are very close to it. The Newtonian theory works fine for satellites around moons and moons around planets. The theory also works fine for planets around stars if the planetary orbits are very large compared to the radius of the star. But Newton's theory of gravity is not correct for a planet in a very small orbit around a big star, like Mercury in its orbit around our sun.

The orbit of Mercury is not circular. It has a large eccentricity of 20 percent, which makes the orbit distinctly elliptical. Because Mercury has an orbital period of only 88 days, the astronomers have been able to follow it through hundreds of revolutions around the sun and have been able to measure the parameters of the orbit to high accuracy. The major axis of the orbital ellipse of Mercury shifts a little each revolution—5599.74 $\pm$ 0.41 seconds of arc per century, to be exact (about three or four degrees of total precessional shift since people started measuring a few centuries ago). Calculations using the Newtonian theory of gravity indicate that the perturbations introduced by the other planets in the solar system cause most of this shift, but not all of it. Even after many refinements, the maximum calculated orbital shift due to the planetary perturbations was found to be 5557.18 $\pm$ 0.85 seconds of arc per century, leaving a discrepancy of 42.56 $\pm$ 0.94 seconds of arc per century between the measurements and predictions of the Newtonian theory of gravity.

Finally, along came Albert Einstein with a new theory of gravity. Using his new theory, Einstein calculated the orbit of Mercury and found that in his theory the major axis of the orbital ellipse of Mercury should precess an additional 42.9 seconds of arc per century, in excellent agreement with the measurements. Other competing theories of gravity, when applied to the precession of the orbit of Mercury, give an incorrect value or even the wrong sign.

Einstein's theory of gravity is more complex than the two previous theories of gravity. In a simplified form it can be expressed as:

"A mass causes space to curve. Other masses move in that curved space."

In the Einstein view of gravity, mass does not cause gravity. Instead, mass curves space, and curved space causes gravity. In this picture, what Newton called the gravity force is force-free motion in curved space. A good analogy is to imagine a rubber sheet stretched over a frame. If you put a heavy ball bearing in the center of the rubber sheet, the weight of the ball would cause a curved depression. The mass of the heavy ball bearing has "curved" the rubber sheet "space." If you then drop a tiny marble on the curved rubber sheet, the marble would immediately start to roll toward the center as if the large ball were attracting it. But there is no direct attraction between the ball bearing and the marble; the ball bearing is curving the rubber sheet and the marble is responding to the curvature of the rubber (and the gravity of the Earth). If the marble were tossed properly into the curved depression in the rubber sheet, it would go into an "orbit" around the heavy ball bearing at the center.

Because Mercury is close to the sun, the space curvature caused by the sun has two effects on the motion of Mercury. First, the curved space produced by the sun causes Mercury to move in an orbit about the sun, just like all the other planets do under the influence of the curved space caused by the sun. But in addition, the space near the sun where Mercury orbits is *so* curved that some of the space is missing!

A circle drawn around the sun out near the orbit of Earth has a full 360 degrees of angle in it. But a circle drawn around the sun in near the orbit of Mercury does not have a full 360 degrees in it; it is missing roughly 0.1 seconds of arc. So every time Mercury orbits the sun, it comes up short by that much. After a few centuries, this missing piece of angle in Mercury's orbit adds up to a noticeable precession. The prediction and confirmation of the existence of this tiny little amount of missing space by the Einstein theory of gravity has led to many other and more dramatic predictions by the theory, such as the Big Bang, black holes, gravitational waves, space warps, time machines, and even gravity control. Some of the predictions, such as the Big Bang and black holes, now seem to be verified –

by observation. The others are still future magic, but we are beginning to envision how they might turn into future reality.

One of the major improvements of the Einstein theory of gravity over the Newtonian theory of gravity is that the Einstein theory properly handles the problem of the time it takes for a gravitational influence to propagate from one place to another. In the Einstein theory of gravity, it takes a finite time for gravity to travel from the generating mass to the detecting mass. Also, in Einstein's theory it is possible for gravitational forces to travel as waves, just like radio waves. These gravitational waves would be generated by rapidly oscillating masses, just as radio waves are generated by rapidly oscillating electric currents moving up and down a radio tower. Like radio waves, which keep on traveling even after the radio station is turned off (or the disk jockey has switched to a different record), these gravitational waves will keep on going even after the generating masses stop oscillating.

To make a significant amount of gravitational radiation it would be necessary to oscillate very large, very dense masses at very high speeds. The only masses that are large enough, dense enough, and moving fast enough to emit detectable amounts of gravitational radiation are rotating, binary, neutron star pairs and exploding supernovas. Detectors have been built to search for the interstellar gravitational radiation from these sources, with as yet inconclusive results. Although we have very sensitive detectors for gravitational waves, there are as yet no good ideas for generators of gravitational radiation that can emit waves strong enough to be sensed by the present detectors. Communication with gravitational waves is still future magic.

Since we do not yet have a gravitational communication system, the speed of propagation of gravity waves has not been measured directly. There is indirect evidence, however, that the velocity of propagation of gravitational waves is the same as the velocity of propagation of radio waves or light—300,000 kilometers per second (186,000 miles per second).

The Einstein theory of gravity has two constants in it. When the Einstein equations are arranged to describe the static attraction of one mass on another mass, then only one constant remains and it turns out to be the Newton constant of gravity G, which tells how much force (in newtons, pounds, or whatever) is produced for each amount of mass (in kilograms, troy ounces, pounds, or whatever). When the Einstein equations are arranged to describe gravitational waves, the second constant shows up in the wave equation where the velocity of propagation of gravity should be. When the Einstein equations are then rearranged to describe the precession of the orbit of Mercury, then both constants show up in the solution. The correct answer for the amount of precession of 42.9 seconds of arc per century is obtained only if the numerical value for the velocity of propagation of light is used for the constant that describes the velocity of propagation of gravity. This is our only "proof" that gravity propagates at the same speed as light. There are other good theoretical reasons why gravity and light should travel at the same speed, but it is important for a direct measurement to be made as soon as it becomes technically feasible.

The Einstein theory of gravity also solves the riddle of why the solar system has not run down due to the delay in propagation of the gravity from the sun to the Earth. In the mathematical equations of the Einstein theory of gravity, two terms that depend upon the propagation velocity of gravity interact with each other in a complicated way. When the relative motion of the masses making the gravity field is slow (such as the year-long motion of the Earth around the sun), then these two terms compensate each other and there is no net time delay observed in the gravity interaction between the two bodies. It is only when the relative motion of the masses is rapid, so that the gravitational wave associated with that frequency is comparable to the separation distance between the two bodies, that any phase-delay effect can be noticed.

Because the Einstein theory of gravity is more complex than the Ug or Newton theories, it can give us more handles by which we can control gravity. There are at least two ways that we can use Einstein's theory to negate the gravity field of the Earth. There are also two ways we can use his theory to make a mass push instead of pull.

The Einstein theory of gravity has a number of different facets to it. It is like a precious jewel that shines forth glitter after glitter of insight as we examine it—first from one viewpoint and then from another. One facet is that gravity can travel as waves; another facet is that the curvature of gravity can be so strong it "swallows" space; still another facet is that gravity behaves very much like electricity, although more weakly.

In the scientific studies of electricity, it has been found that electricity and magnetism are related. If you change or move electricity you make magnetism, and if you change or move magnetism you make electricity again. This transformation between electricity and magnetism is used to make your automobile run. The electricity in your car battery is only 12 volts, not strong enough to run your spark plugs. This low-voltage electricity is used to create magnetism in the spark coil. The magnetism temporarily stored in the coil is then released very rapidly when the points open. This rapidly changing magnetic field then generates the powerful, high-voltage sparks that are used by the spark plugs. By using the magnetic field as an intermediate step, the automotive engineers have found a way to convert weak electric forces into strong electric forces.

The Einstein theory of gravity says that gravity behaves the same way as electricity. If you take a mass and the gravity field that surrounds it, and move the mass very rapidly, you can create a new field, the gravitational equivalent of magnetism. It is not magnetism, but a completely new field that is part of our future-magic inheritance. If you can then cause that new field to change, you can create a stronger gravity field than you started with. More important, that stronger gravity field can be made to appear at a place where there is no mass, and can be either attractive or repulsive.

Conceptually, there are a number of ways that such a gravity machine could be made. One idea is to roll up some hollow pipe to form a long coil, like the curly cord on a telephone (see Figure 7). We then bend the long coil around until the two ends meet to form a curly closed ring. If the pipes are filled with massive liquid and the liquid is moved back and forth in the pipes rapidly enough, then an alternating push–pull gravity field will be generated at the center of the ring. If the machine were big enough, and the liquid were dense enough and moving fast enough, then we would have a gravity catapult that could launch and retrieve rocket ships from space by its gravity repulsion and attraction.

How big? How dense? How fast? Unfortunately, the machine has to be as big as the distance over which you want the gravity effects to operate. The liquid has to be as dense or denser than white-dwarf-star material, and the speed of the flow has to be so high that the ultradense liquid will approach the speed of light in a few milliseconds.

I am afraid that it will be some time before we have all that gravitational technology well in hand. But we do have the theory

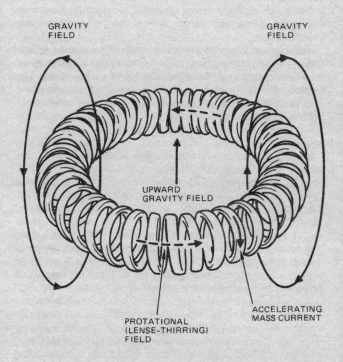

GRAVITY FIELD

GRAVITY FIELD

UPWARD GRAVITY FIELD

PROTATIONAL (LENSE-THIRRING) FIELD

ACCELERATING MASS CURRENT

HUGHES AIRCRAFT CO.

Figure 7. Machine for producing a repulsive gravity force.

needed to design our gravity catapult, and in some future-magic time in the long distant future we will have college classes full of bright students taking their first course in Gravitational Engineering, studying the turbulent flow in ultradense matter and producing more and more efficient designs for the gravitational attractor and repulsor beam intensities to minimize passenger discomfort during the launch or retrieval of an interstellar passenger liner.

The Einstein theory of gravity can give us yet another future-magic way to control gravity. One of the strangest facets of the Einstein theory of gravity is the concept of curved space. The method by which a massive object causes a curvature in space is difficult to really comprehend. It is as if the mass had grabbed hold of space and pulled space into it. This grip of mass on space is still maintained when the mass is moving. The space seems to move along with the mass. This effect, called the "dragging of the space–time coordinate frame," is the basis for another future-magic type of antigravity machine.

If you are near a rapidly moving dense mass, you will find yourself "dragged" along in the direction of the moving mass. One could envision a "lift" shaft, lined with pipes full of rapidly flowing ultradense fluid that wafts you rapidly up to the top of a mile-high building. But more likely this "drag" effect will be used in space as a gravity catapult for shipping purposes within the solar system. This machine would again be in the form of a ring of ultradense matter, but this time the ring would be uniformly whirling from inside out like a gigantic smoke ring.

If a spaceship entered such a toroidal gravity catapult through the hole from one side, it would be expelled out the other side of the hole with a greatly increased velocity. If the spaceship were falling in toward the sun from the asteroid belt with a high velocity, it would be gently stopped in Earth orbit by threading the torus in the opposite direction. Since the forces on the spaceship during acceleration and deceleration are gravitational forces acting equally on every atom in the ship, all the atoms in the spacecraft are stopped at the same rate and at the same time, so that even though the accelerations and decelerations can be at rates equivalent to hundreds of Earth gravities, the passengers on those spacecraft will not even have to turn in their martini glasses for "landing" in the Earth–moon system, much less buckle their seatbelts, stow their overhead luggage, raise their seatbacks, and secure their tables.

As unbelievable as these machines for controlling gravity might seem, they at least use a form of matter that we know exists, even if it is currently found only in the interiors of far distant stars. There are speculations that there might exist another type of matter. It has very strange properties. If it ever could be found or made, then a whole new era of future magic in gravity control would open up.

All the matter that we know of is the type called regular (positive) matter. Yet both the Newton and the Einstein theories of gravity allow the existence of an opposite form of matter, called negative matter. According to the theories of gravity and motion, an atom of negative matter would repel all other matter (including other atoms of negative matter).

Now, the first thing to realize about negative matter is that is is *not* "antimatter" or "mirror matter." Mirror matter is different from regular matter in its quantum mechanical properties, not its gravitational properties. Although it has yet to be proven experimentally, we are fairly sure that antimatter attracts other forms of matter, just like normal matter. Negative matter, however, would repel other forms of matter.

We do not know how to make negative matter. But when we do, we will discover the future-magic result that it will not cost us any energy to make that negative matter. Because the rest mass energy of a particle is proportional to its mass ($E = mc^2$), the rest mass energy of a negative mass particle is negative! That means that if we always create equal amounts of positive and negative matter at the same time, it will cost us no net energy to do so!

One can imagine a future-magic scene in some huge laboratory, where great machines apply intense electric, magnetic, and gravitational forces to some microscopic point in empty space. The energy levels of the fields are raised higher and higher until "empty space" itself is ripped apart into a ball of regular matter and an equal-sized ball of negative matter, the whole process using no net energy except for the losses in the generating machines.

Once we have our negative matter, we can start using it to make antigravity machines. But we must be very careful how we handle the negative matter. Unlike a chunk of regular matter, which responds to your push by moving away, if you push on a chunk of negative matter, it will come *toward* you! (If, by mistake, you try to push some negative matter, and it starts to move toward you, you must quickly run around behind it and give it a slap on the rear to bring it to a halt!)

Now that we have learned how to control our working material, the simplest antigravity machine that we can make is to form the negative matter into a dense disk and lay it on a good strong floor. If the disk is dense enough and thick enough, then the repulsive gravity field on both sides of the disk will be one Earth gravity. That negative gravity field from the disk would then cancel the gravity field of the Earth. In the region above the disk, the gravity attraction would be zero and you could float there in free-fall.

The negative gravitational field of negative matter can also be used for gravity propulsion. If you place a ball of very dense negative matter near a similar dense ball of regular matter (which is incidentally attached to your spaceship), you will find that the negative matter ball will repel the regular matter ball, which in turn will attract the negative matter ball. Then, in a nearly unbelievable form of future magic, the two dense balls will start to move off in a straight line at a constantly increasing speed. The acceleration will be the strength of the gravitational attraction of one ball for the other, with the negative matter ball chasing after the positive matter ball and the positive matter ball bringing your spaceship along with it.

You might at first worry that you are getting something for nothing. First there were two balls of matter, both standing still, with no kinetic energy. Then, after a while, they are both moving off together at speeds approaching that of light with no propulsion energy being expended to get them up to speed. You might think that would prove that negative matter is impossible, since it looks like the law of conservation of energy is being violated.

But if you look very closely, you will find that negative mass propulsion does not violate any laws of physics. It is true that the ball of regular mass gains speed and increases its kinetic energy [$E = \frac{1}{2}(+m)v^2$], so it looks like it is getting energy out of nowhere. But while it is doing so, the ball of negative matter at the same time is gaining *negative* energy [$E = \frac{1}{2}(-m)v^2$] and the total energy of the two masses is zero, just as it was when they were standing still. Thus, negative mass propulsion does not violate the law of conservation of energy.

By the same types of argument, you can also show that negative-mass propulsion does not violate that other important law of physics, the law of conservation of momentum. For while the momentum of the positive ball of mass is increasing, the momentum of the negative ball of mass is decreasing, resulting in zero net momentum, even though the two balls started out standing still and now are moving off at high speeds.

So far as we know, negative matter does not exist. We don't know why it doesn't. After all, both the positive and negative forms of electricity exist, so why not the positive and negative forms of mass? Perhaps there is some yet unknown law of physics that prevents it from forming. But even if we can never obtain this future-magic material, we can still devise ways to control gravity with just regular matter, if we just work hard and use enough energy and intelligence.

The Einstein theory of gravity is now serving the human race well, and will until a better theory of gravity is discovered. We do not know the correct theory of gravity yet. The correct theory of gravity must include quantum mechanics—the theory of the behavior of atoms and elementary particles. The Einstein theory of gravity, despite all its recognized grandeur, ignores quantum mechanics. Because it does not recognize the world of the small, someday it will be replaced. Many brilliant people are now working hard to find a new theory of gravity that will retain all that was good in Einstein's theory, yet will add the new features of gravity effects into the microcosmic world of the atom.

The new quantum theory of gravity will be even more complex than the Einstein theory of gravity. The strange Einsteinian concepts of curved space will be mixed up with the even more exotic zoo of "elementary" particles, with their strangeness, beauty, charm, and color. Yet we should not despair because the theories become more complex. For it is their very complexity that will be the tools that the gravitational engineer of the future will use to invent, design, build, test, and make work the machines that will give us control over our common burden, gravity.

Can we really make an antigravity machine? The answer is yes. There are many ways to make a machine that will cancel the gravitational attraction of Earth. It is also theoretically possible to make a machine out of massive bodies that will repel a massive object instead of attracting it. The technology required to build such machines is not here right now, but as we gain control over more energy and move into space where we can manipulate large masses without having to contest Earth for their control, we will move into the realm of future magic in the field of gravity control. When that day comes, the children of the human race (or whoever the human race has evolved into by then) will control gravity as easily as our littlest children now control the awesome power of lightning with the flick of a wall switch.

Black Magic

Another magical result that came out of research in the science of gravity has been the prediction and then the discovery of that bizarre enigma, the black hole. It is truly a hole, in that anything dropped into it falls forever. It is truly black, in that nothing comes back out, not even light. Even the identity of what went into the black hole is obliterated by the blackness. The power of the black hole is so awesome that it even swallows space and warps time.

Black holes are forms of matter predicted not only by the Einstein theory of gravity, but many other theories of gravity. We now have good astronomical evidence that they really exist out in space. In our Milky Way galaxy there are probably millions of black holes containing the mass of a large star, while at the very center of the galaxy there is probably a huge black hole containing the mass of a million stars. This supermassive black hole would be about 3 million kilometers across, twice as large as our sun.

We don't have to worry about falling into these monsters of space–time, however, for they can only pull on us at long range with their gravity field, and that field is many times weaker than the gravity field of the sun. So we will stay tied to the sun, keeping comfortably warm, while the sun orbits around the black hole at the center of the galaxy. After a nearly uncountable number of years, the orbit of the sun will decay and the sun will finally join the big black hole at the galactic core, but that will take place long after the sun and all the rest of the stars in the galaxy have burned out. We and our robots will have left this worn-out galaxy long before that time and continued life in a new, fresh galaxy that we will have designed to suit our tastes.

The reason that a black hole is black is that the gravity field of the black hole is so large that the escape velocity of the black hole is greater than the speed of light. The escape velocity of an object like a planet is the velocity a rocket must have to leave the surface of the planet and coast off into space without need for additional propulsion. For the Earth the escape velocity is 11 kilometers per second; at the surface of Jupiter it is 61 kilometers per second; and for the sun it is 620 kilometers per second (0.2 percent of the speed of light). As long ago as 1795, it was noticed by the famous astronomer and mathematician, Pierre Simon, the Marquis de Laplace, that at the surface of a planet with the density of Earth and a radius some 250 times that of the sun, the escape velocity would be equal to the speed of the corpuscles that light was thought to be made out of at that time. Laplace thus concluded that such a planet would be dark. This was the first speculation on the concept of a black hole.

Black holes became more than speculation in 1915 when Albert Einstein formulated the equations for his theory of gravity, the General Theory of Relativity. Only months later, Karl Schwarzschild found one of the first solutions to those equations. Called the Schwarzschild solution, it describes the motion of a small test particle near a nonrotating uncharged massive object. The Schwarzschild solution is the relativistic replacement for the Newtonian equations that describe the orbits of the planets about the massive sun.

Like many mathematical solutions to equations that describe the behavior of fields, the Schwarzschild solution is only valid in the region *outside* the mass forming it. To describe what happens inside a massive object requires the use of other solutions to the Einstein theory of gravity that take into account the type of matter involved, its temperature, its pressure, etc. But outside a spherically symmetric mass, only one solution applies, the Schwarzschild solution, and all the solution needs to know about the object is its mass. The rest of its parameters, like temperature, pressure, even whether it is made of matter or antimatter, are irrelevant.

The Schwarzschild solution gives the same results as the Newton theory of gravity for a test particle near a mass when the test particle and mass are far apart. But when the gravitating mass is very dense, so that the test particle can get very close, there are differences between the predictions of the Newton theory of gravity and the Schwarzschild solution to the Einstein theory of gravity. One of these differences causes an extra precession in the orbit of the planet Mercury. Another causes light passing by the sun to be bent inward. (By a slight modification, one can get a light-bending effect from the Newton law of gravity, but it is wrong by a factor of two from the experimental measurements, while the Einstein theory of gravity agrees with experiment.) Another difference causes light signals passing by the sun to take longer to travel because time runs slower near the sun. This has been checked by tracking time signals from spacecraft as they pass in back of the sun. Another difference is that photons of light "get tired" as they try to climb up a gravitational field. Unlike a stone, which slows its speed as its energy becomes less, photons, which must travel *at* the speed of light, are gravitationally redshifted to a lower frequency. The lower the frequency of a photon, the lower the energy. This gravitational redshift effect was measured by sending gamma-ray photons up a tower at Harvard and measuring their decrease in frequency as they climbed up out of Earth gravity.

Because we have measured all these effects, we know that the Schwarzschild solution to the Einstein General Theory of Relativity is the best description of the gravity field outside a large mass, but that solution predicts some bizarre behavior when the mass is either very large or very dense, so that the test particle can get close to it. One of those bizarre predictions is the black hole.

A mass turns into a black hole when the escape velocity of the mass equals that of light. For a given mass M this occurs when all the mass is concentrated inside a radius R called the "Schwarzschild radius" ($R = 2GM/c^2$). The mass disappears from view and its place is taken by the "event horizon." The event horizon separates the outside universe from the miniature universe inside. It is a one-way membrane, in that objects can fall in through the event horizon, but things inside the event horizon cannot get back out. It is also the infinite redshift boundary, since light emitted from an object at that radius is infinitely gravitationally redshifted to zero energy. In essence, the event horizon is a black shield that prevents anyone from seeing what is going on inside. (It is interesting to note that *Schwarzschild* means "black shield" in German.)

After the event horizon is formed by a collapsing star, the collapse of the star continues in the same manner as it did before the event horizon formed. The star gets denser and smaller in radius as it collapses. The event horizon, however, stays constant in size after it has formed, with a radius equal to the Schwarzschild radius.

One of the problems in discussing black holes is to define what is meant by the word *radius* or *diameter* of a black hole. The diameter of a normal sphere can be obtained either by measuring the internal distance from one side to another, or by measuring the circumference of the sphere and dividing by pi (pi = 3.14159 . . .). The strong gravitational field of a black hole curves the space so strongly near the black hole that its diameter is no longer related to the circumference by pi. In fact, since an outside observer cannot make any measurements inside the black hole, the diameter cannot be measured, or even calculated for that matter. Thus, when we talk about the diameter of a black hole, what is meant is the distance given by dividing the measured circumference by pi.

Theoretically, black holes can come in many different sizes and densities. The typical black hole that one reads about in the Sunday supplements is the very dense black hole that is a few kilometers across and has the mass of a number of suns. It is a large star collapsed into a volume the size of a large mountain. The density is 10^{18} times that of normal matter and even 1,000 times that of nuclear matter. A stellar mass black hole is probably spinning fairly rapidly, since the original star that formed it was likely to be rotating somewhat. During the collapse of the star to form a black hole, the angular momentum in the original star was conserved, leaving the black hole spinning rapidly. The collapsing star increases its spin speed for the same reason that an ice skater increases her spin speed when she pulls in her outstretched arms during a toe spin.

The solution to the Einstein gravity equations that describes a rotating black hole was found by the mathematician Roy Kerr in 1963, almost fifty years after the solution for the nonrotating black hole. The Kerr solution reduces to the Schwarzschild solution when the rotation of the black hole is zero. Recently, other mathematicians have shown that these two solutions describe the only stable configurations for an uncharged black hole.

The black hole could have lost more electrons than protons during the collapse process, so it could have a modest electric surface charge, and since the black hole is spinning, that rotating electricity would produce a magnetic field. The solution for a charged, rotating black hole ring was found by Newman in 1965 as a solution to the combined Einstein gravity equations and Maxwell electromagnetic equations.

One important characteristic of a black hole is that after it is formed, the only things you can measure about the final configuration are its mass, angular momentum, charge, and magnetic field—nothing else. A black hole made out of a dying star looks exactly like a black hole made out of a dying antimatter star, or for that matter, a black hole made out of a few solar masses of televisions, moldy cheese, or anything.

You will all be relieved to know that our sun is a little too small to turn into a black hole all by itself. When it uses up all its energy it will turn into a white dwarf star. All of its mass will collapse into an object about half the size of the Earth with a density that is a million times larger than that of normal matter. It will sit there glowing whitely from the heat of its collapse, slowly turn redder, and then turn dark as it cools off over billions of years. If our sun had been two or three times more massive, the collapse would not have stopped at the white-dwarf-star stage, but would have proceeded to the neutron-star stage, where the mass of a star is compressed into a volume some 20 kilometers across with a density of a hundred trillion times that of normal matter. If our sun were larger than three solar masses, however, then the neutron-star stage would not be stable.

In 1939, J. Robert Oppenheimer and his student showed that the nuclei in a collapsing star are not strong enough to resist the gravitational crushing forces if the initial mass of the star is large enough. Their paper was little noticed because of other things going on in the world in 1939. Oppenheimer became involved in those other things and it was not until after World War II that scientists came back to look at black holes. They found that there was no way to avoid the conclusion that the end point of the evolution of a star with a mass greater than three solar masses has to be a black hole.

One convincing candidate for a black hole is the X-ray source Cygnus X-1. Because it is a source of rapidly varying X rays, it must be a compact star—either a white dwarf, neutron star, or black hole. The X-ray source is in orbit around a companion star that is a typical blue supergiant with a mass of about 20 solar masses. The orbital period of 5.5 days obtained from the X-ray data then gives us an estimate for the mass of the X-ray source of eight solar masses. Since stellar theory puts an upper limit on the mass of a neutron star of three solar masses, and this source is well beyond that limit, it must be a black hole.

The model for the Cygnus X-1 system is that the blue giant and the black hole are in close orbit around each other, with the black hole only a few stellar radii away from the surface of the supergiant. The gravity tides from the black hole pull the supergiant into a big blue egg, with the elongated end pointing at the black hole. The outer gaseous envelope of the blue supergiant is dragged from the pointed end of the supergiant star to spiral about the black hole. The infalling gas first forms an accretion disk circling the black hole. As the gas spirals through the accretion disk, it gets more concentrated and hotter due to friction between the gas molecules, until it reaches a temperature exceeding ten million degrees. At this temperature X rays (as well as lots of heat radiation) are produced. The orbits of the gas molecules become unstable when the orbital radius is less than three Schwarzschild radii. The extreme tides of the black hole then pull the gas from the inner edge of the accretion disk into the black hole.

Another candidate for a black hole is the X ray–emitting binary star system SS 433. The present model for this system is that it consists of two stars, both greater than ten solar masses, in a binary orbit with a period of 13 days. One of the stars is still a normal star, although a rare type called a Wolf-Rayet star that has a tendency to emit mass. The other is the suspected black hole. The accretion disk is so hot that it is brighter than the nearby normal star.

By some as-yet-not-well-understood process, the collection of the gas from the accretion disk onto the black hole creates a self-excited dynamo. The system generates strong electric and magnetic fields near the surface of the black hole, producing twin jets of gas ejected at about 25 percent of the speed of light along the axis of the black hole. These jets emit light and radio waves that are detected on Earth. The jet that is pointed toward us is strongly blueshifted by the Doppler effect, while the jet pointed away from us is Doppler redshifted.

The rapid spin gives the black hole an oblate shape. The spin axis of the black hole is tilted at about 20 degrees from the orbital plane of the binary system. The tidal action of the normal star on the oblate shape of the tilted black hole causes the black hole "top" to precess with a period of 164 days. Thus the jets emitted from the poles of the black hole squirt out in a spiral pattern along two oppositely directed 20-degree cones. Similar twin-jet structure has been seen coming from quasars, indicating that SS 433 might be a miniature model of a quasar.

Large black holes exist not only in the center of our galaxy, but probably exist in the center of every galaxy. Our evidence for them came from the study of quasars. When they were first observed, quasars were thought to be a strange sort of star. But as more and more of them were found and studied, it was realized that they were much larger and much farther away than first thought. First, by examining their spectra, strongly redshifted emission lines were found. In general, the fainter the quasar, the greater the redshift. The pattern of redshifts indicated that the redshifts were not gravitational in nature, but that the quasars were outside our Milky Way Galaxy and were partici- pating in the general outward expansion of the Universe. The redshifts on some quasars were so large that the quasars were estimated to be more than halfway across the Universe. To be seen at all on Earth from those distances, they would have to be the brightest single objects in the Universe. Second, the optical and radio output of the quasars would vary rapidly, typically changing significantly in brightness in days or even minutes. This gives an upper limit on the size of the quasar, since different portions of a large object cannot simultaneously change intensity faster than a triggering signal can be sent from one side to the other. Even if somehow all portions of a large object could be changed at the same time, an observer would see a delay between the change in the part of the object closest to him and the part farthest from him. This means that the quasars must be very small, the size of the solar system at most.

Because of the small size of the quasars, it is easily shown that nuclear reactions cannot produce the observed large energy output. The energy source must be the conversion of gravita- tional potential energy into heat as mass is dropped into a deep gravitational potential well—a giant black hole. Calculations show that up to 50 percent of the rest mass of infalling matter can be converted into radiation that can escape the black hole. At this rate, a few solar masses per year of infalling gas is suffi- cient to power a typical quasar.

Quasars seem to be much more numerous in the early universe, because their numbers reach a peak at a redshift corre- sponding to a time some 70 percent of the way back toward the

Big Bang. The size and luminosity of quasars indicate that they are supermassive black holes of about 10^8 solar masses (about $\frac{1}{1000}$ the mass of a large galaxy) fueled by radiating, infalling matter. Nearly all the quasars have also been found to be embedded in a fuzzy nebulosity that usually has the size, shape, and barred or spiral structure of a typical galaxy. Thus, quasars seem to be nothing more than a much brighter version of the more common Seyfert galaxies, which have a bright inner core. Thus, there is little doubt left that quasars are just especially bright cores of galaxies and that most, if not all, galaxies have central black holes of a similar sort, with a wide range of masses and luminosities. Recent evidence also indicates that the brighter quasars are found in galaxies that are in the process of swallowing another galaxy, or stripping a passing galaxy of its gas by tidal forces. The new gas from the other galaxy is the fuel that is feeding the supermassive black hole in the center, causing the quasar to flare up in brightness.

Many quasars have also been observed to emit twin jets of matter moving at close to the speed of light. Some of the jets shoot straight out from the galactic core for millions of light-years, well past the outskirts of the galaxy. This indicates that whatever the "engine" is in the center of the galaxy, it has maintained its pointing direction for millions of years. A spinning black hole "gyrocompass" fits the model well. Other jets show similar length, but a dual-spiral pattern, indicating that the source of the jets is precessing with periods of the order of 10,000 years. Such precession could be caused by a binary pair of supermassive black holes in the central core.

What does a black hole look like? As a star turns into a black hole, the time it takes for it to turn black is very rapid. In a few milliseconds it goes from full luminosity to less than a billionth of full luminosity. For a human observer, a collapsing star essentially disappears instantaneously. An observer near a collapsing black hole can be one of two kinds, a static observer who sits at rest in the external field of the black hole supported by a powerful rocket or a skyhook from infinity, or a free-fall observer who falls into the black hole along with the stellar matter.

When either observer is far from the black hole and looks in the direction of the black hole he sees a black disk. Around that black circle he can see the normal star pattern, except near the black hole the star pattern is distorted. The black hole does not cover up the star pattern as it passes in front of it; instead, the black hole disk seems to "expel" the points of light from that region of the sky. A star image moves to one side or the other of the black disk and slides up and over. If the star image and the center of the black hole disk exactly coincide, then the star image momentarily breaks up into a bright ring of light around the black disk where the photons from the star in back of the black hole have been bent by gravitational focusing. (There are actually a number of rings—one where the photons circled the black hole once before they flew off toward the observer, one inside that where the photons circled twice before they flew off, etc.)

As the static observer moves closer and closer to the horizon the black hole disk gets larger and larger and completely fills the sky. Then all the infalling radiation from the rest of the Universe is observed as a very tiny, highly blueshifted, incredibly bright spot in the "up" direction. The reason the light is so bright is that the static observer is "accelerating" toward the light in his rocket ship instead of free-falling along with the light.

For a free-fall observer, the view toward the black hole is also black, and it grows in size as the observer falls toward the black hole. But unlike the static observer, the dark patch in the forward direction of the sky never extends around into the back hemisphere. Half of the free-fall observer's sky (or more, in the early stages far from the black hole) is always filled with the external star pattern. Because the Doppler redshift of the free-fall observer moving away from the distant stars more than compensates for the gravitational blueshift, the photons from the distant stars are redshifted everywhere, except in a bright band near the observer's equator where they are blueshifted. The free-fall observer notices nothing unusual when he falls through the event horizon. All the observing stops, of course, when the observer hits the singularity at the center of the black hole.

The fact that the observer *must* hit the singularity at the center of the black hole is strongly emphasized by the mathematically oriented physicists who study black holes. They point out that although Einstein showed us that space is equivalent to time, there is a major difference between a spacelike dimension and a timelike dimension. If you get far away from everything and don't do anything, then you can stand still in space—but you can't stand still in time. You can slow down time by flying off into space in an ultrafast rocketship or by setting up house-keeping on a very massive planet, but you can't stop time. You keep on moving inexorably through time (t), in one direction only (+t), until you come to the end of time (t = ∞).

In the Schwarzschild solution to the Einstein gravity equations, there are three space dimensions and one time dimension. But at the magic boundary called the one-way event horizon that delineates the surface between the inside of the Schwarzschild black hole and the outside, the radial space dimension takes on the behavior of a time dimension, while the time dimension takes on the behavior of a space dimension. That means, that once inside the one-way event horizon, despite all the rockets, all the forces, all the future magic you can command, you keep on moving inexorably through space in the radial direction (r), in one direction only (−r), until you come to the end of space at the singularity (r = 0). From this mathematical point of view, you can no more increase your radial distance from the center of the Schwarzschild singularity than you can turn back the hands of time.

These very powerful mathematical arguments should temper any speculations about what might or might not be possible inside a black hole. Yet the mathematical arguments are not without possible loopholes. First, the mathematics leads to infinities, and we know that although mathematics permit infinities, nature objects to them. Something will happen to prevent the infinite density singularities from forming. What it is, we do not yet know. Second, many of the theorems of black holes make "reasonable" assumptions, such as: causality is not violated; the Universe contains no "naked singularities"; and there are no primordial connections to other universes. Yet there are many counterexamples of solutions to the Einstein gravity equations (admittedly quite contrived) that allow one or more of these things. It is the existence of these counterexamples that allow for future-magic speculation concerning black holes, large and small.

Not all black holes have high density. The larger a black hole, the smaller the density. We are probably living inside a black hole—the Universe. The Universe is very massive, so it doesn't have to be very dense to form a black hole. In fact, if you calculate the density of a black hole the size of the Universe, you find that the density required is one atom per cubic centimeter, very close to the average density of space in our galaxy.

Present estimates by astronomers of the average density of the visible mass in the Universe, however, leave us a factor of ten short. This has led to a search for the so-called "missing matter" that is needed to bind up the Universe into a nice neat package. Many candidates for the missing matter, such as massive neutrinos, brown dwarfs, miniature and supermassive black holes, and massive "axion" particles have been proposed, but whether the Universe is closed or open is still an open question. If the Universe is closed and is therefore a black hole, then one could ask why it isn't collapsing. It is, or at least it is trying to, but for some unknown reason the Universe got started with a big bang that has all the matter flying outward. After a long enough time, the gravitational pull will overcome the initial momentum and the Universe will collapse at the singularity where $r = 0$.

One could have a black hole that is galactic in size. The average galaxy has about 100 billion stars. If you crammed all those stars into a volume with a radius of about 2,000 times that of the distance between the Earth and the sun (an astronomical unit or AU), you would form a black hole. Although this black hole is only about 11 light-days in radius, the spacing between the stars would still be large enough, almost one AU, that collisions between the stars would be infrequent. If our solar system fell into such a galactic-sized black hole, the tides from the miniuniverse would be strong enough to separate the planets from the sun, but they would not be strong enough to do damage to the planets or the sun itself. The difference in gravity across the diameter of the Earth as the Earth approached the event horizon of this incipient black hole universe would be insignificant, about 40 microgravities. You wouldn't feel a thing as the Earth fell into a black hole of this size. From the viewpoint of an observer inside the miniuniverse, you would pop into view out of nowhere into the middle of space. Once you fell in, however, you could never find your way back out. You could look in vain for the "edge" where you came in, but everywhere you looked, all you would see would be the stars in the miniuniverse. It would be possible for a human being to survive in such a black hole in a well-shielded rocket ship.

What would it be like to live in a miniature closed universe like this? You will only have a few days to look around, since this miniuniverse is 11 light-days in radius and is collapsing at nearly the speed of light, but let us imagine that you have at your disposal a rocket ship with a faster-than-light warp drive.

You take off from your home planet in your rocket ship on a journey into the unknown like a future-magic Magellan to explore this compact universe only 4,000 AU in diameter. You would leave going in a straight line away from your planet, always keeping it in sight through a telescope pointed directly behind. After you had traveled about one-third the way across/around your universe, the view through the rear telescope would show a greatly magnified view of your planet because the strong gravity of all the stars between you and the planet would curve the light rays, giving a magnified image. At the halfway point in your journey, the image of your planet through the rear telescope would have expanded to fill practically the whole rear hemisphere of view. At the same time, a lookout peering through a front telescope would see the same magnified view of your home planet, but of its backside. As you completed your journey, the view through the rear telescope would continue to expand and become fainter, while the view through the forward telescope would shrink until it coincided with the view of the real thing through the forward porthole as you return triumphantly back home, having circumnavigated the universe while always traveling in a straight line.

It is as difficult for us to imagine living in a closed, finite, curved universe as it was for early man to comprehend living on a closed, finite, curved world. If there are only six continents and seven seas on the Earth, then when you come to the last continent there *has* to be an edge to the world somewhere. But we now know that there is no edge anywhere on the globe. In the same manner in our galactic-sized miniuniverse, even through there are a lot of stars, there are a finite number. As you go to each one and look around, each star seems to be at the "center" of the universe, with equal numbers of stars in all directions. There is no edge, there is no way out, and alas, the singularity approaches.

Besides black hole universes, it is also possible to conceive of black hole worlds. One example of a black hole world, conceived by Gerald Nordley, would be a black hole that a human being could live *on*, instead of *in*. It would be built as a spherical shell of very strong, but very low density material. Diamond foam or that famous science-fiction material "duralightium" would be possible candidates. The radius, thickness, and density of this hypothetical world would be adjusted so the surface gravity would be one Earth gravity. Thus, a human being could live comfortably on the surface and yet the gravitational potential is so high, that for all practical purposes the world is a black hole.

Since the mathematicians tell us that once the conditions for a black hole have been reached, collapse is inevitable, we will want to stop just short of conditions for a black hole. The critical point is reached when the escape velocity equals the speed of light. We will stop adding mass to the shell when the escape velocity V is 99.5 percent that of light. The Newtonian gravity acceleration on the surface of a spherical shell with a mass M and a radius R is $a = GM/R^2$, but the gravity acceleration predicted using the Schwarzschild solution is greater by a factor of $(1 - 2GM/Rc^2)^{-\frac{1}{2}}$ or $(1 - V^2/c^2)^{-1/2}$. If we assume that $V = 0.995$ c, then the amplification of the Newtonian acceleration is a factor of 10. Note that as the escape velocity gets even closer to that of light, the relativistic amplification of the Newtonian gravity acceleration rises to infinity, even for a finite mass.

It turns out that the two requirements—that the world have a surface gravity of one Earth gravity, and that at the same time it be almost a black hole—define a unique radius for the black hole world. This radius turns out to be almost exactly five light-years. By choosing a thickness of the shell as a quarter of a light-year and a density of the diamond foam at about one-billionth that of water, we can produce a surface gravity field of one Earth gravity on the surface of the shell without excessive pressures inside. With the radius, thickness, and density known, the mass required is also then uniquely determined. Unfortunately for those considering making their own private black hole world where they could literally get away from it all, the mass of diamond foam needed turns out be be equal to the mass of 150 galaxies! It would be some time before we could build such a world, even if we could make diamond foam.

What bothers the inventor of this world is that there is no way to get off his world. Since the gravity field is only one Earth gravity, it would seem that it should be possible to somehow climb up through the one Earth gravity field and escape the black hole. But the mathematics of black hole theory says that escape is essentially impossible. If you tried to use a rocket to escape, the escape velocity of this world is, by design, so close to the speed of light that no rocket can make it. If you tried to climb a very long, very strong stepladder, you would use up more energy in the climb than there exists in rest mass in your body. If you attempted to take along a sack lunch to supply more energy to your body, the amount of energy you could get from lunch, even assuming your stomach used a future-magic form of digestion to convert the entire rest mass of the lunch into energy, would be less than the energy you used to carry it up. It would not even work to make future-magic electric boots and connect them by a long extension cord to a power plant on the surface of the black hole world. As you used the electric boots to climb up the ladder, the frequency and energy of the electricity coming through the wires would diminish with altitude until your boots stopped working. It is essentially impossible to get off the black hole world.

What would you see if you lived on such a black hole world? If you looked down, you would see your feet and the ground below. If you looked to one side, you would see those people and objects off to that side, except it would look like they were on slightly higher ground than you. That is because the light coming from them is being pulled down by the gravity field of black hole world. Because of the gravity pull, only those light rays that started from their bodies in a slightly upward direction are able to reach your eyes. Those light rays that went straight out were pulled down by the gravity and hit the ground somewhere between you and the person you are looking at. Since the light rays from that person are curving downward as they reach your eye, it looks like the person is above you.

To look even farther off into the distance, you will need a good telescope (don't forget that this black hole world is 5 light-years in radius). With your telescope you can see distant buildings and cities, but instead of being below the horizon as they would be on Earth, they would be above the horizon. Objects halfway around black hole world would be halfway up into the sky, and when you finally turned your telescope straight upward you would see the opposite pole of black hole world. Visually you would be living in a hollow world with no escape to the rest of the Universe. (It is no wonder you can't get off the black hole world. You can't find the way to "up.")

Although large black holes have interesting properties and characteristics and are fun to speculate about, it will be a long time, if ever, before we could attempt to make them in order to extract some form of future-magic technology. But black holes can come in many sizes, and the smaller ones involve masses that are small enough for the human race to dream about making and using to make future-magic machines.

Small black holes were first discussed in the scientific literature by Stephen Hawking. It had long been known that for a black hole to form spontaneously by gravitational collapse, the amount of mass involved had to be larger than the mass of the sun. Hawking speculated that miniature black holes much smaller than the sun could have been formed by the Big Bang at the beginning of the Universe when the pressure of light and other matter was very high. They could be any size, from solar masses down to about 10 micrograms.

These small black holes are very dense and very interesting. One might be able to use them as tools, if we can find or make them. They have very small diameters, most of them much smaller than an atom, with the smallest, the 10 microgram mass version, being only 10^{-35} meters across. The miniature black holes would be attracted by the Earth, the other planets, and by the sun into orbital trajectories. Most of these orbits would be elliptical orbits out in space around the sun. Since the miniature black holes are so tiny and so dense, however, they could even be in an orbit that passed right through the sun or a planetoid.

Although they are small in size, the miniature black holes would have a significant gravity field. In passing through a body made of normal matter, a miniature black hole would produce powerful tidal forces at atomic ranges that would cause drag to take place. After bouncing back and forth through a planetoid a number of times, the miniature black holes would slow down and be captured. There could be swarms of them in the center of the sun and planets, slowly eating them up an atom at a time. The rate of capture is very small since the miniature black holes are so small they can only swallow one atom at a time.

A few years after Stephen Hawking invented the concept of miniature black holes, he found a way to make them disappear! While going through some detailed calculations about the interaction of the ultrastrong gravity field of these ultradense objects on the space–time vacuum near their surface, he discovered that his newly invented miniature black holes were *not* black. They glow instead.

Stephen Hawking has developed a picture one can use to attempt to understand the reason why black holes look like they are emitting radiation. According to the theory of quantum mechanics, what we call vacuum is not empty, but is full of pairs of "virtual particles" that are created temporarily out of nothing, exist for a while, then merge back into nothing (see Figure 8). While the particles exist, the law of conservation of energy is being violated since the particles have an energy ΔE. But the duration Δt of the violation of the law of conservation of energy is very short.

In quantum mechanics you cannot measure an energy change ΔE in a time shorter than Δt if $\Delta E \, \Delta t < h$, where h is Planck's quantum constant. Since the duration of the violations of the law of conservation of mass energy are shorter than that given by the equation, quantum mechanics allows them to happen. (You can break any law, even a law of nature, as long as you don't get caught at it!)

Most of the virtual particles in the vacuum are low-energy photons, but even charged particle pairs like electrons and positrons occasionally appear for a short period of time. If a small black hole were placed in this emptiness full of energy, its powerful gravitational field would swallow one of the virtual particles if it got too close. With no partner to recombine with, the other member of the virtual-particle pair would be promoted to the status of a "real" particle and leave. To an onlooker, it would seem as if the black hole had "emitted" the particle.

In this model of the interaction of a miniature black hole with the vacuum, the black hole emits radiation and particles as though it had a temperature. The temperature is inversely proportional to the mass of the black hole. A solar mass black hole is very cold, with a temperature of about 10^{-7} degrees above absolute zero. The temperature rises as the mass decreases. When the mass of the black hole is about 10^{14} kilograms (the mass of a large asteroid), the temperature is less than a billion degrees, so only photons, neutrinos, and gravitons are emitted.

According to Donald Page, who carried out lengthy calculations on the subject, such a hole should emit approximately 81 percent neutrinos, 17 percent photons, and 2 percent gravitons. When the mass becomes significantly less than 10^{14} kilograms, the temperature increases until the black hole is hot enough to emit electrons and positrons as well as radiation. When the mass becomes less than 10^{12} kilograms (the mass of a small asteroid), the temperature now approaches a trillion degrees and heavier

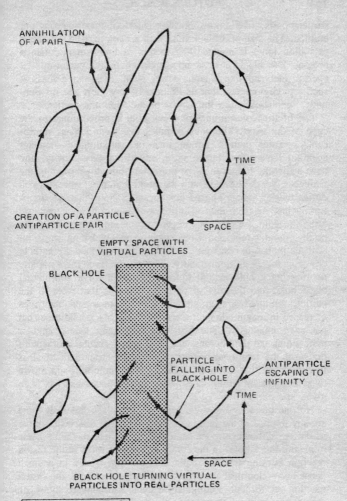

ANNIHILATION
OF A PAIR

TIME

SPACE

CREATION OF A PARTICLE-
ANTIPARTICLE PAIR

EMPTY SPACE WITH
VIRTUAL PARTICLES

BLACK HOLE

PARTICLE
FALLING INTO
BLACK HOLE

ANTIPARTICLE
ESCAPING TO
INFINITY

TIME

SPACE

BLACK HOLE TURNING VIRTUAL
PARTICLES INTO REAL PARTICLES

HUGHES AIRCRAFT CO.

*Figure 8. Virtual particles of vacuum near
a black hole.*

particle pairs, like muons, kayons, protons, and neutrons are emitted. The size of a black hole with a mass of 10^{12} kilograms (a billion tons) is about 10^{-16} meters, a little smaller than a proton. The black hole is now emitting 6,000 megawatts of energy, the output of a large power plant. It is losing mass at such a prodigious rate that its lifetime is very short and it essentially "explodes" in a final burst of radiation and particles.

The lifetime of a miniature black hole is proportional to the cube of the mass. Those black holes that have a mass significantly greater than a billion tons (a one-kilometer-diameter asteroid) have a low temperature, are losing mass slowly, and have a lifetime longer than the present 15-billion-year age of the Universe, so they would still be around if they were formed during the Big Bang. Those miniature black holes that are significantly less massive than a billion tons would have a temperature exceeding a trillion degrees, be radiating energy in prodigious amounts, and would have evaporated long since.

If the miniature black hole is rapidly rotating, then the particle emission increases dramatically. The power level for a rapidly rotating black hole is 300 times larger than for a nonrotating black hole, and the mix of particles shifts so that most of the particles emitted are gravitons, with photons and neutrinos increased in magnitude over the nonrotating black hole case, but not as dramatically. The gravitons with their spin-2 angular momentum and the photons with their spin-1 angular momentum drain off the rotational angular momentum faster than the loss in energy, so that a rapidly spinning black hole will spin down to a nearly nonrotating state before most of its mass has been given up.

No one has found any evidence of tiny black holes. If there are any trapped in the Earth or sun, it would be difficult to prove it. There is, however, one indication that there might be some miniature black holes in the center of the sun. Most of the fusion reaction burning that takes place in the sun occurs in a small dense hot region near the center. According to theory, the fusion reactions go through a complicated cycle that converts hydrogen atoms into helium, then burns the helium to produce carbon, oxygen, nitrogen, and the other elements up to iron. The theoretical calculations, backed by atom–atom collision experiments on Earth, are now able to predict the present size, temperature, and burning rate of the sun quite accurately. They also predict that the fusion reactions at the center of the sun should produce a large flux of neutrinos. The neutrinos, being able to pass through light-years of lead without being stopped, immediately leave the center of the sun, while the heat and light generated in the core of the sun takes ten million years to get out through the optically opaque outer layers of the sun.

There are so many neutrinos coming from the sun that it is possible to detect them on Earth despite their low interaction rate. A detector for solar neutrinos has been operating for many years now. It consists of a large tank of carbon tetrachloride (cleaning fluid) underground in a salt mine to keep out the cosmic ray background. When a neutrino hits a chlorine atom in the liquid carbon tetrachloride, it turns the chlorine atom into a rare radioactive isotope of argon with a half-life of 35 days. Argon, being an inert gas, is then swept out of the liquid carbon tetrachloride by flushing it with helium gas. The single atoms of radioactive argon are then detected with a counter. For the past decades, significant numbers of solar neutrinos have been detected using this apparatus, but the number of detected neutrinos has been one-third that predicted by the otherwise successful solar fusion theory.

One explanation for the low number of observed neutrinos is that there are miniature black holes in the center of the sun helping along the fusion process. That means the normal fusion process doesn't need to be as active and as a result emits fewer neutrinos. There are other explanations for the shortage of solar neutrinos, but most of them are just as speculative as the miniature black hole explanation.

If it turns out that small black holes really do exist, then I propose that we go out to the asteroid belt and mine the asteroids for the black holes that may be trapped in them. If a small black hole were in orbit around the sun in the asteroid belt region, and it had the mass of an asteroid, it would be about the diameter of an atom. Despite its small size, the gravity field of the miniature black hole would be just as strong as the gravity field of an asteroid and if the miniature black hole came near another asteroid, the two would attract each other. Instead of colliding and fragmenting as asteroids do, however, the miniature black hole would just penetrate the surface of the regular asteroid and pass through to the other side. In the process of passing through, the miniature black hole would absorb a number of rock atoms, increasing its weight and slowing down slightly. An even more drastic slowing mechanism would be the tides from the miniature black hole. They would cause stresses in the rock around the line of penetration and fragment the rock out to a few micrometers away from its path through the asteroid. This would cause further slowing.

After bouncing back and forth through the normal matter asteroid many times, the miniature black hole would finally come to rest at the center of the asteroid. Now that it is not moving so rapidly past them, the miniature black hole could take time to absorb one atom after another into its atom-sized body until it had dug itself a tiny cavity at the center of the asteroid. With no more food available, it would stop eating, and sit there and glow warmly for a few million years. After years of glowing its substance away, it would get smaller. As it got smaller it would get hotter since the temperature rises as the mass decreases. Finally, the miniature black hole would get hot enough to melt the rock around it. Drops of melted rock would be pulled into the miniature black hole, adding to its mass. As the mass of the black hole increased, the temperature would decrease. The black hole would stop radiating, the melted rock inside the cavity would solidify, and the process would repeat itself many centuries later. Thus, although a miniature black hole left to itself has a lifetime that is less than the time since the Big Bang, there may be miniature black holes with the mass of an asteroid being kept alive in the asteroid belt by a symbiotic interaction with an asteroid made of normal matter.

To find those asteroids that contain miniature black holes, you want to look for asteroids that have anomalously high temperatures, lots of recent fracture zones, and anomalously high density. Those with a suspiciously high average density have something *very* dense inside. To obtain a measure of the density you need to measure the volume and the mass. It is easy enough to get an estimate of the volume of the host asteroid with three pictures taken from three different directions. It is difficult to measure the mass of an object in free-fall. One way is to go up to it with a calibrated rocket engine and push it. Another is to land on it with a sensitive gravity meter. There is, however, a way to measure the mass of an object at a distance without going through the hazard of a rendezvous. To do this, you need to use a mass detector or gravity gradiometer. This is a device that measures the gradient or the changes in the gravity attraction with distance. These gravity gradient forces are the tidal forces by which the moon causes tides to rise on the Earth, even though both the Earth and the moon are in free-fall. There are a number of different ways to make a gravity gradiometer. The one that I invented uses two dumbbell-shaped masses connected together at the center in the shape of an X (see Figure 9).

When a single dumbbell is placed near a gravitating body such as an asteroid, one mass or the other on the dumbbell will be closer to the asteroid. Since the gravity field of the asteroid gets stronger with decreasing distance, the near mass of the dumbbell will be pulled harder than the far mass, causing the dumbbell to ultimately align itself with the direction to the asteroid. This natural alignment of a long object in orbit around a gravitating body is used by many Earth-pointing satellites and by the Space Shuttle during resting periods. By building my gradiometer with two crossed dumbbells at right angles to each other, one dumbbell is torqued clockwise while the other is torqued counterclockwise. The amount of differential torque between the two arms is measured by determining the change in angle between the two arms. This is a lot easier than trying to measure the angle of one arm with respect to some reference direction.

I use one more trick in the operation of the gravity gradiometer instrument that I invented. I deliberately rotate the sensor at 15 revolutions per second. In this rotating reference frame, the tiny differential angles between the two arms turn into tiny differential vibrations, and it is a lot easier to measure vibrations than angles. My gravity gradiometer could detect the mass of my fist at 30 centimeters (a foot), me at two meters (I mass over 100 kilograms), and an asteroidal-sized black hole at 1,000 kilometers.

Once you have found a suspiciously warm asteroid that seems awfully massive for its size, then to extract the miniature black hole, you give the surface of the asteroid a strong shove and push the asteroid out of the way. The asteroid will shift to a different orbit and where the center of the asteroid used to be, you will find the miniature black hole. The black hole will be too small to see, but if you put an acoustic detector on the asteroid you will hear the asteroid complaining as the black hole comes to the surface. Once the black hole has left the surface you can monitor its position and determine its mass with a mass detector.

It is not too dangerous being near a black hole if you are careful. A modest-sized one, with a mass equivalent to that of a 250-meter-diameter asteroid made of rock, would have a

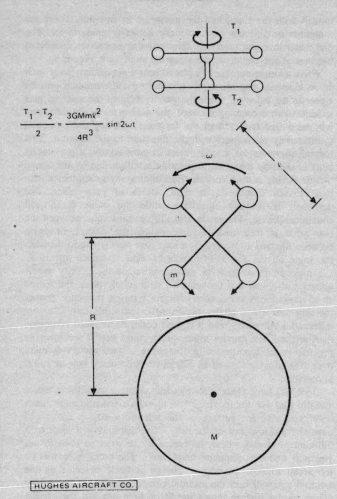

$$\frac{T_1 - T_2}{2} = \frac{3GMm\ell^2}{4R^3} \sin 2\omega t$$

HUGHES AIRCRAFT CO.

Figure 9. *Method of operation of rotating gravity gradiometer.*

gravity field of about one Earth gravity at a distance of 30 centimeters (a foot). If you approached this miniature black hole by yourself, you would be in danger unless you carefully put yourself in orbit about it ten meters or more away (your orbital period at ten meters distance would be about four minutes). Two people could get right up next to the miniature black hole if they put their hands and knees together to make a space between them. Their combined center of mass is now in the space between them, and if they carefully arrange their approach so that the trajectory of the black hole does not intersect either of them, they can put the black hole between them where they can both take a close look. The gravity forces they would experience would be about the same as if they were crawling on their hands and knees on a floor back on Earth. A black hole the size of an asteroid is smaller than an atom, so you can't see it directly. It will cause bending of light rays passing by it, however, so you could see it by placing an illuminated grid in back of it and looking through a microscope to find a flaw in the grid. The flaw will be caused by the bending of the light by the black hole floating in front of the grid.

The next step in corralling the invisible black maverick is to put some electric charge on it. This means bombarding the position of the miniature black hole with a focused beam of ionized particles until the black hole has captured enough of them to have a significant charge-to-mass ratio. The upper limit will depend upon the energy of the ions. After the first ion is absorbed, the black hole will have a charge and will have a tendency to repel the next ion. Another upper limit to the amount of charge you can place on a black hole is the rate at which the charged black hole pulls opposite charges out of the surrounding space. You can keep these losses low, however, by surrounding the black hole with an electrostatic shield.

Once a black hole is charged, you can apply forces to it with electric fields. If the charged black hole happens to be rotating, you are in luck, for then it will also have a magnetic field and you can also use magnetic fields to apply forces and torques. The coupling of the electric charge to the black hole is very strong, so the black hole will not let go. You can now use strong electric or magnetic fields to pull on the black hole and take it anywhere you want to go.

If the black hole were very small, only boulder-sized, and you were successful in getting and keeping a lot of charge on it, you could conceivably bring the charged miniature black hole down to Earth and keep it there. The force that can be applied to a maximally charged black hole by a reasonably strong electric field of a few hundred thousand volts is more than enough to levitate a boulder-sized black hole in the gravity field of the Earth. The chances of losing the black hole due to a power failure or other accident would be high enough, however, that it would be better if black holes were left in high orbit.

Once you have charged black holes that you can manipulate at will, then you can use them in a number of ways. By putting them in a mixture of deuterium and tritium gas, you can cause fusion reactions to take place without having to have the D–T mixture at high temperatures and pressures. The black hole will act as a catalyst for the fusion reaction. The density of the D–T gas near the black hole will be greatly increased by the gravity forces of the black hole and the fusion rate in that region will increase dramatically, creating a "hot spot." Most of the reaction products will come out of that region and deposit their energy in the rest of the gas and the usual shielding around the fusion reaction chamber. The resultant heat can then be used to power a thermal power plant. A few deuterium and tritium atoms will be lost to the black hole, but those losses should be small.

Energy can also be extracted from a black hole if it is rotating. A rotating black hole has two surfaces where interesting things take place. The outside surface is called the surface of infinite redshift. This is where an outside observer sees the infalling objects slow in time and the light from them becomes infinitely redshifted. Inside that surface is another surface, called the one-way event horizon. Once an object has passed through that surface it can never return. The one-way event horizon is separated from the surface of infinite redshift except at the poles of the rotating black hole. The region between those surfaces is called the ergosphere, since energy can be extracted from that region. The ergosphere disappears when the spin goes to zero.

The original energy extraction process thought up by Roger Penrose involved sending two closely coupled bodies in a close orbit around the equator of a spinning black hole. After the two bodies had entered the ergosphere, but were still outside the event horizon, they would be separated. One would be kicked outward while the other was kicked inward. The infalling body would spiral into the spinning black hole, slowing it down, while the other body would leave with more energy than the two bodies had originally. A future civilization might obtain its energy using such a technique on a rotating black hole. A spaceship containing useless rubbish would fly into a carefully selected orbit entering the ergosphere. While inside the ergosphere the spaceship ejects its rubbish into the hole in such a direction that it subtracts from the angular momentum of the black hole. The spaceship escapes again to a large distance from the hole. If done properly, the kinetic energy of the spaceship can increase by more than the total mass-energy of the rubbish. In the process, some of the rotational energy of the black hole has been converted into the kinetic energy of the escaping spaceship. Up to 29 percent of the mass-energy of a spinning black hole could be extracted this way. It is not even necessary to use physical bodies or rocket ships. If an electromagnetic wave of just the right frequency and direction were scattered off a rotating black hole, the scattered wave would have a greater amplitude than the incoming wave due to a process called superradiant scattering. The rotation of the black hole would, of course, decrease during the process.

If the spinning black hole is small, then there will be a spontaneous emission of radiation and particles. This is because the vacuum surrounding the black hole is not empty, but spontaneously generates photon and particle pairs. Some halves of the photon and particle pairs will find themselves to have just the right energy and direction and be in just the right place to act as the two-stage rocket ship to extract energy by the Penrose process or act as the electromagnetic wave in the superradiant process. This "spin down" radiation of miniature spinning black holes is in addition to the "thermal" Hawking radiation.

Even if miniature black holes are never found and the only black holes we ever have are large stellar- and galactic-sized collapsed masses, these large black holes may still be very valuable in directing us toward some still-unknown form of future magic. For by merely observing these objects in detail as they interact with the matter around them, we will be observing phenomena that we cannot replicate on Earth, or even in our solar system—phenomena involving warped space, distorted time, and contorted ultradense matter that will test our theories as we stretch them to cover these bizarre happenings. We are learning, and will continue to learn, as we attempt to model what we see, and out of that learning will come new, better theories that will be the spells we need to invoke new forms of future magic.

Then, if we can find (or make, by using our new theories) miniature black holes, we will have the magic wand that we will need to bring new forms of future magic into being. Gravitational communication, limitless sources of energy, space warps, time machines, and more, might be ours. Some of these new technologies we may see in the near future, some we may see in the far future, some may never be in any future: all would be magic to us today.

It is interesting to note that given all the well-known facts about black holes, it is easy to prove that black holes don't exist! As a black hole starts to form, we see the massive objects that are going to make up the black hole falling inward. As they approach the combined infinite redshift and one-way event horizon, they slow down in time and become infinitely redshifted. To an outside observer the mass that is going to make up the black hole never quite reaches the event horizon and stays there suspended for an infinitely long time. We also know that all black holes have a finite temperature and are emitting particles. The larger black holes are not very hot and are emitting particles very slowly, but after a long enough period of time (less than an infinitely long time) they will have emitted all of their energy as radiation and will no longer have any mass and will cease to be a black hole. Thus, from this point of view, there is no such thing as a black hole. Only *incipient* black holes exist and even they ultimately evaporate away before they become *real* black holes.

Time Magic

One of the most magical things I see in our future is the ability to travel in time. If a present-day scientist were confronted with a real time machine, he would certainly say that the machine had to be run by the rules of magic. His argument would go like this: Science is based on logic. Anything that produces logical paradoxes is not science. Time machines produce logical paradoxes. Therefore, if time machines exist, they must use magic, not science.

Yet, two of the most respected and tested theories of physics, both the Einstein Special Theory of Relativity and the Einstein General Theory of Relativity, allow time to be manipulated. Although we are currently far from being able to control the energies and masses that will be required to make a time machine suitable for human use, these theories give us the physical principles behind time travel.

In the far future when our present technology evolves and makes possible what we now see as future magic, our gravitational and time engineers will construct time-phones and time-craft as easily as we now construct space-phones and spacecraft. One of these days, instead of being a slave to the ever-ticking clock, we will be able to send our time-craft on a journey through 60 minutes of time into the past or future as easily as we now send our spacecraft through the 60 light-minutes of space to Saturn.

How do we make a time machine? What are the problems? And what will we do about the paradoxes that time machines bring? What most people don't realize is that one type of time machine already exists. Various versions of these machines can be found in university and government laboratories. They are used every day by the scientists there, but they do have some

limitations. They are only good for one-way time travel, and
they can only handle a few atoms at a time. These present-day
time machines are based on Einstein's Special Theory of
Relativity, and to understand how they work we need to know
a little bit more about this remarkable theory that is now almost
a law of nature.

Einstein's Special Theory of Relativity should really be called
the Einstein Theory of Mechanics at High Velocities. The
Einstein theory replaces the old Newtonian theory of mechanics.
The Newton theory described how matter moves through space
and time. The matter would gain and lose energy as various
forces acted upon it, but nothing else happened to the matter.
The Newtonian laws work very well for objects moving at
ordinary speeds, but they are not adequate when the velocities
of the masses began to approach that of the speed of light. The
newer Einstein theory correctly predicts the behavior of matter
and energy, while Newton's old law fails when the amount of
energy in a particle becomes large and the particle is moving
near the speed of light.

The Einstein theory is called a theory of relativity because that
is the way that Einstein stumbled onto the correct theory of
mechanics. In his usual insightful manner, Einstein didn't try to
think about planets in orbit, or falling spheres, or billiard balls,
or the other mechanical things that occupied the thoughts of
Newton and other theorists thinking about mechanics. Instead,
he asked a more personal question: "What does a person see
and sense when he is moving?"

Einstein knew that experiments had shown that there was no
way for a person to tell he was in motion, as long as it was
constant motion. For example, suppose we had two observers:
Jill in a rocket ship and Jack floating lazily in space. Jill turns
on her engines for a while and accelerates up to a high velocity
toward Jack, then turns the engines off. She is left floating in
free-fall just as Jack is. She looks out her cockpit window to
see Jack flashing past. It is obvious to both Jack and Jill that
they are in motion relative to each other, but since both are
floating in free-fall, neither can prove who is moving and who
is standing still. They can both look out and see the stars, and
perhaps Jill is moving with respect to the stars and Jack isn't.
Jack might argue that he's the one who is standing still, because
he sees the stars stationary. To Einstein, however, each observer
is just as important as the other. It doesn't matter that all the

stars in the universe would have to be moving to make Jill stationary.

To the genius mind of Einstein, an observer like Jill was just as important as the rest of the universe. This was no time for a democratic vote as to who was moving and who was not. The only thing that counts is a physical measurement, and since there was no method of measuring absolute velocity, both Jack and Jill's points of view were equally valid. Jill in the rocket ship could be moving, with the universe sitting still; or Jill could be standing still, with the rest of the universe in motion. All points of view and all frames of reference are equally valid. Everything is relative—and that's where the name *relativity theory* came from.

At first glance, the Einstein Special Theory of Relativity doesn't seem to follow common sense. Of course Jill's rocket ship is moving and the rest of the universe is standing still. But Einstein just continued on in his methodical way, saying, "But suppose it *is* true that we can't tell the difference between a spaceship moving one way and the whole universe moving the other way?"

In his usual technique of thinking unthinkable thoughts, he then asked himself, "What would I see if I could travel at the speed of light and were to look at a light wave traveling alongside of me?" If Einstein used the Newton picture of the way things worked, the answer would be that he would see the electric and magnetic fields in the light standing motionless—not vibrating. Yet it was the vibration of the fields that gave the light beam its frequency . . . its energy . . . its very existence. According to the laws of electromagnetism, unless a light beam vibrates, it cannot exist. Newton's law led to a paradox.

He thought other unthinkable thoughts. "Suppose I were traveling at nearly the speed of light and I sent out a beam of light ahead of me. Being light, it would seem to me to be moving at the speed of light, but since I am sending it off from a moving platform, would not some other observer see the light beam moving *faster* than the speed of light?" Yet the velocity of light coming from fast-moving stars had been measured by astronomers and was always the same, no matter what the velocity of the star was—another paradox.

To Einstein, the only consistent answer to any of these questions was: "No. No matter how fast or slow I am going, the result of any experiment (especially a measurement of the

speed of light) must be the same for all observers whose frames
of reference are moving at a constant velocity, no matter what
that velocity is.''

Now, according to any reasonable extrapolation of Newton's
laws, this was impossible. Different observers should measure
different velocities of light, depending upon whether the motion
of their frame of reference added or subtracted from the motion
of whatever was being observed. Yet Einstein accepted his own
"impossible" answer and proceeded to produce a set of mathematical equations describing space, time, matter, and energy that
would produce the desired result of a constant velocity for light
no matter what speed the frames of reference of the observers
were moving at.

The equations that Einstein came up with were awkward.
They even involved square roots. Ignoring their strange looks,
Einstein proceeded to examine the implications of those
equations. The results predicted by those strange set of equations
are astounding in their abandonment of common sense, yet all
of the predicted results have been proven to be true time and
time again.

They are: Space can be converted into time—and vice versa.
Mass can be converted into energy—and vice versa. As you
travel near the speed of light: space shrinks, time expands, and
mass increases. If you travel at the speed of light: space shrinks
to nothing, time increases to eternity, and your mass (if you had
any to start with) increases to infinity.

The impossibility of the last means that it is impossible for
any material object (like Einstein himself) to attain the speed of
light because it would take an infinite amount of energy to
accelerate an infinite mass. Light, being a form of pure energy,
has no rest-mass per se, and so can (and to exist—must) travel
at the speed of light. Yet what a queer universe the photon lives
in. Since its space has shrunk to zero and its time has expanded
to eternity, the photon exists everywhere along its trajectory at
all times!

The most amazing result from Einstein's Special Theory of
Relativity that is hardest for people to accept is the slowing
down of time at high velocities. This is best illustrated by the
famous twin paradox: There are two astronauts, Jack and Jill.
They are twins. One astronaut, Jill, travels off on an interstellar
spacecraft and spends a long time traveling at nearly the speed
of light, while her twin, Jack, stays at home. Upon the return

of the traveler, Einstein's equations say that while the stay-at-home Jack has aged considerably, Jill is still young since she has been traveling in her time machine, the relativistic space-craft.

Thus, one way to make a time machine is to find a way to move at velocities close to that of light. Unfortunately, this special-relativity time machine only works one way. It can allow you to go into the future at a slower rate than normal, but you cannot go back in time. Still, this kind of time machine would have its uses. If you were sick and there was no cure for your disease, a short sojourn in a relativistic rocket ship could keep you from dying until the medical researchers could find the cure for what was ailing you. If you had a rich but very healthy aunt, then a few days spent at 99.99998 percent the speed of light could ensure that you would be able to enjoy your aunt's inheritance while you were still youthful.

These special-relativistic time machines are being used today. In many of the laboratories studying the properties of the atomic nucleus, there are large machines called "atom smashers" that use electric, magnetic, and radio fields to accelerate tiny charged particles to very high velocities. These particle beams are then shot into metal foil targets. Most of the high-speed particles pass right through the foil, but occasionally one of the particles plows head-on into the nucleus of one of the metal atoms, smashing the nuclei into bits.

Some of the "bits" are very interesting, since they are particles that exist inside the nucleus, but we normally don't see them because they have a very short lifetime. Some of the particle lifetimes are so short—a trillionth of a second—that the particles would travel less than a millimeter before they decayed if it were not for the time machine that kept them alive. For the atom smasher is also the time machine.

The energy that the atom smasher puts into its beam is so high that the bits of smashed nuclei that come out of the miniature explosion are moving at nearly the speed of light. Since the bits are moving so fast, their lifetimes are increased 10,000 times or more, and instead of living only a trillionth of a second, they now live a few hundred millionths of a second and can travel tens of meters from the highly radioactive target chamber out through the steering magnets and into carefully designed instruments that measure the mass, charge, spin, and other exotic properties of that short-lived bit of nuclear stuff.

When the time-machine properties of the Einstein special theory of relativity were first discussed, many people refused to believe that such a thing could happen. How could one twin stay young while the other grew old? If such a thing could be done, it wouldn't be done by scientists, but by magicians using some magical youth potion. But the true magical elixir of eternal youth was brewed by a scientist, Einstein, who gave us a new picture of the basic fabric of the Universe, the space and time we live in.

The reason that the paradox of the twins is hard for us to believe comes from our limited experiences with high velocities. Our supersonic jets and rockets may go fast enough for most of us, but even our fastest rockets, boosted to their highest speeds by close encounters with the rapidly moving planets of Jupiter and Saturn, still travel at only one ten-thousandth of the speed of light. Unfortunately, the unusual effects predicted by Einstein's Special Theory of Relativity only become significant when you are traveling at speeds greater than half the speed of light. Because of this limited experience with high velocities we have developed a "common sense" that says that time is some absolute quantity that ticks the same way for all things.

This strong, but erroneous belief in "common sense" is often backed up by people trying to use the principle of "relativity" to prove their point. If "everything is relative," they would say, "and all points of view are equally good, then the idea of the traveling twin Jill living longer than the stay-at-home twin Jack leads to a logical paradox."

Their argument goes like this: "Jill takes a ride on a relativistic rocket ship, while her lazy twin Jack stays curled up in front of his fireplace on Earth reading *War and Peace*. Jill returns some decades later just as Jack is reading the last page. (Jack is a slow reader.)

"According to Einstein, Jill will be young and perky, having aged but a few years, while Jack looks and feels like Rip Van Winkle.

"Well, if everything is relative, and Jack's point of view is just as good as Jill's point of view, then according to 'relativity' it would be equally good to say that while Jack was reading in front of the fireplace, the earth was taking *him* on a relativistic ride, while Jill sat cooped up in her motionless rocket.

"The situation would be even more symmetric if we imagined

Jack and Jill meeting out in empty space in two identical rocket ships, then flipping coins to see who travels and who waits.

"Since the 'all points of view are equally good' relativity principle says that we can either assume that Jack is moving while Jill is standing still, or that Jill is moving while Jack is standing still, then the Einstein time dilation effect leads to the paradox that depending upon which point of view you choose, Jack ages slower than Jill, or Jill ages slower than Jack. These results are mutually contradictory, thus there is a logical paradox generated. Since the Einstein idea of time dilation is what caused the paradox, it must be wrong, and the time that a person lives does *not* depend upon his velocity."

The resolution of the "twin paradox" comes when we carefully consider and keep track of three things. The first is the concept of "points of view," better called "frames of reference." The second is the concept of "constant velocity." The third is the concept of "comparing clocks."

The principle of relativity, that all points of view are equally valid, is only true for frames of reference that are moving at constant velocity. This means that the frame of reference must remain in constant motion at the same speed and in the same direction *for all time*. Those points of view that stop or start, or that go at constant speed but change direction (going in a circle, for instance), are not the "frames of reference" that relativity applies to. They are different because of their acceleration. So let's make sure that we give Jack and Jill the proper frames of reference to travel in—those which have constant velocity.

To compare clocks, Jack and Jill must be at the same place at the same time so that they can put their clocks side by side and both agree that they read the same. To arrange that at the beginning of the relativistic aging experiment is easy (although a little tricky if Jill is whizzing by Jack at 99.9 percent of the speed of light). It is obvious, except for that one point in space and time where they meet, that if Jack and Jill stay in their constant velocity frames of reference their paths will never cross again. Since they can never meet to compare clocks, the question of who is older is moot.

You might argue that there are other ways to compare clocks. For instance, Jack and Jill might exchange radio signals that carry the ticking sounds of their respective clocks, and they each can compare the ticks broadcast from the other with the ticks from their own clock.

It turns out that in relativity theory you cannot compare clocks this way. They must be at the same place at the same time. Any attempt to compare clocks by sending signals produces ambiguous results whose interpretation depends upon the observer. For instance, since Jack and Jill are moving apart at high speeds, then the ticks on Jack's radio beam are slowed because Jill's rocket ship has moved farther away after each second, and succeeding ticks have a farther distance to travel. In the same way, Jill's radio sends out ticks to Jack, but drops them off into space at a constantly increasing distance. Thus, to both Jack and Jill the other's clock seems to be running slower. At first this sounds paradoxical, but both Jack and Jill are smart scientists and know about the Doppler effect due to the constantly increasing distance between them, so they expected this result. (The lowered tone of the whistle on a departing train is a similar effect.) All they can say is that any attempt to compare clocks using radio or other signals will give ambiguous results. It will be necessary for one or the other of them to do something to bring their clocks back together again so they can be compared side by side.

To resolve the Twin Paradox problem, let us set up a carefully designed experiment. Jack climbs into his rocket ship *Frame 1* (short for Frame of Reference 1), and goes out into space and turns off his rocket so he is no longer accelerating and is moving at a constant velocity. Once he has stopped the engines, the name of his rocket ship now means something real—the unique frame of reference in which Jack resides. Jill also takes off in her rocket ship *Frame 2* and, after getting up speed relative to Jack, she aims her vehicle carefully at Jack's spacecraft so that their side portholes will pass facing each other. She then turns off her engines, leaving her floating in space. They both swim down from their cockpits and go to the side portholes. They set up their cameras and clocks (digital quartz chronometers with microsecond accuracies and large numbers on the readout). Fortunately Jill is a good pilot and the ships pass each other with a relative velocity of 99.9 percent of the speed of light and with their portholes within a few centimeters of each other. There are simultaneous clicks of their two cameras and each sees that the readouts on both clocks indicate the same time.

Jill now continues off into space, and within a few hours is out in the outer regions of the solar system on her way to the stars. They compare clock ticks by radio signals, but they both know that you can't tell anything definite by that technique, for both think that the other's clock is slow.

The resolution of the paradox comes at the turnaround point. Up until that point, special relativity says that the aging question is ambiguous. In order to compare the relative times of the two clocks (or the ages of the two twins), they must both be at the same place. Now instead of having Jill turn on the rocket engine in *Frame 2* and destroying the validity of her rocket ship's name, let's have her hitchhike back. For the purposes of the experiment, we have sent David out earlier in his rocket ship *Frame 3*. David went out a few light-years, then turned around and headed back into the solar system at 99.9 percent light speed, right next to the track Jill would be coming out on. Jill contacts David and arranges for a ride back in on *Frame 3*. As they pass, Jill hops off *Frame 2* and onto *Frame 3*, carrying her clock with her. *Frame 2* continues on its way out into the starry sky, keeping true to its name.

(One might think it would be difficult for Jill to make the transfer from a frame of reference moving at +99.9 percent of the speed of light to a frame of reference moving at −99.9 percent of the speed of light carrying a heavy quartz chronometer, but Jill, like Jack, is quite nimble.)

Jill rides back in with David in *Frame 3*, and when David zips by Jack, Jill is down at the side porthole, her youthful face grinning in exuberance as she snaps a picture of her gray-haired twin Jack and his aging quartz chronometer with a time indicated on it that is many years later than the time on Jill's clock.

We know that Jill will be the younger twin because she is the one that violated the "principle of equivalence of reference frames" by jumping off *Frame 2* and coming back on *Frame 3*. By abandoning her original coordinate system that she started with, Jill can no longer claim "everything is relative." The stay-at-home twin Jack is still with his original coordinate system *Frame 1* and thus has not moved, paying a price for this stodginess by aging at a precipitous rate compared to the traveling twin.

Suppose David had gone the other way, and had arranged to pass by Jack at 99.9999 percent of the speed of light, and Jack and his chronometer had left *Frame 1* and jumped on *Frame 3*.

Then sometime later, when *Frame 3* had caught up with and passed Jill in *Frame 2*, it would have been Jack that was younger. (At 99.9999 percent of the speed of light, Jack is aging slower than Jill, who is moving at 99.9 percent of the speed of light.)

Except for a few who still cherish the idea of an inviolable, unchangeable time, the human race has absorbed this unusual behavior of nature at high velocities, and has learned not only to live with this "one-way" time machine, but to use it. There is yet another type of "one-way" time machine. You are living on it—the earth! This type of time machine uses one of the magical properties of gravity predicted by the Einstein theory of gravity, the General Theory of Relativity. According to the general theory, a high gravity field causes time to run slower, just as high velocities do. The amount of time slowing in the field of the earth is not very much, although it is measurable if you have an accurate enough clock. A clock in the basement of a building will run slightly slower than one on the top floor of the building. To get a significant amount of slowing, the gravitational field has to be very strong.

One way to obtain a strong gravitational field is to find a neutron star or a black hole and send your spacecraft into a close orbit around the mass. You are now down in the gravitational potential well of the star and are living slower than those farther away. Since you are in a free-fall orbit, the strong gravitational forces pulling on you are canceled by the centrifugal force of your orbital rotation. The problem is that when you are in orbit about a dense star, the only place where the gravity and centrifugal forces exactly cancel is at the center of mass of the spacecraft (or you!). The other points are not quite in free-fall and are subject to the tidal forces due to the change in the gravity field of the star with distance and angle. For an orbit around a neutron star or black hole, these tidal forces can reach hundreds of earth gravities per meter. These tidal forces are strong enough to literally tear you limb from limb. If you go even closer, the tides will be strong enough to straighten out the helical twist in your DNA!

In the very distant future, however, it may be that our future magicians will be able to make a one-way gravitational time machine that won't kill you with its crushing tidal forces if you try to use it. This time machine would be a hollow ball of ultra-dense material. The gravitational potential inside such a hollow ball is uniform. It can be quite high, giving a strong time-slowing effect, yet because there are no variations in it, there are no gravitational forces, since it is the variations in the gravitational potential that cause the accelerations.

Many people think that the slowdown of time in gravitational fields and for fast-moving objects has only been confirmed for high-speed elementary particles. In one of the better justified boondoggles in the annals of science, however, nothing can beat parlaying a test of Einstein's theories of relativity into a trip around the world. In 1971, American physicists Hafele and Keating borrowed two identical, highly accurate portable clocks from the U.S. Naval Observatory, and obtained a grant from the Office of Naval Research to pay for three around-the-world tickets (one seat for each of them and a seat for one of the clocks). The twin clocks were set to the same time in Washington, D.C. One clock-twin stayed in Washington, where it was only subjected to the slowdown in time due to its position in the gravity field of the earth. The other clock-twin took off at a speed of 1,000 kilometers per hour (600 mph) and went in a round-trip journey around the earth at an average height of ten kilometers (six miles) above the earth's surface.

The time as measured by the moving clock twin was slowed down by the fact that it was moving at a velocity close to that of light (well . . . it was closer to the speed of light than the stay-at-home twin). The time as measured by the stay-at-home twin was slowed by the fact that it was subjected to a much greater gravitational field than the elevated twin (well . . . it was 1.0016 times greater). However, the velocity effect was larger than the gravitational effect, so upon return to Washington, the moving clock was found to be slower by exactly the amount predicted by the two theories of relativity.

Just to check, the scientists and the world-traveling clock went back around the earth the other way, where the rotational speed of the earth subtracted from the airplane's speed rather than adding to it. Again the scientists got the correct result. (This was probably the cheapest test of relativity ever made; it only cost $8,000, of which $7,600 was spent on airfares.)

Scientists have already built a magic time machine that stretches the lifetimes of tiny particles by 10,000 times. When will we be able to build a time machine big enough to keep large particles (like us) forever youthful? We have already built and are using the first model of that magic time machine. It's called the Space Shuttle.

The Space Shuttle is a great space-travel machine, but as a time-travel machine this first version leaves something to be desired. The orbital velocity of the Shuttle is nearly eight kilometers per second (26 millionths of the speed of light). If you stayed in an orbiting space shuttle for a year, you would age more slowly than your twin on the ground, but only by about one-hundredth of a second.

To make real time machines out of our space-traveling rocket ships, we need to make them go at nearly the speed of light. It will be difficult, but we can see the technology to build these magical time machines coming in our future.

Einstein has given us one-way time machines that allow us to slow our rapid progression into the future. What about a time machine that will allow us to go into the past as well as the future? For that we turn again to Einstein's General Theory of Relativity.

The Einstein General Theory of Relativity should really be called the Einstein Theory of High Accelerations. The theory is mostly about gravity, which causes the accelerations, but it also contains the Special Theory of Relativity which is about high velocities. Thus, the general theory describes what happens when either the velocity or the acceleration of an object is very large.

We are only just beginning to understand all of the ramifications of this theory of gravity that Einstein gave us. There are many marvels that have already appeared as we study these equations, magical things such as gravitational waves that can travel all the way through the earth without hindrance, curved space that distorts the light beams coming from the constellations of stars in the heavens, and black holes that swallow everything that comes near them. But the most amazing of the magical things that are predicted by the Einstein gravity equations are the two-way time machines. Yes, plural, for the Einstein General Theory of Relativity has already given us tentative engineering designs for a number of time machines that allow us to travel both backward and forward in time. The theorists may complain about the stability of some of the designs, and the environmentalists may be appalled at the resources that will be needed, but the gravitational engineers of the future will build these time machines if they are given the mandate, the money, and the mass.

Einstein's gravity theory allows many shapes for a time machine. In fact, it seems that any rotating object that is dense enough to produce a region with a twisted ultra-gravity field can produce time-confusing regions. There are some shapes, however, that can produce time-travel regions that might be usable by humans. One gravitational mass configuration that can act as a time machine is a large, rapidly rotating, dense object that is collapsing to a black hole just as its spin speed is rising to that of the speed of light. This extreme version of a spinning, collapsing star can be described quite accurately by a mathematically rigorous solution to the full, nonlinear Einstein gravity equations. No approximations are used. This solution is called the Kerr metric, after the theorist Roy Kerr, who probably was dismayed when he found that the mathematical beauty that he had discovered not only described something physical, but also something that might have some future application.

The Kerr solution describes the twisted shape of the space–time on the outside of some collapsing, rotating mass that is approaching high density. Large stars are rotating masses, and as they reach the end of their short lives, they collapse into dense rotating black holes. Large stars, however, are usually rotating fairly slowly. (The sun rotates about once every 25 days.) The speed of the material near their surface is well below that of the speed of light. The amount of angular momentum in a large star is considerable, however, and the momentum is conserved as the star collapses. In fact, the angular momentum in most stars is sufficient to bring the surface of the star up to light speed long before it has reached black hole densities.

Left to itself, a collapsing star will find ways to shed its angular momentum, either by throwing material off from its rapidly spinning equator, or by breaking up into two or three smaller bodies orbiting about each other that emit gravitational radiation. With the excess angular momentum gone, the star will finally form into an elliptically shaped black hole.

However, it is possible (and given the human race's proclivity for fooling around with nature, probable), that this pancake-shaped collapse could be induced to form a doughnut-shaped collapse, with all the dense mass out in the rotating ring. Once such an object were formed, then the Kerr solution to the

Einstein equations says that the empty region in the center of the doughnut can be the gateway to a time machine!

The numbers from the Kerr solution indicate that as you come down from overhead and start to approach the plane of the ring, the strong gravity field of the ring starts to change your space and time compared to that of an observer far away. Your space becomes smaller and your time becomes longer. The spinning of the dense doughnut causes even stranger things to happen. The twist that the rotation puts into your space–time converts part of what you would call space into what the outside observer would call time, and converts part of what you would call time into what he would call space.

The Kerr solution then says that as you pass through the plane defined by the dense ring, the space–time conversion becomes complete. Your forward space dimension has been turned into a time dimension while your time dimension has turned into a space dimension.

What is more amazing is that when you go through the hole in the ultradense doughnut, you don't come out on the other side! Instead, you find you have entered a strange type of hyperspace. In this hyperspace you feel perfectly normal, even though one of your three space directions has been interchanged with time. If you go in the hyperspace up near the rotating ring and move in the direction against the rotation of the ring for a number of rotations, you will observe nothing unusual happening to you. In your travels near the rotating ring, however, you have traveled backward in space (the forward direction being determined by the direction of rotation of the ring). If you then return back through the hole in the ring, your time and space dimensions will be restored to normal. But don't forget that while in hyperspace you went backwards in space and what used to be space is now time. Although you have returned back to your original position in space, you will find that your position in time has moved backwards a number of years!

This magical result obtained from the Kerr solution to the Einstein equations can be found in a highly mathematical paper published by Brandon Carter in the 1974 volume of the *Physical Review*, the most prestigious scientific journal in the field of physics. In that paper Carter concludes, "To sum up, . . . the central region has the properties of a time machine. It is possible, starting from any point in the outer regions of the

space, to travel into the interior, move backwards in time
. . . and then return to the original position."

Now, there are many mathematical theorists who insist that
such a special shape for a rotating mass cannot happen. There
have been scientific papers written to show that even infinitesimal deviations from the special doughnut-shaped symmetries of
the Kerr solution (such as would be caused by the presence of
a spaceship trying to use the time machine), would drastically
alter the structure of the Kerr solution. The authors conclude that
nature will not allow such mass configurations to form and
therefore time machines are impossible. Yet, when you read
these papers that purport to prove the impossibility of time
travel, you find that they use assumptions such as "realistic
collapse," "normal matter," and "stable configurations,"
assumptions that greatly limit the generality of the proofs. A
review by Stephen Siklos in the science magazine *Nature* is an
example: "Unfortunately, this [Kerr's] solution . . . does not
represent a *realistic* collapse."

There are many things in our present world that are not in a
"realistic" or "stable" state that would be normally allowed by
nature. A transistor is an unnatural miracle—an ultrapure silicon
crystal. A liter of liquid helium, a laser, a pure-bred poodle, a
geostationary orbit communication satellite—all are "unnatural"
oddities kept stable by their human makers.

This uncomfortable situation for the theorists is best illustrated by a paper published by Frank Tipler. Tipler concluded
his paper with a carefully chosen, deliberately pontifical statement: "The demonstration that no possible combination of
known substances, known forms of machinery, and known forms
of force can be united in a practicable machine by which men
shall [travel back in time], seems to the writer as complete as
it is possible for the demonstration of any physical fact to be."
(The brackets were in Tipler's original paper.) With the excep-
tion of the words in the brackets, Tipler's quotation is identical
to a statement published by Newcomb in 1906 at the conclusion
of his classic paper proving the impossibility of heavier-than-air
flying machines. In Newcomb's paper, the words in the brackets
were "fly through the air." Newcomb was proven wrong by the
Wright brothers in 1903, *before* his statement reached print. One
feels that Tipler deliberately hedged on his "impossibility
proof" by his choice for the form of his conclusion.

It may be true that nature will not naturally form a Kerr-metric time machine from a collapsing star, but with a little guidance and some future-magic technology applied by our far-future ancestors, perhaps a star bigger than our sun can be made into a ring-shaped time machine 100 kilometers in diameter—and maintained despite the fact that it would not be stable if left alone. At a size of 100 kilometers, the gravitational tides from the dense mass of the ring are weak enough that they will not cause damage to people and well-built spacecraft passing through the center of the ring. A time machine of this size would be big enough and safe enough to send an entire rocket ship back in time.

The Kerr time machine does have the problem that in order to get the time-travel effect, the mass in the spinning ring has to move at a speed equal to that of light, and that can never be attained, just approached. There are other solutions to the Einstein field equations, however, that improve upon the Kerr solution. One of these describes the collapse of a rapidly rotating dense mass with an electric charge on it. These solutions show that the addition of an electric charge to the mass relaxes the speed-of-light requirement. A rapidly spinning dense doughnut with a large electric charge on it will form a time machine even when the speed of the mass in the ring is below that of the speed of light. Since the original star has enough rotational energy to reach near-light speeds after collapsing from a diameter of 10 million kilometers to a diameter of 100 kilometers, all our far-future magicians have to do is make sure that the star stays highly charged as it collapses and it will form a time machine.

Even if it turns out that the Kerr time machine can't be built, it isn't all that important. A spinning ring is not the only shape for a time machine. Another configuration for a time machine is a spinning cylinder. Described by Frank Tipler in 1974, the theoretical model for this time machine uses a mathematical approximation, so it is not as rigorous as the Kerr model. The approximation used is to assume that the long spinning cylinder is infinitely long. It is equivalent to saying that you are concerned only about the gravitational fields near the middle of the cylinder and the ends of the cylinder are so far away that the slight differences in the gravity field due to the fact that the cylinder is finite are not large enough to worry about.

The reason for using the approximation is that the formula for the gravitational field of an infinitely long cylinder is very simple, while that for a truncated cylinder is mathematically quite complicated. By making the assumption that the cylinder is infinite in length, instead of finite, the simple cylinder mass formula can be used in the complicated Einstein equations and the equations solved to find out what the gravity field of the cylinder is doing to the space and time near the middle. Any electrical engineer can attest that the infinitely long approximation works well in electromagnetic theory and accurately predicts the electric and magnetic fields near the middle of a long, but finite, wire. The approximation should work equally well in gravitational theory. Any lingering doubts about the validity of the results should be overcome by the fact that the Kerr solution was rigorous and resulted in a time machine, so it shouldn't surprise us if the Tipler solution results in a time machine, even if the solution is not rigorous.

Tipler's time machine is a long cylinder of ultradense mass with a spin speed at its surface that is one-half that of light (see Figure 10). The time-mixing region is near the midpoint of the cylinder, but *outside* the mass of the cylinder. The important feature of the Tipler Two-Way Time Machine is that it allows travel both backward and forward in time (depending upon whether you circle with or against the spin of the cylinder), and neither the time traveler nor the time machine has to move at velocities close to that of light. In his now-famous paper, "Rotating Cylinders and the Possibility of Global Causality Violation," published in the 1974 volume of the *Physical Review,* Tipler concludes, "In short, general relativity suggests that if we construct a sufficiently large rotating cylinder, we create a time machine."

This time machine, however, like all the time machines that use the Einstein laws, can only take you backward in time to the moment that the machine is turned on, and forward in time to the moment that the machine is turned off. Einstein's laws do not allow a future time-machine maker to go back into time to tell himself how to make the machine. Thus, at least one of the possible time-machine paradoxes is avoided.

Once we have a time machine that allows us to go both forward and backward in time, then paradoxes arise that are even more confounding than the twin paradox. Exhuming an old cliché: "What is to prevent you from going back in time and killing your grandfather before he has any children?"

There are other paradoxes brought about by the assumption of the existence of a two-way time machine, but they all boil down

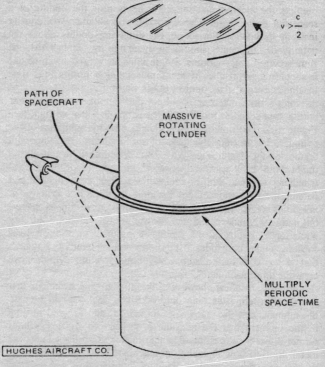

Figure 10. The Tipler two-way time machine.

to the violation of a strict time-ordered cause-and-effect relationship. There are those who would argue that this alone is enough. The very fact that causality would be violated means that time travel is impossible. Nothing more needs to be said. ("I'm sorry, young man, I can't buy your story that you came from the future to warn us about an asteroid about to strike the ocean off the East Coast. You are logically impossible. Go away!")

It doesn't take time travelers to cause trouble. Even messages sent back and forth in time can produce logical paradoxes. For instance, you could send a message to your future self asking it to send a message to your past self telling you not to send any messages in the present. If you sent the message, you would have been told in the past not to send the message, so you wouldn't, but then the future wouldn't have told you not to send the message so you would have . . . and another logical paradox arises.

Yet . . . we learned to accept the truth of Einstein's special-relativity mathematics, despite its insistence that time was not the same for all, but could be stretched and compressed. In the future, we may learn to accept Einstein's general-relativity mathematics, which says that not only can time be stretched and compressed, but time can be made to run backwards.

I don't know how the logical paradoxes brought about by time travel will be resolved. I suspect that just as we were forced to realize that time-rate is not absolute, but depends upon your experiences with space vehicles, we shall be forced to realize that time-order is not absolute, but can vary according to your experiences with time vehicles. Once a time machine exists, then decisions made at one point on the time line of an individual can affect not only the future of that individual, but also the past of that individual.

Suppose there *were* a time machine. Suppose it were something as simple as a time-phone, a telephone that allowed messages to be sent into the past. The time-phone would only be used after the occurrence of some disaster, such as an asteroid hitting the earth. After the disaster had occurred, a message could be sent into the past to warn the people of the impending problem so that they could evacuate the affected area and at least save lives. In the future, the evacuation has already taken place, the asteroid struck, and the people have come back to rebuild. One of their first jobs would be to send the evacuation message back in time, for if it is not sent, then they would all be dead.

Although there might be some thoughts about testing the paradox by *not* sending the message, I'm sure in this case it would be sent, for the consequences of not doing so would be too great. Thus, the sending of the message in the future is the "cause," while the evacuation is the "effect," yet the effect precedes the cause in time. Yet, from a logical viewpoint that neglects temporal order, the evacuation "effect" was a direct consequence of the message "cause"; it just happened to be transferred by a time-phone that sent it backwards in time.

A time-phone will also give us a broader perspective of events before any major political or social decision is made. As a result of the existence of a time-phone, we will have an "awareness" that extends further into the future than the merest instant that you and I are currently limited to. By using the time-phone, we can be made aware of future events and avoid their consequences. Just as modern airplanes use long-distance radar to search the space ahead of them for storms, and change their routes to avoid them, so time machines will allow the pilots of the nations to search the time ahead of them for disaster and avoid their consequences.

Time machines will also raise philosophical questions. If you in the future send a message back in time to yourself in the past, does the "you" in the future have any free will? For you know that you must and will send the message at the proper time in the future.

Yet, "free will" has always been limited by the laws of nature. For instance, if your past self has made the decision to jump off a bridge, your future self is bound by that decision. When time machines exist, your future decisions, in the same way, can bind your past self to the consequences of that "yet-to-be" decision.

It may be tens of thousands of years before the human race has turned what is now future magic into future technology. It will be a long time before our engineering technology can control collapsing stars in order to make a time machine big enough for a vehicle loaded with human time travelers. Long before that time, however, our gravitational engineers may be able to make miniature time machines with the mass of an asteroid and the dimension of an atomic nucleus that will allow messages encoded on pulses of laser light to be sent backward and forward in time.

To make a time-phone we would take a fairly large asteroid

about a kilometer in radius (a little larger than the sun-grazing asteroid Icarus) with a mass of about 15 billion metric tons, and compress it down until it reached the densities needed to create a small time-confusing region. The asteroid would now have the dimensions of an atomic nucleus—a superheavy, superdense nucleus. If we extract electrons out of the asteroid as we compress it, the resulting super-nucleus would end up highly charged. Although the amount of charge we can put on the black hole is limited, it is large enough to give us a "handle" on the black hole so we can "hold" on to it and "manipulate" it.

Once we have made an electrically charged black hole, then whirling electric and magnetic fields can push the charged super-nucleus like the rotor on a motor and get it spinning. The spinning charged particle will then create a north and south magnetic pole at its spin poles. A superstrong magnetic field can then pull on the magnetic poles until the nucleus is stretched out into a long spinning cylinder. This would be a time machine for nuclear-sized time travelers, extremely short pulses of gamma rays with wavelengths smaller than the time-transfer region. A message would consist of a small number of gamma rays, each at a slightly different frequency corresponding to its "code word" in the message. At these high energies, gamma-ray detectors are quite efficient, and the decoding of the cluster of photons that emerged a few weeks in the past or future would be relatively easy.

These "time-phone" time machines may exist within 100 years if there are breakthroughs in our understanding of elementary particles and ultradense matter. Some of us now living may owe our lives to the warnings brought to us from the future by these "magical" paradox producers. Then, after the crisis is over and we have time to reflect, we will wonder about those ancient philosophers of the twentieth century who worried so much about those "time machine paradoxes."

Warp Magic

There are two basic ways to get from here to there in a hurry. One way is to find some future-magic method for moving through the space between here and there faster than the speed of light. The other way is to obey the cosmic speed law but find some future-magic method of getting from here to there without having to go through all that dreary empty space in between. To do that, what you need is that good old science-fiction plot-speeder-upper, the space warp.

If future-magic time machines are theoretically possible, then future-magic space warps should be, too. It is an axiom of relativity, where time and space are treated on an equal footing, that a faster-than-light space-warp system is operationally equivalent to a time machine. If one observer sees you moving from one place to another through a space warp faster than the speed of light, say entering the space warp at Sol and arriving at Alpha Centauri one hour later, a different observer, who just happened to be passing by in a rapidly moving spacecraft, would swear that you arrived at Alpha Centauri *before* you left Sol. In fact, if that observer could see inside the space warp, he would see three yous. He would see you back at Earth walking toward the entrance to the space warp before you started your journey, he would see you at Alpha Centauri walking away from the space warp exit after you had completed your journey, and he would see you in the space warp traveling backward from Alpha Centauri to Earth (getting younger as you traveled) to meet yourself walking into the entrance to the space warp in preparation for the start of your journey.

It would be ideal if we could find or build a space warp that was big enough to accommodate a large spacecraft with plenty of room inside for a human crew. A tiny space warp would still be useful, however, even if it could only pass through a tiny robotic probe, or one photon or elementary particle at a time. Such a space warp could serve as a faster-than-light communication system, or a "Federal Express" overnight package delivery system, keeping the bureaucratic machinery of the United Star Systems of the Milky Way (USSMW) creaking along.

It turns out that there are a number of possibilities for space warps based on the curved space–time theories of Einstein. These space warps are "bridges" or "tunnels" that shortcut through higher dimensions from one point in our space to another. All of these space-warp concepts have some theoretical problems since they involve singularities due to the extreme mass densities and extreme space–time curvatures that are involved. Yet those problems might not be insurmountable for a sufficiently advanced technological civilization and it might be possible to build a space warp using the Einstein General Theory of Relativity.

Yet we know that the Einstein General Theory of Relativity is not adequate for describing the real Universe. The Einstein theory does not properly contain the behavior of matter in the small. Ultimately it will have to be replaced by the "Unified Field Theory" for which Einstein and many others have searched for many years. The Unified Field Theory is supposed to be a theory that combines all the known forces: electromagnetic, gravity, strong nuclear, and weak nuclear. At the same time, it will have to use the complex number mathematics that are necessary to describe the strange quantum mechanical behavior of mechanics in the small. When the correct Unified Field Theory is found, then perhaps it may give us clues for even better future-magic possibilities for the construction of space warps. The Penrose Twistor Theory is one candidate for this Unified Field Theory. Space warps are also possible in the Penrose Twistor Theory. The Penrose space warps don't work by building a tunnel or bridge from one point to another; instead, the underlying twistor space is given a "twist" that temporarily eliminates the space between here and there during the time you want to travel.

The Einstein Theory of Gravity has produced three types of space warps to date. The first is the Wheeler Wormhole, which was postulated by John Wheeler as a warping of empty space that is predicted by his Theory of Geometrodynamics (Wheeler's version of the Einstein Theory of Gravity). In this attempt to combine some of the aspects of quantum mechanics with the Einstein curved-space picture of gravity, Wheeler looked at the probable behavior of space–time in the very small.

In the Wheeler Theory of Geometrodynamics, the Planck length plays a pivotal role. This fundamental length only involves the velocity of light c, the Newtonian gravitational constant G, and the Planck quantum constant h. The Planck length is very small, only 1.61×10^{-35} meters. This fundamental length is so much smaller than the size of atoms (10^{-10} meters) or particles (10^{-15} meters) that it obviously has nothing to do with determining the size of either. John Wheeler feels that the Planck length is our connection to the quantum theory of gravity, for when empty space is examined at characteristic dimensions comparable to the Planck length it begins to lose its smoothness and starts to develop a foamlike consistency.

The reason that space–time begins to loose its smoothness in the Wheeler Theory of Geometrodynamics is that in quantum mechanics there are certain limits on what can be observed. In order for you to observe something in a region that is very small in dimensions, that something must have a high momentum. (If it didn't have a high momentum before, the very act of observing it will give it a high momentum.) A high momentum implies a high energy and a high energy implies a high mass and a high mass implies a high gravity field and a high gravity field implies a high space curvature. At distances as small as 10^{-35} meters, the energy densities associated with this space–time "foam" can be estimated to be of the order of 10^{94} times that of normal matter. At these densities, the amount of energy existing in a region with the dimensions of a Planck length is sufficient to form a quantum singularity with the radius of a Planck length and an effective mass of 10^{-8} kilograms, about the mass of an amoeba.

The space-curvature fluctuations at these dimensions are so chaotic that space–time itself turns into a foam made of bubbles, bridges, and tunnels. The bubbles are like miniature black holes that form, then evaporate away again. The bridges and tunnels are tubes of space–time, with the tunnels being wormholes going from one space–time point to another.

A Wheeler Wormhole would allow travel from one point in the Universe to another point in the Universe without going through the Universe. If the distance through the wormhole were smaller than the distance between the two ends of the wormhole in this Universe, it would be possible to travel from one place to another faster than the speed of light. Unfortunately, a Wheeler Wormhole is very small, some 10^{-35} meters in diameter. It is much too small for a spacecraft, but it conceivably could be used to send a message from one place to another in this Universe faster than the speed of light.

The wormholes are dynamic, constantly changing in size with time. A wormhole starts out pinched at the waist into a singularity of highly curved space–time. From a distance it looks like a black hole caused by a mass. As time goes on, the wormhole opens up and reaches a maximum diameter that is twice the Schwarzschild radius of the equivalent mass. The diameter of the wormhole then shrinks and finally pinches off again to form another singularity.

It would seem likely at first glance that since the diameter of a Wheeler Wormhole is 10^{-35} meters, that the distance spanned by the wormhole would be of comparable dimensions. This is probably true, but it could be that at the other end of the wormhole opens up at some distant point in this Universe, or perhaps in some other universe. There could then be other wormhole connections to points far distant in our Universe.

After Wheeler invented the wormhole, he assigned a student the task of calculating the time it takes to travel through the wormhole. Unfortunately, the student found that the extreme warpage of space–time inside the Wheeler Wormhole affects not only space, but time. The time dilation experienced in the wormhole makes it take just as long (or longer) to go through a Wheeler Wormhole as it does to travel from one end to another through the outside flat space of the Universe. Also, the dynamic behavior of the wormhole means that you must arrange your start time and speed so that you are going through the wormhole while the throat is open. The mathematics also indicates that to avoid getting caught in the singularity, it is necessary that you have a faster-than-light space drive on your spacecraft, otherwise you will get trapped in the singularity when the wormhole pinches off. If you planned on sending messages through the Wheeler Wormhole instead, normal photons would not do since they too would be trapped by the singularity. Instead you would have to use a communication system that transmitted tachyons, hypothetical particles that always travel faster than the speed of light. So, as currently understood,

Wheeler Wormholes are not a way to violate causality (unless you can already violate it by having an FTL drive or tachyon radio). If ever made and used, however, they might be a way to send messages directly from one part of the Universe to another without having to use lots of radio power and large transmitting and receiving dishes.

The mathematical structure of the Wheeler Wormhole is the same as that of the mathematical structure for a Schwarzschild black hole caused by a dense mass. The Schwarzschild mathematics thus contains within it the prediction that a black hole can form a large wormhole in space. The Schwarzschild solution to the Einstein equations, however, is only valid for the region outside the collapsing mass of the star. In a real black hole formed by a collapsing star, the mass that formed the black hole only allows us to observe just part of the total mathematical structure of the Schwarzschild solution. The only parts of the solution that can be experienced from our portion of the Universe are the event horizon (which we can fall through), the interior of the event horizon (which we must fall through), and the singularity (where we stop falling). The throat of the Schwarzschild wormhole and the other universe on the other side, all of which are incipient in the mathematics of the Schwarzschild solution, are blocked by the presence of the matter in the collapsing star.

If the collapsing star is electrically or magnetically charged, however, then the Schwarzschild solution goes over into the Reissner-Nordstrøm solution. This solution, found shortly after the Schwarzschild solution in 1918, describes the structure of space–time outside a massive object that also contains an excess of charge. In this mathematical solution, there are now two event horizons. There is an outer event horizon, which is slightly inside of where the event horizon would be if the collapsing mass were not charged. Then just outside the singularity is an inner event horizon. The larger the charge, the greater the radius of this inner event horizon.

A spaceship could follow the mass of a collapsing charged star and pass through the outer event horizon (provided it could withstand the tidal forces). Once inside the first event horizon, the radial space dimension has taken on timelike qualities, in that the spaceship must inexorably continue moving inward to constantly decreasing radial dimensions, following the collapsing charged mass down toward the singularity. As the collapsing mass becomes smaller and smaller, a second event horizon will form. The spacecraft will then pass through this inner event horizon. Once inside the inner event horizon, the collapsing mass will continue falling inward toward the center under its self-gravitation, where it will form the singularity. Inside the inner event horizon, however, time and space have once again reversed roles and it is now possible for the spacecraft to turn on its rockets, halt its motion in the radial direction, and go into orbit about the singularity.

The mathematics then says that, if the spacecraft has enough energy, there is no mathematical reason why the spacecraft cannot then go back out through the inner event horizon and the outer event horizon to emerge back into the outer universe again. The mathematics also tells us that the universe that the spacecraft emerges into is not the universe it left. The spacecraft has traveled through the charged black hole space warp or Chargewarp, and emerged somewhere else.

If such a trip were really possible, the actual maneuver of the spacecraft would be to dive into the Chargewarp, building up speed by using the gravitational attraction of the collapsing mass. The spacecraft would pass through the outer event horizon, then through the inner event horizon, now nearly at the speed of light. It would then apply a little bit of side thrust so that the trajectory of the spacecraft would pass to one side of the singularity. The spacecraft would whip around the singularity and then head back out again with enough kinetic energy to travel back up through the gravitational potential well, through the inner and outer event horizons to emerge from the Chargewarp in the other universe.

Usually when people discuss charged black holes, it is assumed that the charge being discussed is electrical charge. It is quite possible that real black holes have some electrical charge on them. Electrons, which have negative electrical charge, are some 2,000 times lighter than protons, which have positive electrical charge. It is thus easy to imagine some process or other occurring during the collapse of the star that would result in a black hole preferentially collecting one type of charge over the other. This condition would not go too far in the real world, however, for after the black hole had built up just a small amount of charge (compared to its mass), the electric fields around the black hole would become strong enough that they would start to collect the oppositely charged particles from the space around it with higher efficiency, limiting the charge buildup.

The Reissner-Nordstrøm solution does not care, however, what kind of charge is used. The solution applies equally well to black holes that have magnetic charge. If magnetic monopoles are real, and if our future-magic technology allows us to manufacture them in sufficient quantity, then it might be possible to make a Chargewarp using north or south magnetic monopoles. Since the real world does not seem to contain large quantities of magnetic monopoles, then a magnetic Chargewarp would not suffer the self-canceling features that an electric Chargewarp would. It would be a major technological challenge to construct a black hole solely out of a few thousand solar masses of north magnetic monopoles to build a Chargewarp tunnel from Sol to Tau Ceti. But to a true future-magic civilization, it may be equivalent in difficulty to the current project to build a tunnel between England and France.

The third space-warp concept that uses the Einstein gravitational equations is based on the Kerr solution to the full field equations of the Einstein Theory of Gravity for a dense, spinning mass. Like the Schwarzschild solution, the Kerr solution is only valid in the empty regions of space outside of the spinning mass. If you assume the star is very dense and spinning very rapidly, however, then you find out that what the Kerr metric is describing is not a spinning oblate sphere, but a spinning torus or ring of dense mass. All the mass is in the ring. The gravity tides are strong near the surface of the ring and it is dangerous to approach the ring too closely. There is no mass in the center of the ring, however, so there are no gravity tides there. If you go through the center of this massive rotating ring you do not come out the other side (see Figure 11).

Instead, as you pass through the ring in either direction, you will enter a hyperuniverse. The Kerr solution to the Einstein field equations describes a space warp—a Ringwarp. In this hyperuniverse the space–time has different properties from the normal space–time of this Universe. Mass in the hyperuniverse is negative and repels instead of attracting. Also, as you enter the hyperuniverse, what was the time dimension in our Universe turns into a space dimension in the hyperuniverse, and what was a space dimension in our Universe turns into time in the hyperuniverse. To get out of the hyperuniverse back into our

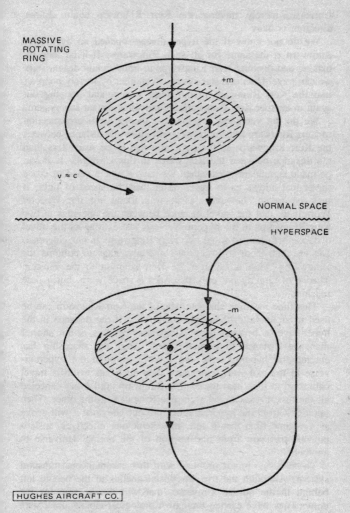

MASSIVE
ROTATING
RING

+m

$v \approx c$

NORMAL SPACE

HYPERSPACE

−m

HUGHES AIRCRAFT CO.

Figure 11. The Kerr metric space warp.

Universe, merely traverse the Kerr Ringwarp again. Either direction is okay.

We do not know if the hyperuniverse opened up by a Kerr Ringwarp is the same for all such Ringwarps. If it is, then by making and opening Kerr Ringwarps in orbit around distant stars we can travel from one star system to another by merely popping into the Kerr Ringwarp in our solar system and popping out again in another Kerr Ringwarp around some distant star system.

We do not yet know whether the theory for interconnection of Kerr Ringwarp hyperuniverses will allow the distance between the Kerr Ringwarps in the hyperuniverse to be made less than the distance between the Ringwarps in this Universe. If it can be made significantly less, then we have a new method of space travel that allows us to travel faster than the speed of light. It may be found, however, as it was found for the Wheeler Wormhole, that the travel distance between the openings in two Kerr Ringwarps in the hyperuniverse is just as long as the travel distance between the same two Kerr Ringwarps in our Universe. Despite this, there still may be some advantage to building the Ringwarps. That is because the Kerr solution to the Einstein Theory of Gravity not only describes a space warp, but a time machine.

This time machine characteristic of the Kerr Ringwarp can be used to attain faster-than-light travel even if the distance in the hyperuniverse between Kerr Ringwarp openings is not shorter than the distance in normal space. After the spaceship has entered the hyperuniverse and traveled through the hyperuniverse to the exit Kerr Ringwarp, then all it has to do is travel backward in time near the exiting Ringwarp until it has canceled all the time it took to get from one Ringwarp to the other. Then upon exit from the hyperuniverse into our Universe it will arrive at the same time that it left, thus achieving effectively instantaneous transport from one portion of the normal Universe to another.

There is one minor problem with this instantaneous transport system. Although the trip was instantaneous to the people left behind in the normal Universe, that will not be true for the crew. They have carried their own biological clocks along with them and have aged not only during the long journey from one star system to another, but also while they were circling boredly under the exiting Kerr Ringwarp while traveling backward through time. Fortunately, they would be able to use the time dilation experienced in a relativistic rocket ship to keep them from aging too much faster than their comrades at home.

Even though a Kerr Ringwarp may not be the solution for transporting humans from here to there faster than the speed of light, it may be the solution for transmitting messages over interstellar distances faster than the speed of light. A robotic message probe capable of carrying out the complex flight plan would not be hard to build for a civilization capable of making a Kerr Ringwarp.

Any of the space-warp concepts that involve singularities in space–time will always have problems. The mathematically oriented physicists that study the exotic behavior of black holes can easily show that even minor perturbations, such as that caused by a spacecraft trying to use a space warp, should cause the space warp to distort or collapse. The mathematicians are probably correct, and it is very unlikely that the currently conceived versions of space warps can ever exist. Yet it is very interesting that our best theory of the way the Universe operates does allow for the theoretical existence of such future-magic machines as space warps, albeit under extremely idealistic conditions. As the Einstein General Theory of Relativity is replaced by a better theory, we can hope that this future-magic aspect of the Einstein theory remains in the new theory. Then if we are lucky, we may find that the new theory shows us how to make a space warp that really works.

The Wheeler Theory of Geometrodynamics and the Einstein General Theory of Relativity are not the only theories of the structure of space–time that give us clues to space warps. There is another theory, called the Penrose Twistor Theory, which is also attempting to come up with a description of the universe, but from a completely different point of view. If the Penrose Twistor Theory turns out to be a better description of reality than the Einstein relativity theories, then this multidimensional form of future magic could unveil a completely new set of rules of nature. This could create a new technological explosion that will be more revealing, more astounding, and more magical than all of our past technological advances combined. For example, the Penrose Twistor Theory has in it the potential for warping (in this case, twisting) space so that you can go from here to there without having to go over all the points in between.

In the Penrose Twistor Theory, the Universe that we observe is an illusion, a simplification, of a much more complicated

universe controlled by the equations of the Twistor Theory. If
you think about it, the world we observe is an illusion. When
your brain "sees" some distant three-dimensional object with
your eyes, all your brain "really" senses is the pattern of light
hitting the curved two-dimensional light-sensitive surface that
covers the back of your eyeballs. That light pattern in turn has
been transmitted from the distant three-dimensional object to
your two-dimensional retina by massless spinning particles of
light called photons.

Where does the illusion stop? Is the three-dimensional world
that we derive from our senses "real"? It turns out that in the
Twistor Theory, our Universe is just a three-dimensional illusion
of some "realer" universe of a higher number of dimensions,
transmitted from this higher dimension to our three-dimensional
existence by massless spinning objects called twistors.

This dependence on a higher number of dimensions for the
Universe is a major characteristic of the Penrose Twistor
Theory. In Twistor Theory, space is not three-dimensional, or
four-dimensional, or five-dimensional, but eight-dimensional.
Penrose's research arises in response to one of the most bother-
some dichotomies in physics today: In all the mathematical
calculations involving the macroscopic world, from designing
toasters to calculating the distances to the farthest stars, real
numbers are used. But real numbers are not adequate to describe
the submicroscopic world of the atom. To solve the equations
of quantum theory, a different system of numbers, called
"complex numbers," is required.

Roger Penrose feels that this dichotomy is wrong. Since
everything material is made of atoms, and all energy exists as
discrete bundles called quanta, and since both atoms and quanta
require the use of complex numbers instead of real numbers,
Penrose feels that all our calculations about the Universe should
use complex numbers. But to do this completely means refor-
mulating all of the other major theories of physics—such as the
Einstein Theories of Relativity and the Maxwell Theory of
Electromagnetism—with new mathematical formulas that use
complex numbers instead of real numbers.

To develop these ideas, Penrose has created his Twistor
Theory. From this he hopes to produce a unified view of all of
physics and thus create an entirely new vision of reality.
Complex numbers are an essential aspect of this new twistor
universe. While some of the mathematics is standard, the

important and crucial part of the theory is the use of complex numbers and the effect of the orderly nature of these numbers on the theory.

Complex numbers are made from a combination of two number systems—the familiar real numbers and the "imaginary" numbers. Imaginary numbers were invented by mathematicians to define the square root of a negative number. (A square root of a number n is that number which when multiplied by itself will produce n.) There is no real number that when multiplied by itself will result in any negative number, including minus one. Such numbers just do not exist.

Just because a number is nonexistent does not stop a good mathematician. When the mathematicians find out that the world does not give them enough numbers to play with, they merely invent new ones to suit themselves. Waving their magic pieces of chalk, they chant, "Let there be a number which when multiplied by itself gives minus one." Lo, it exists! Now the mathemagicians can proceed with their logical games, unhampered by reality.

The imaginary number that the mathematicians invented to handle calculations that involve the square root of minus one is given the symbol i. By the definition given to it by the mathematicians, $i \times i = -1$. In creating this nonreal number, the mathematicians also created a complete new set of nonreal numbers, for the i can be of any size, from $0i$ to $1,000,000i$, and beyond. It can go negative, as $-8i$, and can have values in between, like $\frac{1}{3}$ or 0.33333333 . . . i. All of the possible numbers that use i are called "imaginary numbers," an imaginative name that the mathematicians invented.

After playing with the imaginary numbers for a while, the mathematicians then combined the imaginary number system with the real number system. They found that they had invented a new type of number. It was a very strange-behaving number that was very complex to deal with. With their usual imaginative command of language, they called them "complex numbers." Some typical complex numbers are $A = (a + ix)$ and $B = (b - iy)$, where a, b, x, and y can be any real number, including zero. It is the orderly behavior of complex numbers that is crucial to the Penrose Twistor Theory.

Normally when two different entities are mixed together, the result is nothing more than two things jumbled together. There is nothing new about 100 apples and 100 oranges mixed together, except for the need for a bigger box to keep them in. When you mix real numbers and imaginary numbers together to form complex numbers, however, the amount of "jumbling" allowed in the resultant complex numbers is limited, if you require that the complex numbers behave as a decent number.

In order for a set of numbers to be useful they should behave in such a way that $A + B$ gives the same answer as $B + A$, and $A \times B$ gives the same answer as $B \times A$. When the mathematicians used these rules to define how to carry out the operations of addition and multiplication on complex numbers, they found that the real part of the complex number was controlled by the imaginary part of the complex number. This control comes about because two imaginary numbers multiplied together will produce a real number. Crossing two oranges will never produce an apple, but multiplying the imaginary number i times the imaginary number $-i$ produces the real number 1.

To understand something about the way complex numbers work, the analogy of a weaving loom is appropriate: The real numbers are the parallel woof threads attached to the top of a loom. The possible mathematical operations that can be performed on those numbers are all the braided crossovers that can be made with the loose ends of the threads. If the mathematical operations are complicated, the number threads can end up in a snarled tangle. For example, by use of what they call "pathological" functions, mathematicians can change a simple smooth reordering, such as the doubling function $2a = b$ ($1 \rightarrow 2, 2 \rightarrow 4, 3 \rightarrow 6, 4 \rightarrow 8 \ldots$) into a pathological reordering with results like ($1 \rightarrow 2, 2 \rightarrow 4, 3 \rightarrow 999999, 4 \rightarrow 8 \ldots$).

Although such "pathological" functions are allowed by the rules of mathematics, they do not exist in the real world. Physicists know that no matter how abrupt a physical change seems to be, there is always a smooth transition from one value to another. What is intriguing, and is an essential part of Twistor Theory, is that the very nature of complex numbers is such that only smoothly varying answers are allowed. The pathological functions the mathematicians can impose at will on the real number system are not allowed by the complex number system. Thus, complex numbers seem a better candidate for a mathematical description of our Universe than the ordinary real numbers, which do not exhibit this intrinsic smoothness.

When the imaginary numbers are added to the mathematical loom to make the complex numbers, they are like the warp threads woven at right angles across the real-number threads. If the two separate types of numbers are to be properly combined to make complex numbers that are ordered and obey the simple rules of arithmetic, the two types of numbers must be interwoven like the warp and woof threads in finished cloth. Once this bolt of complex number "cloth" is woven, it can be "crumpled" by various mathematical operations, but the interwoven nature of the real and imaginary numbers prevents the tangled snarls that were mathematically possible when the real-number threads were left loose.

For a long time, the complex numbers were thought to be just another toy of the mathematicians and had no relationship to the physical world. But then the realm of the atomic particle and the photon of light was discovered. It was found that in order to describe the behavior of these tiny atoms and concentrated bundles of energy, we needed a new theory of mechanics, called quantum mechanics. This new theory not only included the four-dimensional space–time of the Einstein Special Theory of Relativity, but replaced the old Newton billiard-ball picture of mechanics with a new concept of how particles move and interact with each other.

What is most amazing, is that unlike the Newton Theory of Mechanics, which uses real numbers to describe what happens, the new Quantum Theory of Mechanics requires complex numbers. Even the equations for the mechanical interaction of one particle on another must contain the imaginary number i to properly describe what happens in an atom. It is as though nature was impressed by the orderly behavior of the complex numbers and, wanting some degree of order in the universe, chose them instead of the more unruly real numbers.

But the Penrose Twistor Theory goes beyond the use of the orderly complex numbers to describe the mechanics of the Universe. At the present time, the space–time that we live in is described using real numbers. Roger Penrose thinks perhaps that even this is wrong. Maybe the seemingly solid space and time around us is just a real-world illusion of a more complex universe that uses the logical, highly controlled system of complex numbers for the same reason that the Quantum Theory of Mechanics does.

The universe described by the Penrose Twistor Theory is a strange but logical one. In place of the Einstein universe, which describes three space dimensions and one time dimension by four real numbers, the Penrose universe is described by four complex numbers. Since each complex number has a real part and an imaginary part, there are a total of eight numbers that can be used to describe things. Inhabiting this complex eight-dimensional space are Penrose's fundamental entities that are the building blocks of his universe, the twistors. The eight quantities of the new twistor space describe: the three dimensions of the twistor position in space; the two angles that describe the direction of the twistor motion along the space–time light cone through that point; and the energy, spin, and polarization of that motion.

Twistors are not "particles" *in* space–time. Nor are they the "points" *of* space–time. Instead, they are something that lies somewhere between the concepts of "particle" and "point." From a geometrical point of view, a twistor can be thought of as a "fuzzy" particle, although it is not identical to a particle. Mathematically, a twistor is closer to being a "square root" of a particle. Yet, in theoretical calculations, a twistor is mostly used in a way that makes it more nearly analogous to the usual concept of a "point" in space–time.

One way of trying to visualize the geometric view of a twistor is to imagine a small hunk of complex space shaped like a twisted rope ring or quoit that travels along its axis at the speed of light. If the twistor has a lot of energy, then it is a tiny, localized, tightly wound loop of thread with a strong influence in the immediate region around it. If the energy in the twistor is low, then it is a large, fuzzy ring of yarn whose weak influence extends for a considerable range around it.

We, of course, not being atomic-sized beings, cannot see a twistor or the complex nature of space. We only see the part that is described by real numbers. Yet the real-number behavior that we observe is controlled by the hidden complex-number structure of twistor space—through the orderly interrelated behavior of the complex numbers.

Although we only see the "real" part of the Universe, there are many types of elementary particles that experience the full complex nature of the universe since complex numbers must be used to describe their behavior. In fact, there seem to be too many different types of "elementary" particles to believe that they are all really elementary. In an attempt to explain the myriad different kinds of particles that are observed, it is usually assumed that all the particles must be made up of combinations of a small number of more fundamental objects. In the Penrose Twistor Theory, those fundamental entities are the twistors.

Penrose and his co-workers have been able to demonstrate that combinations of certain types of twistors produce objects that behave like the various elementary particles. A single twistor (in its various guises) can produce one of the known massless particles that always travel at the speed of light, such as a photon, neutrino, or graviton. Two twistor combinations produce things like electrons. Three twistors in various combinations can theoretically produce the building blocks of the nuclei of atoms, the protons and neutrons, while higher numbers of twistors can produce even more exotic particles. What is even more remarkable, in the Penrose Twistor Theory, not only are particles constructed from twistors, but even the points in space and time are constructed from twistors!

A point in four-dimensional space–time is generated by the collection of eight-dimensional twistors representing all possible light paths through that space–time point. Due to the uncertainties inherent in quantum calculations, however, the space–time points generated by the twistors are "fuzzy." Thus, although there will be only a finite number of space–time points in an interval, space–time will look continuous to us because of the fuzzy nature of the points.

There are indications that Roger Penrose is on the right track with his Twistor Theory. One intriguing feature of his eight-dimensional twistor space is that it is so controlled by the natural mathematical behavior of the complex numbers that the twistors in the eight-dimensional Penrose universe only permit one kind of four-dimensional space–time to exist—and that space–time is exactly the kind that we live in!

Penrose and his co-workers are now embarked on what will be a decades-long program of mathematical and physics research to explore the implications of this complex twistor space. They have already had some successes. Besides making the eight-dimensional twistor space generate the observed space–time, they have also been able to generate a complex kind of gravity theory. In the Einstein Theory of Gravity, gravitational effects are caused by the warping of space and time by matter. In the Twistor Theory of Gravity, gravity is also caused by mass causing a curvature in space, but instead of just a warpage in four-dimensional space–time, it is a warpage in eight-dimensional twistor space. Ultimately, Penrose hopes to show that different types of deformations in twistor space will produce all the different known forces—not only gravity, but also electromagnetism, the weak nuclear force, and the strong nuclear force. There may even be other possible distortions of twistor space that will produce new types of forces that are but future magic to us now.

Other startling revelations have come out of the studies of the Penrose Twistor Theory. If twistor space is only slightly distorted, then the distortions show up as forces in our perceived Universe. If, however, twistor space is strongly distorted (by intense gravitational fields or perhaps by some future-magic machine), then that strongly distorted portion of twistor space no longer has the smoothly varying mathematical order needed to make a proper space–time.

According to the Penrose Twistor Theory, that portion of space–time in our perceived universe that used to be defined by that now-distorted section of twistor space no longer exists! Thus, by suitable distortions of the eight-dimensional twistor space, it is possible to just eliminate those tiresome long distances from here to there. Instead of producing a space warp, the Penrose Twistor Theory produces a space eliminator.

Let us imagine we are in the far future. The Penrose Twistor Theory has evolved from its primitive mathematical state into a fully developed engineering technology. You are in an interstellar Twistorwarp ship drifting in space in the outer regions of the solar system (the warping of twistor space is difficult to control when the space is already warped by the mass of the sun and planets). The pilot checks his orientation and turns on the Twistorwarp drive. You feel no motion as the engines build up their terrific tensions that distort the very foundations of the Universe.

You are staring out the porthole at the distant light of the sun, waiting for something to happen, when suddenly through the porthole on the opposite side of the ship comes the light from other suns—three of them! You turn and look out the opposite porthole to see the triple-star pattern of the Alpha Centauri star system. It contains a close binary pair of stars, one of which is very much like the sun, and, circling much farther out, a small reddish dwarf star—Proxima Centauri. You look from one porthole to another: the 4.3 light-years between the solar system and the Alpha Centauri system has vanished! It has been eliminated by a strong distortion of twistor space.

The Twistorwarp engines that have been holding the twistor space in its distorted condition now relax their hold, but in such a way that the distortion smooths out in the opposite way from how it was formed. As the whining of the generators drops below the audio range, the image of the sun zooms away into the expanding starry sky, leaving the spaceship in the Alpha Centauri system as the Universe relaxes back into its undisturbed state. Then, for the first time since you left Earth orbit, you feel a sense of motion to your star-spanning travels as the antimatter rockets roar into life, taking you on the last leg of your journey to the newly colonized planet around Alpha Centauri A.

Future Speculations

Scientists are only human. Although they have been trained to always try to think objectively about the world around them, there are limits. There are some topics that many scientists will refuse to even discuss. Which topics are taboo varies somewhat with the scientist. For instance, there are still some scientists who refuse to accept the strong theoretical and observational evidence for black holes. Other scientists, for good reason, have a difficult time believing that Nature will ever allow us antigravity, space warps, time machines, or faster-than-light communication. They admit that certain mathematical solutions to the Einstein equations allow these anomalies under certain drastic assumptions, but they firmly believe that some version of "cosmic censorship" will ultimately prevail and Nature will prevent us from ever exercising those solutions.

There are other scientists who have a hard time believing in the feasibility of the extreme versions of space flight such as interstellar travel or huge Skyhooks, Space Fountains, and Rotavators. Usually, however, they are at least willing to admit their doubts are based on economic or engineering feasibility, not physical feasibility. I, personally, have been told in loud and no uncertain terms by a Nobel laureate that *any* attempt to even *discuss* the possible practical use of antimatter was "crazy."

I too have my doubts about the reality or attainability of many concepts, but I try to maintain an open mind. In my opinion, if science is to be any good to us at all in describing the behavior of the Universe, then *everything* must ultimately be describable in scientific terms. To give an extreme example, either God exists or he does not. In my view of science and the way scientists should operate, if God does not exist, then it is the job of science to attempt to prove that he does not exist. If God does exist, then he must come under the purview of science and it is the job of the scientist first to prove he exists, and then to build up a body of experimental, observational, and theoretical knowledge that will ultimately enable the human race (or whatever the human race has evolved to by then) to understand him.

God is an extreme example of a taboo topic that most scientists will refuse to discuss in an objective, scientific manner. There are many others. The reasons why most scientists refuse to get involved in a serious discussion of these taboo topics is that the very phrases that describe those topics are ill defined and laden with decades, if not centuries, of emotion-riddled, crackpot-oriented, yellow-journalistic baggage. They do not want their names or reputations associated in any way with these phrases.

They also have a legitimate scientific reason for avoiding discussion. The taboo topics have been dreamed up by naive human minds, and just because someone can think of a concept and give it a name does not make it real. These skeptical scientists do not see any "handles" by which they could grapple with these ill-formed concepts in order to understand them from a logical scientific point of view. Without that understanding, it is impossible to prove or disprove the reality of the concept.

I believe I have found some ideas that may give us a handhold on some of these slippery concepts *if they are true*. It is important that you realize that, in my opinion, all of the following topics are wishful thinking, *not* scientifically valid concepts. But if they are real, perhaps these speculations will help us bring these concepts under the umbrella of scientifically acceptable topics open for discussion. Then, if the scientific method can be applied successfully, perhaps these currently taboo topics can graduate to future magic and thence to future reality. The taboo topics I will attempt to shed light on are free energy, reactionless drives, extrasensory perception (ESP), and life after death.

FREE ENERGY

One of the goals of every backyard inventor is to invent a source of free energy—a battery or perpetual-motion machine that produces energy and does work, but never runs down. It is probably too much to hope that our future-magic technology will allow us to get "something for nothing," but it may be possible, using the theory of quantum electrodynamics to do something almost equivalent to that—extracting energy from the vacuum.

The Theory of Quantum Electrodynamics is the theory for describing the microscopic behavior of electricity and magnetism. It is one of the more successful physical theories, since it has been checked experimentally many times and found to be accurate. In quantum electrodynamics a region of space is divided into a large (infinite) number of modes of potential oscillation for the electromagnetic field. The state of the electromagnetic field is defined by counting the number of photons in each mode. The "vacuum" state is defined as that state where there are no photons in any of the modes. Yet, according to quantum electrodynamics, each mode of oscillation, even when the space is at absolute zero, has in it a zero-point oscillation with an energy equal to "half" a photon. This residual electromagnetic field produces fluctuating electromagnetic forces that have observable consequences.

One place where the effects of the electromagnetic fluctuations show up is in the calculation of the energy states in a hydrogen atom. The electric fields of the quantum fluctuations cause perturbations to the orbit of the electron around the proton. Even though the perturbations average out over the orbit, the electron moves in a slightly shifted orbit compared to that calculated from the electric field of the proton alone. This produces most of the shift in the energy levels of the hydrogen atom that was experimentally observed in 1947 by Willis Lamb and Robert Retherford.

Since, according to quantum electrodynamics, each mode has on the average a zero-point energy of half a photon, and since there are an infinite number of modes, this means that empty space has an infinite amount of energy. Richard Feynman, examining this paradox, tried to put a bound on this infinity by assuming some physically reasonable cutoff for the shortest wavelength mode, such as the Compton wavelength of a proton (2×10^{-16} meter). Even this cutoff gives an energy density of 10^{15} times that of water for the vacuum. This density is comparable to the density of the proton itself. The paradox remains. Feynman and others found a way around the infinities by a mathematical technique called renormalization, but no one has a good explanation why the extremely high predicted energy densities don't have a large gravitational effect.

In summary, there is a theoretically infinite source of energy in the electromagnetic fluctuations of the vacuum, and it is theoretically possible to interact with the electromagnetic fluctuations and obtain energy. One technique involves the use of small black holes.

In the Theory of Quantum Electrodynamics, the vacuum is not empty, but is full of "virtual" particles that are created out of nothing, exist for a while, then merge back into nothing. Most of the particles are low-energy photons, but even charged particles like electrons and positrons occasionally appear for a short period of time. Stephen Hawking showed that if a small black hole were placed in this emptiness full of energy, its powerful gravitational field would swallow the virtual particles if they got too close. With no partner to recombine with, the other member of the virtual particle pair would be promoted to the status of a "real" particle and leave. To an onlooker, it would look as if the black hole had "emitted" the particle. Thus, it would seem that the black hole had extracted energy from the vacuum.

In the details of Hawking's theory, however, it is shown that a virtual particle swallowed by the black hole has "negative" energy, so the total energy–mass content of the black hole is *decreased* by the addition of the virtual particle. So although it looks like the black hole allows us to get something out of the nothing called the "vacuum," in reality the energy came out of the mass of the black hole, rather than the vacuum.

The work of Hawking and others on developing relations between black hole physics, quantum theory, and thermodynamics will eventually produce a good theory of thermodynamics in the quantum domain. I suspect that once such a theory is developed we will find out that the vacuum fluctuation energy is unusable because of some quantum version of the Second Law of Thermodynamics.

It is well known that there is plenty of (low grade) energy in the warm waters of the ocean. We would not be violating the First Law of Thermodynamics by trying to build a boat with an engine that would use this energy for propulsion. But unless we provide the engine with some heat sink that is colder (has less energy density in it) than the ocean, the Second Law of Thermodynamics will see that the engine doesn't work. In the same manner, I suspect that the same type of thing will prevent the utilization of the vacuum fluctuations as a source of unending "free" energy. We need to have a "heat sink" for the quantum energy engine. What can have less energy density in it than the nothing that makes up the vacuum?

Since there is yet no theory that proves it is impossible to extract energy out of the vacuum, and the example of the "hot" black hole seems to show that it might be possible, there has been a lot of speculation on space drives that somehow use the energy of the vacuum for propulsion. So far, the best explanation of the operation is in Charles Sheffield's science-fiction novel *The McAndrew Chronicles*.

I have found a way, however, to extract a small amount of energy from the electromagnetic fluctuations of the vacuum. It is a vacuum fluctuation "battery" and it is based on the Casimir effect.

In addition to the well-known Lamb-Retherford shift in the hydrogen atom, there is another, lesser-known, effect of the electromagnetic vacuum fluctuations called the Casimir force. The Casimir force is a short-range attraction between any two objects caused by the presence of the electromagnetic fluctuations in the vacuum. A calculation by Casimir of the force between two conducting plates showed that the conducting plates restrict the number of normal modes that can exist in the vacuum between them. Although there are an infinite number of modes between the two plates, that infinity is smaller than the infinite number of modes that would be allowed if the plates weren't there. In a straightforward calculation of the number of normal modes and the zero-point energy in those modes, Casimir predicted that the electromagnetic vacuum fluctuations between the plates would have a negative energy density that was proportional to the third power of the spacing between the plates. There thus would be an attractive force between the plates that was proportional to the fourth power of the spacing. The force was independent of the material in the conductors.

Later, the analysis was broadened by Lifshitz to include dielectrics. It was found that any two plates, whether conductors or dielectrics, would experience a fourth power force law, but one that was also proportional to the dielectric constant of the plates. The Casimir result for conducting plates is obtained when the dielectric constant of the plates is allowed to go to infinity. The equations describing the Casimir effect are only valid down to a separation distance proportional to the minimum wavelength at which the plates are still a good conductor or the dielectric constant is not unity. For distances closer than that, a different equation takes over. The attractive force will still increase with decreasing distance, but at a rate proportional to the third power of the separation distance. Both Casimir and Lifshitz were aware that these forces due to the fluctuations of the vacuum were known previously as "surface tension," "surface energy," and "van der Waals" forces that occur between uncharged atoms and objects.

Since the Casimir force produces very high force levels at close spacings and, according to Lifshitz, those force levels vary according to the dielectric or conducting state of the plates, it is conceivable that one day the Casimir force could be a significant factor in the operation of microcircuits with submicrometer dimensions.

The experimental measurement of the Casimir force has been carried out a number of times with varying degrees of success. Usually the experiment is carried out between a curved dielectric lens and a flat dielectric plate. The first successful measurements were carried out in the 1950s by some Russian scientists on quartz, with separation distances down to 1,000 angstroms (about 300 atoms).

Other dielectric plate experiments were carried out with slowly improving precision. The closest separation distance obtained was 14 angstroms (about 5 atoms) with two crossed cylinders of mica. That data shows good agreement with the $1/a^4$ Lifshitz law from 300 angstroms to 200 angstroms, with a break in slope at 150 angstroms, changing to the $1/a^3$ law from 100 angstroms down to 14 angstroms. At 14 angstroms, the measured force between the two mica cylinders was over 10 tons per square meter! Although experiments on dielectric plates are in good agreement with theory, there are no good experiments to date on metal plates down to the spacings that will show the deviation from the $1/a^4$ retarded field law to the $1/a^3$ nonretarded field law. With the advances in microcircuit technology, including the development of molecular beam epitaxy "atomic spray guns" that can lay down monolayers of atoms, it should now be possible to prepare samples of metals that are flat enough to carry out Casimir force experiments at separation distances less than a nanometer.

The Casimir force has some of the properties of the gravity force since it is purely attractive, is independent of the material in the plates, and is a function of the inverse power of the separation distance, although the variation with separation distance goes as a higher power than the gravity force. Although there is no rigorous proof known that the vacuum fluctuation field is a conservative field like the gravity field, it is highly probable that it is. Otherwise, it would be possible to design machines using the Casimir force that would allow an infinite amount of energy to be extracted from the vacuum.

Even if the vacuum fluctuation field is a conservative field, that does not mean we cannot use it to obtain energy. The gravity field of the Earth is a conservative force field and yet hydroelectric dams extract energy from the gravity field by using water coming from a region of high gravitational potential. In reality, of course, the energy extracted from a hydroelectric dam came originally from the sun, which evaporated the water from the oceans at a low-gravitational potential and placed it in lakes at a high-gravitational potential. The hydroelectric dam is then seen as a mechanism that uses the gravitational force of the Earth as a "catalyst" to convert the gravitational potential energy of the water into kinetic energy that can in turn be converted into electricity by the turbines. Hydroelectric dams are also used for energy storage. During times of low electrical demand, electricity can be used to pump water back up to a lake at high gravitational potential.

In the same manner, I have shown that we can prepare a conductor in a foliated state that is in a "high" vacuum fluctuation potential energy state due to its large surface energy, and then use the Casimir force to convert the potential energy into kinetic energy as the foliated conductors cohere into a solid block of conductor that is in a "low" vacuum fluctuation potential energy state. The part of the hydroelectric turbines can be played by any mechanism that can convert kinetic energy into electricity, but we will use the electrostatic repulsion force between two conducting plates with the same polarity of charge.

The general concept for the construction of an aluminum foil "vacuum fluctuation battery" is to take a large number of leaves of ultrathin aluminum foil arranged in a stack with the leaves separated by a few micrometers. Each leaf is connected electrically to an active bidirectional power supply and the shape and position of the leaf is monitored by sensors. The power supply gives each leaf a small amount of positive charge. The positive charge will create an electrostatic repulsion between the plates that will keep the plates separated despite the attempt of the Casimir force to pull them together. This electrostatic suspension system is unstable, of course, so the position of each leaf will have to be electronically stabilized by feedback from the position sensors through the active power supply. Stability may also be enhanced by partial mechanical support of the leaves using frames of insulating material such as aluminum oxide or by unique geometries.

The voltages applied to the end leaf and the next-to-the-end leaf are then adjusted so that the electrostatic repulsion between these two leaves is lowered until the electrostatic force is slightly less than the Casimir force at that distance. The Casimir force will draw the two leaves together, doing work against the repulsive electric field between the plates. By adjusting the electric field to always be slightly less than the Casimir force, the active bidirectional power supply can extract electrical energy out of the kinetic energy of the motion of the plates as they move from large separation distances where the vacuum fluctuation potential energy is near zero, to the minimum separation distance where the vacuum fluctuation potential energy is large and negative. The process is repeated by the next leaf from the end until the foliated conductor is condensed into a solid block. Alternately, all the leaves could be brought together at the same time, like compressing an accordion. Thus, by cohering the multitude of aluminum leaves in a foliated conductor into a single block of aluminum under the careful control of an electronic servo system, it is possible to extract electrical energy from the vacuum.

If the collapse process is halted before the aluminum films cohere, then the vacuum fluctuation battery can be "recharged" by making the applied electrostatic force slightly larger than the Casimir force. The leaves will be pushed apart at the cost of supplying energy from the bidirectional power supply.

Another version of the vacuum fluctuation battery that might be easier to fabricate and have more stability would be a wide flat spiral of foil built along the lines of a Slinky™ toy. Here there is only one conductor to make contact with, and each turn of the spiral acts against the neighboring turns. The spiral configuration allows a substantial compaction of the foil from large spacings to small spacings while maintaining uniform spacing.

Unfortunately for those looking for large amounts of free energy, the numbers indicate that this vacuum fluctuation battery would require significant advances in precision manufacture and

control of extremely thin structures before it would even begin
to approach the watts-per-pound capability of even an ordinary
chemical battery.

The important aspect of the vacuum fluctuation battery is that
it shows that there is at least one way of getting energy out of
the quantum fluctuations in the vacuum. And if there is one
way, there may be other ways that are more efficient. We are
probably not getting something for nothing, however, and the
vacuum does not seem to be a source of continuous "free"
energy. The vacuum fluctuation field is probably a conservative
field, but there is no known proof of that in the literature. Since
the vacuum fluctuation field seems to be the source of what
"holds matter together," it is probably limited in energy density
to chemical energy levels. Still, it is important that I have
identified a nonthermodynamic method of extracting that
chemical energy, as well as a method for getting chemical
energy out of what are normally considered nonreactive chemicals (aluminum foil).

The experimental data on the Casimir force between conductors is of very poor quality. The theory of the Casimir force is
also in a changing state. There is no general proof that the field
is conservative and that you *can't* just keep on extracting energy
if you can think up a clever enough mechanism. In fact, it is
easy to dream up perpetual-motion machines using variations of
the Lifshitz force. As yet, the theory can't prove them wrong.

REACTIONLESS DRIVES

Another dream of the backyard inventor is to invent a
reactionless space drive—some collection of gizmos in a box that
when energized will make the box rise into the air and speed
off to the stars. Usually the gizmos are gyroscopes, for nearly
everyone at one time or another has held a gyroscope in their
hand and watched it perform its magic feat of levitation. With
one end sitting on your finger, the rest of the gyroscope balances
out horizontally, its center of gravity far out away from its single
support point—yet it does not fall!

In their early years, before book learning finally convinced
them it was impossible, practically every space enthusiast,
Robert Goddard and Wernher von Braun among them, has felt
that there *must* be some future-magic way to remove that one
support, yet still have the gyro continue to levitate, or perhaps

drift slowly upwards to the stars. Yet, as each struggled with the concept of a reactionless drive based on gyroscopes, all were forced sooner or later to realize that it would not work. They were beaten by nature's conservation laws.

The law of conservation of energy is not the problem, for a rapidly spinning gyroscope certainly has enough energy to lift itself a considerable distance in the Earth's gravity field. No, it is one of the other conservation laws. The law of conservation of linear momentum.

If you start with a gyroscope sitting on the surface of the Earth, and you end up with a gyroscope moving upwards in the sky with a finite velocity, then by the law of conservation of linear momentum, some other mass must be moving in the opposite direction. The upward moving gyroscope must have had something to push against, like your finger.

The wheel of a gyroscope is spinning furiously. Certainly there must be a way to use that circular motion of the wheel to produce an upward motion of the whole gyroscope. Yet, as many a frustrated inventor has found, when model after model refuses to budge from the floor, there is yet another conservation law standing in the way of progress in future magic—the law of conservation of angular momentum, or spin. But suppose that the conservation laws of linear and angular momentum were not true laws—just approximations . . .

Many years ago BE (Before Einstein), the world was dominated by four conservation laws: conservation of mass, conservation of energy, conservation of linear momentum, and conservation of spin. The physics textbooks of that time insisted that each was always separately conserved despite some unresolved anomalies. For instance, there was that perpetually glowing pitchblende in Madame Curie's laboratory that seemed to indicate that energy was coming from nowhere. Also, calculations of the only known heat source for the sun, gravitational contraction, seemed to give a lifetime for the sun that was less than the age of the Earth, indicating that there might be some other energy source keeping the sun hot.

Suppose you had shown a scientist of that time three one-kilogram bricks on a table, one of frozen hydrogen, one of red-hot iron, and one of room-temperature uranium. If you then asked the scientist which brick had the most energy, the scientist would have first noticed that since all the bricks were at the same height in the Earth's gravitational field, and they all weighed a kilogram, that their gravitational potential energies were the same. If the scientist then measured the temperature of the bricks, he would have said that the hot brick of iron would have more heat energy than the others, and he could even calculate how far that heat energy could lift the iron brick against the Earth's gravity, given an efficient way to convert the heat energy into kinetic energy. Obviously the red-hot kilogram of iron had more energy than the room-temperature kilogram of uranium, and the frozen kilogram of hydrogen ice had the least energy of all.

Then Albert Einstein developed the Special Theory of Relativity to explain what happens to objects traveling near the speed of light. One of the magical but logical consequences of this theory was that the conservation laws for mass and energy were not strictly true! The theory predicted that mass could be changed into energy and vice versa.

The concept must have been mind-boggling at first. Mass is measured in kilograms, and energy is measured in joules. They don't even have the same units. How can you convert one into the other? It would be like turning a sow's ear into a silk purse! The magical conversion of mass into energy does take place, however, and the conversion factor is a phenomenally large one: the speed of light—squared! From Einstein's Special Theory of Relativity comes that famous equation: $E = mc^2$. This equation predicts that if some way could be found to carry out the conversion, a tiny amount of mass will produce an amazing amount of energy—90 megajoules per microgram!

The scientists could now understand what was going on in Madame Curie's laboratory. The nuclei in the atoms of pitchblende were changing from one element to another, and giving off energy in the process. The new element weighed slightly less than the old element and the difference in mass showed up as gamma-ray or particle energy. The scientists then knew that nature was able to violate the conservation laws for mass and energy, but search as they might, there didn't seem to be any future-magic device by which humans could control the conversion.

Albert Einstein told us in 1905 that mass could be converted into energy and he even gave us the conversion equation. But it took 37 years before Enrico Fermi found the future-magic method by which the energy stored in the excess mass of the uranium nucleus could be released. The process ultimately proved to be amazingly simple. You just put two or more large blocks of uranium or plutonium near each other and a chain reaction starts, automatically producing heat (or an explosion).

When Fermi and the other scientists finished their experiments and measurements on all the elements and their isotopes, they found that the very heavy elements, like uranium and plutonium, had an excess of mass per neutron or proton compared to carbon, while elements like iron had a deficiency of mass per nucleon. At the other end of the periodic table, the very light elements like hydrogen and lithium also had a mass excess. If the uranium and plutonium could be fissioned into ironlike elements, the difference in mass would be released as energy. In the same way, if the lighter elements could be sequentially fused together to build up ironlike elements, then again there would be an excess of mass that would be converted to energy.

If you were to ask a modern-day scientist which contains more energy: frozen hydrogen, red-hot iron, or room-temperature uranium, you will now get a different answer. For the modern scientist can see energy sources in those bricks that could not be seen before. The frozen hydrogen, if fused to iron, will release more energy than the fissioning of uranium to iron, and the red-hot iron, which used to be thought the better in the energy sweepstakes, is now seen to be comparatively devoid of energy, despite its high temperature.

Thus, the advent of special relativity produced a new energy source and reduced the number of conservation laws. We now have only three: conservation of mass–energy, conservation of linear momentum, and conservation of angular momentum. The physics textbooks firmly insist that each is always separately conserved despite some unresolved anomalies. For instance, the high-speed jets that are coming from rapidly spinning black-hole quasars seem to indicate that an object which should be sucking matter in, is instead propelling it out. Also, the number of neutrinos being emitted by the fusion reactions in the sun is only one-third of what it should be, indicating that there is still some other yet unknown future-magic source of energy keeping the sun hot.

Einstein did not stop with his Special Theory of Relativity. He next went on to develop his theory of gravity, called the General Theory of Relativity. The Einstein theory of gravity is an extension of the Newton theory of gravity. In the Newtonian theory, gravity is a force field generated by a mass. The gravity field generated by a mass is the same whether or not the mass is hot, moving, or spinning. In the Einstein theory, however, gravity is not caused solely by mass, but is also produced by energy, *and* linear momentum, *and* spin!

In the Einstein theory, the mass of a gravitating body produces the usual Newtonian gravitational attraction that we are familiar with. The heat, stress, and other sources of energy in the gravitating body not only add to the Newtonian attraction, but also produce gravitational stress patterns in the nearby space. The linear motion of the gravitating body also produces a gravitational field, but it is different from the Newtonian gravity. The linear-momentum gravity forces tend to "drag" a nearby test body in the same direction the gravitating body is moving. Similarly, according to the Einstein theory, the angular momentum in a spinning body causes nearby objects to move in curved paths.

If mass, energy, linear momentum, and angular momentum all produce gravity, doesn't that indicate that they are all just different aspects of some more fundamental entity? We scientists studying the Einstein theory of gravity have given this entity a name—the mass–energy–momentum tensor—but just naming something does not mean that we really understand it.

This multi-aspect appearance of the "thing" that causes gravity in the Einstein General Theory of Relativity is reminiscent of the allegory about the blind men and the elephant. One of the blind men felt the trunk and said that an elephant was like a snake; another felt the tail and said that an elephant was like a rope; another felt a leg and said that an elephant was like a tree trunk; while a fourth felt the ear and said that an elephant was like a leaf. They were all partially correct, but none could comprehend the elephant as a whole. Scientists today are in the same predicament. We see aspects of the "mass–energy–momentum tensor," but we still cannot comprehend it as a whole.

Could it be, in some future-magic day, that just as we can now interconvert two of those gravity-producing components of the mass–energy–momentum tensor—mass and energy—that we could interconvert mass, energy, and the two types of momentum?

How could that be? They are different things. Yet, with Einstein giving us the equations and the conversion constants, and Fermi giving us the experimental techniques, we found that a room-temperature brick of uranium could give us more energy than a glowing brick of iron. Could there be other sources of energy hidden in ordinary things that we could extract by conversion of linear momentum and angular momentum to energy? What we need are the right conversion equations and the right experimental techniques.

Suppose we wanted to convert linear momentum to energy. What type of conversion constant do we need? Well, energy is in joules, or kilograms times velocity squared, while linear momentum is kilograms times velocity. To convert linear momentum to energy, we need a conversion constant with the units of velocity. The natural choice is the velocity of light, giving us the conversion equation between energy E and momentum p, of $E = pc$.

Since the numerical value of the speed of light is so high, this equation predicts some remarkable results. A one kilogram mass moving at one meter per second velocity has only one joule of kinetic energy in its motion. Yet, if the speed of light is the correct conversion constant, the linear momentum in that motion, *if* we could find the future-magic method to convert it completely into energy, would produce an additional 300 million joules! (Just stopping the mass will not do. That only transfers the linear momentum to your hand, and thence to the ground. The linear momentum must somehow be destroyed, not just transferred to the Earth.)

But let's go on. To convert angular momentum to linear momentum we need a unit of length. There is a fundamental unit of length, called the Planck length. The Planck length is very tiny, $\Lambda = 1.6 \times 10^{-35}$ meters. This is a trillion, trillion times smaller than the nucleus of an atom.

To convert angular momentum L to linear momentum p, we divide by this very tiny number, $p = L/\Lambda$. That means a very small amount of angular momentum will make a very large amount of linear momentum . . . or mass . . . or energy. The equation for the interconversion would be:

$$E = mc^2 = pc = Lc/\Lambda$$

The smallest amount of angular momentum that you can have is one unit of atomic spin—an electron orbiting a nucleus. If we could find a mechanism to convert that single unit of atomic spin, then the angular momentum destroyed would reappear as either 6.5 kilogram meters per second of linear momentum (a brick flying through the air), 22 micrograms of mass, or the energy of half a ton of TNT!

It may be that someday gyroscopes will take us to the stars. But instead of massive whirling disks of brass or steel, the gyroscopes will be the nebulous whirling particles in the atom. Once we have the proper future-magic technology, we can convert some of those spinning bundles of angular momentum into the energy and momentum that we will need to push a spaceship close to the speed of light.

But we need to find the magic trick that will make the conversion. You don't destroy angular momentum by grabbing a spinning object and bringing it to a stop. When you do that, the angular momentum is merely transferred through your body, to add to or subtract from the spin of the Earth. Unfortunately, we no longer have Fermi around to show us how to convert momentum to energy, as he once showed us how to convert mass to energy.

What we need is a magician—a future magician. Who is the person who will finally be able to "see" this mass–energy–momentum "elephant" that we grope around like blind men? Who will give us a Spin Drive to the stars?

EXTRASENSORY PERCEPTION

My father-in-law, Edwin Dodson, used to be plant supervisor-construction of the C&P Telephone Company of Maryland. One day after dinner he told me about watching one of his maintenance crews while they were looking for an underground cable. The approved company procedure was to get out the low-frequency tone generator and pickup designed by the scientists at AT&T Bell Labs, use the generator to insert a strong electrical signal into one end of the line, then use the ultrasensitive pickup loop to scan along the surface of the ground above the path of the buried cable. Instead of taking out the scientifically and managerially approved AT&T kit, however, the crew made some dowsing rods out of two pieces of pipe and two bent copper wires and proceeded to use ESP to search for the cable. What impressed me about the story was: those same men had to *dig* the hole!

The phrase ESP means different things to different people, including mind reading, foretelling the future, psychokinetics, and dowsing. All of them involve the mind being able to obtain information through extrasensory channels other than the known sensory channels of seeing, hearing, feeling, smelling, and tasting.

Since the people on the repair crew were the ones that had to dig the hole, it must mean *something* that they chose ESP over known technology. I don't believe in ESP, but I am aware that others do. I am constantly looking for some new physical law of nature, or some new way of using a known law of nature to duplicate some of the purported effects of ESP. I think I have found one, a little known quantum-mechanical phenomenon called the Aharanov-Bohm effect.

In the realm of the small, the accepted theory is called Quantum Mechanics. In the theory of Quantum Mechanics, objects like electrons and photons have both particle properties and wave properties. If you take two beams of laser light and shine them on a screen at an angle they will interfere with each other to produce a fringe pattern on the screen. Where the light waves are in phase they augment each other and where the light waves are of opposite phase they cancel each other out. It was a triumphant confirmation of Quantum Mechanics when Davisson and Germer repeated the experiment with two beams of low energy electrons, proving that the electron had a wavelength inversely proportional to its energy.

It was then pointed out by Aharanov and Bohm that the phase of the electron wave was a direct function of the electric or magnetic potential and thus these potentials could be measured directly by merely observing the position of the fringe pattern in a two-electron beam interference experiment. This announcement and its subsequent experimental confirmation for both the electric and magnetic potentials caused considerable flap among conservative scientists. From a classical point of view the potential is merely a convenient mathematical fiction, since it can have any value it wants and the physical results are the same. In classical mechanics, the only observable is the difference between two potentials, not their absolute value. This is why an electrical worker can handle a power line charged up to an electrical potential of 100,000 volts as long as he doesn't let any part of his body touch something at a different electrical potential.

In these interference experiments, however, the potential was found to be directly measurable. The experiments have been done in a number of ways. In one experiment a beam of very low energy electrons was split into two equal beams by a negatively charged wire. The two beams then went off in their separate ways until they were separated by a number of micrometers. There they were deflected back in the other direction by a pair of charged plates. The two beams met again and formed a round bright spot on an electron sensitive screen. Overlaid on the circular spot was a pattern of interference lines.

In the open area between the two beams was a long, thin, tiny electromagnet. A tiny current was passed through the electromagnet, causing a tiny magnetic field to exist *inside* the electromagnet. The electromagnet was so long and so far away from the two electron beams that there were essentially no magnetic forces on the electron beams due to the electromagnet. This was proven since the circular spot did not shift in position. When the electromagnet was activated, however, the fringe pattern inside the circular spot did shift—and by just the amount predicted by Aharanov and Bohm. The two-electron beam system had detected the presence of the magnetic field at a distance. Even when the electromagnet and the electron beams are completely shielded from each other by a perfect superconducting magnetic shield the electron beams can still sense the presence of the magnetic field at a distance. It is this ability of the Aharanov-Bohm effect to obtain information from inside shielded enclosures that makes it an interesting candidate as a possible channel for extrasensory perception.

Different underground bodies have slightly different electric and magnetic potentials. This depends upon the materials they are composed of, their temperature and water content, and their interaction with the Earth's magnetic field and the underground galvanic currents. If the brain has a sensor that can use the Aharanov-Bohm effect to detect the strength and extent of those potentials, even through a shield, then this might be the mechanism for the dowsing aspect of ESP. It is difficult, however, to see how the Aharanov-Bohm effect could be used for the other aspects of ESP.

In all the experiments done to date, the size of the experimental apparatus has been very tiny, micrometers in dimensions. Also, all of the experiments have made the assumption that the quantum phase had to be measured around a closed loop. This limits the usefulness of the technique as a sensing mechanism, since it requires that the measurement path encircle the field to be measured, even though the sensing beams do not have to pass through the field to sense it.

A later publication by Aharanov has hinted that if a reference phase were available that was not affected by the potential, the beam that was affected could be compared with this reference phase without the necessity of the measuring apparatus encircling the field to be measured. One method of carrying out this measurement would be to use two particle states that can interfere but that are acted on differently by the potential fields. The existence of such states is an open question since two states that are acted upon differently by a potential are, in principle, distinguishable from each other and therefore will not interfere.

On the other hand, there is no doubt that something can be learned from the gravitational analog of the Aharanov-Bohm effect. This is the Schiff orbiting gyro experiment. The axis of a gyro in orbit around the Earth will precess due to the warpage of space caused by the mass of the Earth. The change of the direction of the gyro axis can be measured by using an optical stellar inertial reference frame which is negligibly affected by the local space curvature.

If we could somehow find a way to measure potentials directly in a simple manner, then this could lead to completely new sensing technologies for prospecting, communication, and military applications. Then if we can develop sensors that can detect potential, perhaps we can find similar sensors in our brain. These would finally give us a scientific understanding of extrasensory phenomena and remove ESP from the pages of the tabloids and place them onto the pages of scientific journals.

LIFE AFTER DEATH

One of the most magical concepts invented by the human mind is the spirit—a spark of something that is our intellect that is supposed to live on after our body dies. Of all the many types of future magic that might someday come true, one that would be completely unexpected would be a scientific understanding of the spirit.

I believe that in our present, very limited understanding of the Universe and the way it works, there exists a clue, an inkling, of what could possibly be one possible version of what spirit might be. It would have all the magical properties that we envision for the spirit and yet does not violate the laws of nature as we now think they are.

First, I am going to define what I mean by "the spirit": The spirit is an entity that is the animating principle of individual life, especially of individual life in thinking or highly organized beings. The spirit grows and develops as the body grows and develops. However, the spirit is separable from the body at death and is immortal.

Is there any scientific evidence for this definition? To start with, let us see what present-day science has to say about separating the intellect or spirit from the human body. Later, we can discuss how our intellect could exist separate from all matter as an independent, immaterial, and immortal entity. Science is already fairly sure that your intellect is relatively independent of the specific matter in which it resides. When you were born as a baby, your brain had built into it a number of instinctive reaction mechanisms that kept the body alive. But except for those animallike mechanisms, your brain was a blank slate upon which your environment, parents, siblings, pets, and teachers started placing experiences. You learned and grew. You developed response patterns and intelligence. Finally you developed a personality. When this process was completed, your memories, your habits, and your personality were in your brain in the form of coded molecules, coded synapse levels, and coded pathway patterns set up in and among the nerve cells in your brain.

The important thing to recognize is that the information content that currently makes up your intellect is in the *patterns*. Patterns in molecules and patterns in the intercellular nerve interconnections. The nerve cells are the same nerve cells that were in the baby, but now they are arranged into patterns. It is the *patterns*, not the cells, that form your intellect. The patterns would be the same if all the cells and atoms had been replaced by other equivalent cells or atoms.

So far, the only patterns that are complex enough to demonstrate intelligence have been formed in the living nerve cell tissue of flesh-and-blood bodies. Over the years, however, there have been a number of research projects on artificial intelligence, in which attempts have been made to develop intellect patterns in electronic systems rather than in living tissue. Unlike regular computers, which have highly structured designs and make mistakes if they are wired wrong, these neural analog artificial brains are deliberately formed as unorganized structures of. "nerve cells." Care is taken so that the wires from the television camera "eyes" are connected to the "cells" in the "brain" instead of to each other, but at the start it doesn't matter to what part of the brain the wires are connected. The lights that indicate a response are connected to the brain cells instead of to each other or to the television camera, but again, that is all the logic that is built into the device. When the machine is finished, it is a completely imbecilic, randomly wired mess of electronic components that can do nothing.

The researchers, then, acting as teachers, proceed to show things to the television eye, such as pictures of people or the alphabet, and observe the response patterns of the lights connected to the "brain." If the researchers like the response pattern, they push a "reward" button, which sends a signal down the pathways that are being used and increases the likelihood of those pathways being used the next time. If they don't like the response, or they wish to change it, they push the "punish" button, until the machine changes the response to the liking of the "teacher." In this manner, the researchers train the machine, and form patterns of preferred pathways between the electronic nerve cells. These machines have learned, in an elementary and crude way, many things—like running a maze or learning the alphabet. We thus have the first beginnings of an experimental approach to the understanding of intelligence in machines. Right now, the machines only have the IQ of a worm, and there are many problems ahead, but as we gain an understanding of how these machines learn, we begin to gain an understanding of how *we* learn.

Although neural analog machines have been useful in trying to study intelligence, there are problems with this approach to artificial intelligence. To date, the most progress in artificial intelligence has been made with machines that are more highly organized internally. By knowing ahead of time the problems the machines are going to be asked to handle, the machines can be designed to be extremely efficient for that task (although they will usually do more poorly at other tasks). Because they are designed for the specific task at hand, they can outperform the more generalized neural-net thinking machine, including the generalized thinking machine we call the human brain.

Despite the fact that neural-net machines may not be the best solution to the problems of creating an artificial intelligence, they do have much to teach us. There is essentially no difference in the way that the training of these machines forms patterns in the electronic cells and pathways of these machines, and in the way that the training of a baby forms patterns in the protoplasmic cells and pathways of the brain. Perhaps some future-magic day there will be an electronic brain impressed with the patterns copied from a protoplasmic brain. We will then have an intellect in two forms, protoplasmic and electronic. What we will learn then is almost beyond future speculation.

Is pride intellectual? Or emotional? Can a machine envy? hate? love? Or are those reactions found only in human intellects burdened with hormone-driven flesh-and-blood bodies inherited from their animal forebears?

Thus, one part of our question seems to be answered. Science seems to see a future where in a limited way an intellect can one day be independent of the human body. But can the intellect be a spirit—free of all forms of matter? Can it be immortal and exist without any type of body, protoplasmic or electronic, to impress its patterns on? I would like to give one possible way that this could be. It is very speculative (and probably not true), but at least it gives us some clues as to where we might find some form of future magic.

As science learns more about the Universe and the space and time in which we live and move, we are beginning to realize that space and time are not simple things that just exist unaffected by the rest of the Universe. Experiments have shown that space seems to have a structure and characteristics of its own.

To give one example, in high energy experiments on parity nonconservation, in which right-hand spinning and left-hand spinning particles should have been emitted in equal numbers, there was found a strong preference for left-handed particles. The explanation that the mathematics give is that space is not uniform, but has a "left-handed twist" in this part of the Universe. There is also strong evidence that the structure of space is determined by matter itself. There are theories of cosmology that indicate that with no matter or energy, there would also be no space and no time. If you create a small amount of matter, then this matter forms a weak, tenuous space near itself and it begins to take time to do things.

If we have a large chunk of matter and form it into a hollow shell, then inside this miniature universe there forms a relatively strong space and time, and a small particle of matter inside the shell begins to have inertia or mass. You have to give the mass a push to get it moving through the space defined by the large shell of matter, and it takes time to move from one part to another. As the mass of the outer shell is increased, the space gets stiffer and you have to push the little piece of matter harder to get it moving, and it takes longer for it to travel.

Here we see a glimmer of how mass and energy, which are solid, physical things like our body, can influence the structure of space and time, which are ethereal, immaterial things like our concept of the spirit. This effect of matter on space and time is closely related to gravity. In the Einstein Theory of Gravity, space, time, and gravity are all mixed up and are all considered different aspects of the same thing. This is why one sometimes hears that according to the Einstein Theory of Gravity, the sun does not make a gravity field, but instead the mass of the sun curves the space near it. The planets then move in this curved space-time in force-free "straight" lines, which look to us like curved orbits. We attribute this to a force, the gravity force, pulling the planets around in their orbits.

Thus, according to the Einstein General Theory of Relativity, physical things like matter affect ethereal things like space and time, and the space and time in turn affect the motion of the matter. If the matter has patterns in it, these patterns will in turn be impressed on the space and time. If the space and time have patterns, then other matter will react to those patterns. We know that this is true for large bodies like the stars and planets. Is it equally true for small bodies like atoms?

Let us speculate on some future magic. Could it be that as the atoms and molecules in our brain form into the pattern containing our intellect, that these atoms and molecules impress their pattern into the space-time matrix? If so, then we would now have the pattern that is our intellect impressed not only on some material object such as the nerve cells in our brain, but also on an ethereal object such as the space-time in which we live. This ethereal copy of our intellect could be the spirit.

At first glance it might seem that the mass of the atoms and molecules in a human body would be too small to significantly affect space and time. The atoms, however, although small in total mass, have very dense nuclei, and it is *density*, not mass, that counts in curving space. The curvature of space induced by an atomic nucleus near its surface is fifteen trillion times greater than the curvature of space induced by the mass of the entire

Earth! All of these tiny curvature fields from all the atomic nuclei in the atoms in the brain would then form a complex pattern in space–time that is a replica of the pattern of the intellect outlined by our brain cells.

How would these localized points of space curvature behave? We don't know, because there is yet no complete theory of quantum gravity or quantum space–time. Since the space–time curvature effects are limited to a very tiny region near the nucleus of an atom, they cannot have a strong coupling at great distances. But the influence, although weak, can reach out to neighboring electrons and atoms, affecting their motion through ethereal space–time effects.

We must be cautious with these future-magic speculations, however, since a quick calculation will easily show that the nuclear and electrical forces exerted by an atomic nucleus are many, many times larger than the space-curvature effects. Also, no experiment has yet found any evidence of a space-curvature effect. Yet, the theories indicate it is there, and it just may play some part in the operation of our intellect.

How might our brain interact with its "spirit"? The curvature effects are small, but the brain is a unique organ in its drive to find *patterns* in the many-faceted sensory environment impinging upon it. An excellent example of the brain's desire to find patterns is found in the old belief that there were canals on Mars. Mars is covered with craters arranged in random patterns. However, the brain behind the eyes of the first observers of Mars wanted so much to make some sense out of that random dot pattern, that it forced the dots into linear structures, and led the hand to draw the nonexistent Martian canals. This tendency of the brain to pull patterns out of noisy information is one of its strongest attributes. It may be that someday an understanding of this pattern-extraction process will give us a clue to an experiment to demonstrate the existence of an immaterial pattern like the spirit.

We now begin to see how the matter in our body could form a pattern of our intellect in space and time. The ethereal intellect would change and grow as the body changes and grows. In turn, this ethereal pattern in space–time could possibly influence the motion of the electronic and ionic currents in the brain cells. The awareness and influence of the intellect pattern would be strongest in the immediate space–time region where the material particles of the nerve cells exist, but its awareness and influence could extend not only through the space around us, but could also extend into the time around us. Theoretically, this could be all the way to eternity, so that in this magical view, the spirit would be immortal. However, as in the case of space-curvature, I would suspect that as the time interval gets farther and farther away from the period of time where the matter generating the pattern exists, the influence would become weaker and merge into other patterns in the space–time matrix. (Shades of the Force!)

All of this future-magic speculation is very far from currently known, hard, scientific fact. But that only indicates our lack of knowledge about the true nature of intelligence and microscopic space–time interactions.

It now looks like the concept of our spirit as an entity containing our intellect, that is formed by our body, and yet is immaterial and exists after the body is gone, cannot be arbitrarily dismissed as unscientific nonsense. And it may be, that on some future-magic day, rather than denying the existence of the spirit, science will prove that the spirit *does* have a physical reality and that there *is* life after death.

Selected References

For those who would like to read a little more on some of the topics discussed in this book, I have selected a few references out of the many books, research papers, and scientific reprints that I used as background material in preparing the manuscript. The book and magazine references can be found in any good library, but the scientific journal references will require a visit to a nearby university library. Most university libraries allow the public to use the library during certain hours, although they usually do not let the public check out books. Most have, however, extensive (and comparatively cheap) copying facilities.

Chapter 1—Introduction

Arthur C. Clarke's speculations about the future and his three laws can be found in:

Clarke, Arthur C. *Profiles of the Future: An Inquiry into the Limits of the Possible.* New York: Holt, Rinehart and Winston, 1984, pp. 29 and 36.

Many of the ideas discussed in detail in the various chapters of this book were briefly touched upon in a speech I gave to a group of science-fiction writers in 1974. The notes for that speech can be found in:

Forward, Robert L. "Far Out Physics." *Analog Science Fiction/ Science Fact* 95, No. 8 (August 1975): p. 147.

Chapter 2—Future Talk

Benford, Gregory A., D. L. Book, and W. A. Newcomb. "The Tachyonic Antitelephone." *Physical Review D* 2 (1970): p. 263.

Clay, Roger W., and Philip C. Crouch. "Possible Observations of Tachyons Associated with Extensive Air Showers." *Nature* 248. (1 March 1974): p. 28.

Feinberg, Gerald. "Possibility of Faster-Than-Light Particles." *Physical Review* 159 (1967): p. 1089.

Forward, Robert L. "General Relativity for the Experimentalist." *Proceedings Institute of Radio Engineers* 49 (May 1961): p. 892.

———. "Multidirectional, Multipolarization Antennas for Scalar and Tensor Gravitational Radiation." *General Relativity and Gravitation* 2 (1971): p. 149.

———. "Wideband Laser-Interferometer Gravitational-Radiation Experiment." *Physical Review D* 17 (1978): p. 379.

Matzner, Richard. "Low-Frequency-Limit Conversion Cross Sections for Charged Black Holes." *Physical Review D* 14 (1976): p. 3274.

Weber, Joseph. *General Relativity and Gravitational Waves.* New York: Interscience Publishers, 1961, chap. 8.

———. "Method for Observation of Neutrinos and Antineutrinos." *Physical Review C* 31 (1985): p. 1468.

Chapter 3—Magic Matter

Cline, David B., Carlo Rubbia, and Simon van der Meer. "The Search for Intermediate Vector Bosons." *Scientific American* 247, No. 3 (March 1982): p. 48.

Forward, Robert L. "Antimatter Revealed." *Omni* 2, No. 2 (1979): p. 45.

———. "Antiproton Annihilation Propulsion." *Journal of Propulsion and Power* 1 (1985): p. 370.

Martin, Anthony R., ed. "Special Issue on Antimatter Propulsion." *Journal of British Interplanetary Society* 35 (September 1982): pp. 387–424.

Chapter 4—Magic Beanstalks

Bekey, Ivan. "Tethers Open New Space Options." *Astronautics & Aeronautics* 21 (April 1983): p. 32.

Birch, Paul. "Orbital Ring Systems and Jacob's Ladders." *Journal of British Interplanetary Society* I, Vol. 35 (1982): p. 475; II, Vol. 36 (1983): p. 115; III, p. 231.

Clarke, Arthur C. "The Space Elevator: 'Thought Experiment' or Key to the Universe?" Vol. 1 of *Advanced Earth Oriented Applied Space Technology*. London: Pergamon Press, 1981, p. 39.

Forward, Robert L., and Hans P. Moravec. "High Wire Act." *Omni* 3, No. 10 (July 1981): p. 44.

Isaacs, John D., Allyn C. Vine, Hugh Bradner, and George E. Bachus. "Satellite Elongation into a True 'Sky-Hook.'" *Science* 151 (1966): p. 682.

Pearson, Jerome. "The Orbital Tower: A Spacecraft Launcher Using the Earth's Rotational Energy." *Acta Astronautica* 2 (1975): p. 785.

Chapter 5—Magic Starships

Bussard, Robert W. "Galactic Matter and Interstellar Flight." *Astronautica Acta* 6 (1960): p. 179.

Dyson, Freeman J. "Interstellar Transport." *Physics Today* 21 (October 1968): p. 41.

Forward, Robert L. "Roundtrip Interstellar Travel Using Laser-Pushed Lightsails." *Journal of Spacecraft and Rockets* 21 (1984): p. 187.

Forward, Robert L. "Starwisp: An Ultra-Light Interstellar Probe." *Journal of Spacecraft and Rockets* 22 (1985): p. 345.

Jaffee, Leonard D. and co-workers. "An Interstellar Precursor Mission." *Journal of British Interplanetary Society* 33 (1980): p. 3.

Singer, Clifford E. "Interstellar Propulsion Using a Pellet Stream for Momentum Transfer." *Journal of British Interplanetary Society* 33 (1980): p. 107.

Chapter 6—Magic Gravity

Einstein, Albert. *The Meaning of Relativity.* Princeton: Princeton University Press, 1955, p. 102.

Forward, Robert L. "General Relativity for the Experimentalist." *Proceedings Institute of Radio Engineers* 49 (May 1961): p. 892.

———. "Antigravity." *Proceedings Institute of Radio Engineers* 49 (September 1961): p. 1442.

———. "A New Gravitational Field." *Science Digest* 52, No. 3 (September 1962): p. 73.

———. "Guidelines to Antigravity." *American Journal of Physics* 37 (March 1963): p. 166.

———. "Goodby Gravity." *Omni* 1, No. 4 (January 1979): p. 88.

———. "Flattening Spacetime Near the Earth." *Physical Review D* 26 (1982): p. 735.

Kaufmann, William J., III. *Relativity and Cosmology.* New York: Harper and Row, 1973, chap. 11, 12.

Chapter 7—Black Magic

Hawking, Stephen. "Gravitationally Collapsed Objects of Very Low Mass." *Monthly Notices Royal Astronomical Society* 152 (1971): p. 75.

———. "The Quantum Mechanics of Black Holes." *Scientific American* 236, No. 1 (January 1977): p. 34.

Hutchings, J. B. "Observational Evidence for Black Holes." *American Scientist* 73 (1985): p. 52.

Kaufmann, William J., III. *The Cosmic Frontiers of General Relativity.* Boston: Little, Brown and Co., 1977, p. 110.

Penrose, Roger. "Black Holes." *The State of the Universe.* Ed. G. T. Bath. New York: Clarendon Press, 1980, chap 6.

Thorne, Kip. "The Search for Black Holes." *Scientific American* 231, No. 6 (December 1974): p. 32.

Chapter 8—Time Magic

Carter, Brandon. "Complete Analytic Extension of the Symmetry Axis of Kerr's Solution of Einstein's Equations." *Physical Review* 141 (1966): p. 1242.

———. "Global Structure of the Kerr Family of Gravitational Fields." *Physical Review* 174 (1968): p. 1559.

Forward, Robert L. "How to Build a Time Machine." *Omni* 2, No. 8 (May 1980): p. 92.

Kaufmann, William J., III. *The Cosmic Frontiers of General Relativity.* Boston: Little, Brown and Co., 1977, p. 238.

Tipler, Frank J. "Rotating Cylinders and the Possibility of Global Causality Violation." *Physical Review D* 9 (1974): p. 2203.

Chapter 9—Warp Magic

Forward, Robert L. "Spinning New Realities." *Science 80* 1 (December 1980): p. 40.

Kaufmann, William J., III. *The Cosmic Frontiers of General Relativity.* Boston: Little, Brown and Co., 1977, p. 151.

Penrose, Roger. "Twisting Round Space-Time." *New Scientist* 82, No. 1157 (31 May 1979): p. 734.

————. "A Brief Introduction to Twistors." *High Energy Physics (Switzerland)* 1, No. 4 (1980): p. 267.

Wheeler, John A. *Geometrodynamics*. New York: Academic Press, 1962.

Chapter 10—Future Speculations
Free Energy

Boyer, Timothy H. "The Classical Vacuum." *Scientific American* 253, No. 2 (August 1985): p. 70.

Casimir, H. B. G. and D. Polder. "The Influence of Retardation on the London-van der Waals Forces." *Physical Review* 73 (1948): p. 360.

Feynman, Richard P. and A. R. Hibbs. *Quantum Electrodynamics*. New York: McGraw-Hill, 1965.

Forward, Robert L. "Extracting Electrical Energy From the Vacuum by Cohesion of Charged Foliated Conductors." *Physical Review B* 30 (1984): p. 1700.

Harris, E. G. *A Pedestrian Approach to Quantum Field Theory*. New York: Wiley-Interscience, 1972, chap. 10.

Hawking, Stephen. "The Quantum Mechanics of Black Holes." *Scientific American* 236, No. 1 (January 1977): p. 34.

Israelachivili, J. N. and D. Tabor. "Measurement of van der Waals dispersion forces in the range 1.5 to 130 nm." *Proc. Royal Society of London, Series A* 331 (1972): p. 19.

Sheffield, Charles. *The McAndrew Chronicles*. New York: Tor Books, 1983, pp. 72–112, 234–5.

Reactionless Drives

Forward, Robert L. "Spin Drive to the Stars." *Analog Science Fiction/Science Fact* 101, No. 5 (27 April 1981): p. 64.

Extrasensory Perception

Aharanov, Y., and D. Bohm. "Significance of Electromagnetic Potentials in the Quantum Theory." *Physical Review* 115 (1959): p. 485.

Thomsen, Dietrick. "Gauging the Aharanov-Bohm Effect." *Science News* 129 (1 March 1986): p. 135.

Life After Death

Forward, Robert L. "Speculations on the Spirit." *Galileo* 2, No. 3 (November 1979): p. 16.

Acknowledgments

My thanks to Larry Niven, Jerry Pournelle, and Ben Bova, who first encouraged me to write down some of these "crazy" ideas, and to Robert W. Bussard, Carlton Caves, Arthur C. Clarke, Philip Chapman, Edwin Dodson, Freeman Dyson, Rod Hyde, Keith Lofstrom, David K. Lynch, Hans Moravec, Gerald Nordley, Tom O'Meara, Roger Penrose, Charles Sheffield, Frank Tipler, Joseph Weber, and Mark Zimmermann, who helped in a number of technical areas. I also want to acknowledge the long-term support of Dr. George F. Smith, senior vice president and director of the Hughes Aircraft Company Research Laboratories, who for the past 30 years has allowed me to spend part of my time poking at the cracks in the boundaries of scientific knowledge in an attempt to break through. It is hoped that this book will widen those cracks so we can begin to catch a glimmer of the future magic on the other side.

About the Author

DR. ROBERT L. FORWARD is a physicist, lecturer, and writer. He has 34 years of experience in experimental general relativity, gravitational and inertial sensors, advanced space propulsion, low-noise electronics, space sciences, and explaining science to the lay public. He presently spends half his time writing and the other half consulting on exotic space propulsion concepts.

From 1982 to 1987, Dr. Forward was senior scientist on the director's staff at the Hughes Research Laboratories in Malibu, California. From 1983 through 1985 he was on a half-time leave of absence from Hughes as a private consultant to the Air Force, carrying out contracted studies on advanced propulsion concepts, including a major effort on antiproton annihilation propulsion.

From 1978 to 1982, Dr. Forward conducted research on ultra-low-noise systems and invented, demonstrated, and obtained patents on ten novel concepts for removing random noise from both mechanical structures and electronic circuits (electronic damping and electronic cooling). From 1966 to 1978, he was principal investigator on a series of contracts to develop a rotating gravity gradiometer for use in mapping of the earth and moon from aircraft and spacecraft. This novel sensor concept, an invention of Dr. Forward's, utilizes the rotational properties of sensors to distinguish the gravitational effects of a mass from the inertial effects of acceleration. During the same period, he constructed and operated the first wide-band laser interferometer gravitational radiation antenna. The gravitational strain sensitivity he attained in 1973—0.1 femtometer/meter per root Hertz over a 20 kHz bandwidth—was finally equaled by others only a decade later.

In 1967, Dr. Forward founded the Exploratory Studies Department at the Hughes Research Laboratories with 12 people.

When he resigned after seven years to return to full-time research, the department was the largest in the laboratories, with a headcount exceeding 50 people. This was not a single-technology department but had research programs on image processing, artificial intelligence, hologram optics, organic chemistry, advanced space propulsion, vibrational isolation, light valve displays, earthquake prediction, space sciences, and gravitational radiation, as well as major development contracts on light valve displays, hologram optics, and rotating gravity gradiometers.

From 1962 to 1966, Dr. Forward contributed to the theoretical investigation of quantum effects in space laser communication systems and laser modulators and published the first article to suggest the use of lasers for space propulsion. From 1958 to 1962, he was a Hughes fellow at the University of Maryland, where for his thesis he participated in the construction and operation of the first resonant bar antenna for the detection of interstellar gravitational radiation. (The antenna is now on display in the Smithsonian museum.)

Dr. Forward is the author of 65 professional publications on gravitation, gravity sensors, advanced propulsion concepts, and low-noise electrical and mechanical systems. He holds 18 patents on gravitational and inertial sensors, low-noise electronics, laser modulators, holography, and novel communication concepts. In addition to his professional work, Dr. Forward has been involved in the explanation of science to the lay public. He has written over 50 science articles for publications such as the *Encyclopaedia Britannica Yearbook, Science 80, Science Digest, Omni*, the *AIAA* and *IEEE Student Quarterlies, Missiles and Rockets, Analog*, and *Galaxy* and has presented over 100 seminars, after-dinner speeches, and popular science lectures on gravitation, astrophysics, space sciences, and advanced propulsion concepts. He has been interviewed on ten radio talk shows and appeared in three television "science magazine" segments. To educate as well as to entertain, Dr. Forward has written three novels of the "hard" science-fiction genre, where the science is as accurate as possible.

Dr. Forward received his B.S. in physics from the University of Maryland in 1954, his M.S. in applied physics from UCLA in 1958, and his Ph.D. in gravitation physics from the University of Maryland in 1965. He is a fellow of the British Interplanetary Society, associate fellow of the American Institute of

Aeronautics and Astronautics, senior member of the Institute of Electrical and Electronic Engineers and the American Astronautical Society, and a member of the American Physical Society, Sigma Xi, Sigma Pi Sigma, and the Science Fiction Writers of America.

Zecharia Sitchin's
The Earth Chronicles

BOOK I: THE 12TH PLANET
39362-X/$4.50 US/$5.75 CAN

This revolutionary work brings together lost, antediluvian texts, ancient cosmologies, and newly discovered celestial maps to reach the shocking conclusion that we are descendants of a superior race from the 12th planet.

BOOK II: THE STAIRWAY TO HEAVEN
63339-6/$4.95 US/$6.50 CAN

The mysteries of man's pursuit of immortality and after-life with the gods is researched through the astounding conclusions based on names, places, and monuments whose true meanings have been lost for centuries.

BOOK III: THE WARS OF GODS AND MEN
89585-4/$4.50 US/$5.95 CAN

Mankind's earliest records reveal a startling new theory of human origins—and of the "gods" who destroyed the first civilization!

By the year 2000, 2 out of 3 Americans could be illiterate.

It's true.

Today, 75 million adults...about one American in three, can't read adequately. And by the year 2000, U.S. News & World Report envisions an America with a literacy rate of only 30%.

Before that America comes to be, you can stop it...by joining the fight against illiteracy today.

Call the Coalition for Literacy at toll-free **1-800-228-8813** and volunteer.

Volunteer Against Illiteracy. The only degree you need is a degree of caring.

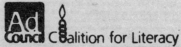

Ad Council ● Coalition for Literacy